Behind the SCENES

RENNIE JONES

SIMON & SCHUSTER

SIMON & SCHUSTER
Rockefeller Center
1230 Avenue of the Americas
New York, NY 10020

SIMON & SCHUSTER and colophon are registered
trademarks of Simon & Schuster Inc.
Designed by Kathryn Parise
Manufactured in the United States of America

10   9   8   7   6   5   4   3   2   1

Library of Congress Cataloging-in-Publication Data
Jones, Rennie.
Behind the scenes / Rennie Jones.
p.   cm.
I. Title.
PS3560.052474B4   1997
813'.54—dc21   97-5804   CIP
ISBN 0-684-80751-3

Prologue

W hat are you doing here? Whatever you want, couldn't it have
waited?"

"No. I've waited long enough."

"I don't appreciate you coming here uninvited. So please turn
around and leave. Now. Before I lose my patience."

"No."

"No?"

"No."

"This is absurd. I want you out. Whatever is troubling you can be
discussed at a more convenient time."

"This is convenient. For me. Frankly, I don't really care whether it's
convenient for you. You see, the truth is that what you want no longer
is going to matter much to anyone, least of all to you."

"What are you talking about? Are you drunk?"

"I am talking about putting an end to your arrogance, to your humiliation of me, to your absolute refusal to listen to me and hear me. I am talking about—" A hand shot out, snapping sharp into visibility like a switchblade. In the hand was a hard object that smacked against the other person's head, stunning him.

"Wha—"

Another hard blow to the side of the head and the person tottered to his knees.

"Stop. We'll talk. Just stop this madness before you do something you'll regret."

"I did something I regret. That's why I'm here now."

And then the hard object dropped to the carpet. The hand retreated to a pocket and this time emerged with something far deadlier.

"It's time. I decided it's finally time."

"Time?" came the breathless gasp.

"Time. To put an end to you."

The six shots from the .32-caliber gun riddled the already weakened body. It was definitely a case of overkill, an irony the murderer appreciated.

One

PART

Chapter
One

Sheila Gainey was surrounded by an audiovisual circus. Four television sets were on, colors primary, voices seductive, messages identical: Buy, buy, buy. Buy a new exerciser, a new blender-chopper, a new insurance program, a guide to your future through numerology. Buy. Buy. Buy.

Usually, Sheila loved to listen to the infomercial competition. Sitting here in her office at Media Gains, the production company to her husband's home shopping network, PCE–TV: Privacy, Comfort, Entertainment, she would jot down notes and ideas and share them with Roger, ideas for new sets, new hosts, new products in the explosive world of electronic retailing that Roger—with her help—had practically invented almost twelve years ago.

But all that Sheila Gainey believed was usual had stopped suddenly two days ago. That was when her husband of twenty years stood in the living room of their spacious Scottsdale, Arizona, home and announced that he had filed for divorce, had booked a room at the Biltmore Hotel for himself, his lawyers would be in touch with the details. And then he had walked out on her and their twenty years together.

Since then, Sheila had been robotic with disbelief, going through the motions of living, anesthetized against life. She could not bear being at home alone, playing the memory tape of her marriage over and over in her mind, getting angrier and angrier with herself for feeling so blindsided by Roger's actions. How could she not have seen it coming? How could she have been so stupid, so trusting? She had not been unaware that his ego had grown exponentially with his success, but the one thing that had always saved Roger from insufferable arrogance was his wonderful ability to laugh at himself, even when he was being a pompous ass. When had that stopped and why hadn't she been paying better attention?

When the questions became too disturbing, she went to her office and turned on all the television sets, oblivious to the colors and sounds and products, oblivious to all that just two days ago she had welcomed with great interest. But three in the morning was less lonely with these strangers than being with her own shattered self.

Three o'clock in the morning was a kind of black hole in the night, made for remembering pain.

"It's time for me to go, Sheila. No other particular female, no male menopause at fifty-one or frightening feelings of time fleeing . . . well, all right, maybe a little. I still love you, Sheil, I do, it's just that it's been twenty years. Twenty years!"

"Have they been bad?"

"No, of course not."

"Then why not try for another twenty?"

"See, that's just it! You don't understand, you can't."

"Did you really expect me to?"

"Yes . . . no . . . oh, I don't know."

"Roger, if it's space you need, we can—"

"It's more than space, Sheil, it's freedom. I just need not to feel so, so scared by the damned predictability of what time is left to me."

"Roger, divorce is not going to change the aging process."

"Maybe not. But I won't know unless I try. At least it might make it more interesting."

"Don't you think I deserve a discussion about this, not a decree? I've been your wife, Roger. Surely you have enough respect for me to discuss this."

But there was no discussion, and Sheila understood Roger's fear of having one. To hear reason, logic, common sense would be to risk changing his mind. Her husband's sense of mortality combined with the luck of being wealthy, successful, a celebrity of sorts, and a very fit, trim, good-looking man had all converged in his mind at the same time, compelling him to use the second and third factors to mitigate the first truth. Nothing must weaken the power of those two factors, and a logical, reasonable discussion could do just that, Sheila now thought bitterly.

The bitterness was short-lived, though. Even two days after Roger's devastating pronouncement, she really did understand what he was going through and could spare only a little anger for him. Most of it was reserved for herself, for taking their future together for granted; for being forty-three years old and not having a clue how to get on with her life without the man who had been her partner since her last year at Arizona State University, when a hotshot Hollywood game-show producer by the name of Roger Gainey gave a guest lecture in her senior communications course and stayed around to marry her three months after she graduated. There were no children to comfort her now, either, since two frightening miscarriages and an ever-more-consuming commitment to career had convinced them they should remain childless. What Sheila was beginning to realize in the brutal clarity of three o'clock in the morning was not only how lonely she felt, but, more paralyzing, how alone. . . .

. . . The alarm was ringing . . . time to wake Roger, put him on his seven-minute snooze alert . . . dammit, why won't the alarm stop that blasted ringing . . . ?

Sheila lifted her head from the desk, opened her eyes, comprehension slowly dawning that she was in her office at five-thirty on Monday morning, that she had fallen asleep at her desk, and the only ringing was the telephone. She did not have to give Roger snooze time. There was no Roger in her bed anymore.

"Hello?" she said groggily.

"Sheil? Thank goodness you're all right."

"Roger?"

"Yes, Roger. Who the hell else would be worried?"

"Why were you worried? I'm not going to kill myself, if that's what you're thinking."

"No, that's not what I was thinking. I was worried about you, okay? Just because we're going to be divorced doesn't mean I've stopped caring about you, you know."

"How reassuring."

"I've been calling you since ten o'clock last night."

"I've been here."

"All night?"

"All night."

"Why? No, never mind, don't answer that. Sheila, are you going to be okay?"

"If I said no, would that change things back?"

"Well . . ."

"Roger, I'm fine, really. The house just seemed overwhelming without you, okay? I didn't know where else to go, so I came here."

"I thought you might have been on a date, or something. Out of spite. Not that you're a spiteful person, but—"

Sheila didn't think she had it in her to find humor in anything, but she was able to manage a slight laugh at his words.

"I admit that was stupid," Roger quickly said. "Freddie had a feeling you'd be there," he added, referring to Freddie Bickford, his longtime friend and former partner, and now lawyer for PCE. "Said another man would be the last thing you'd want. I knew that, too, of course, it's just that . . . under the circumstances . . . hell, I don't know . . . I don't know anything anymore."

Whether it was the familiar gentleness in his voice or the image of him running his hand through his thick salt-and-pepper hair, which she knew he always did in moments of stress, or just the grim realization that she had fallen asleep in her office because her husband was divorcing her and she could not handle being in the empty house—whatever the cause, Sheila suddenly felt crushed by exhaustion, as if a thick drapery had descended upon her, blocking out light and energy.

"Roger, if that's it, I'd like to go now."

"Sheil . . . ?"

"I really am tired, Roger. I want to go home for a few hours. I'll be back for the two o'clock production meeting. That is, assuming I'm still part of Media Gains."

"Sheila, you're *president,* for Christ's sake! You've got fifty-one percent of the business. Of course you're still part of it, why would you think otherwise? This is a divorce of a marriage—everything else stays the same."

"Oh it does, does it?"

"Well, yes. Doesn't it? . . . Can't it? . . . Sheila?"

She had already hung up.

She went home and was able to sleep for about four hours, and when she awoke and had her shower, she looked better, but felt just the same. It surprised her that her dark brown hair had not turned dull and gray overnight, nor that her almost black eyes betrayed no sign of the tears shed. She half-expected to look in the mirror and see a droopy, tired, middle-aged woman, deservedly undesirable. Instead, she looked remarkably untouched by the trauma of a surprise divorce. Small comfort, she thought.

She did not want to attend the Media Gains production meeting this afternoon. Roger and Freddie would be there, as well as others who might know about the divorce. No, they couldn't know, not yet. Roger had only told *her* two days ago. Still, pretending an interest in the meeting's agenda seemed more than she could handle, although she realized that Media Gains and work were her only lifelines out of shock and depression. She loved what she did, loved the meetings with manufacturers or advertising agency executives, pitching a product or a personality or just a concept for possible pickup by PCE, the spot to be produced by Media Gains. She loved the financial meetings, the testimonials meetings, the scheduling meetings, and most of all, she loved the actual production shoot. There was nothing about Media Gains, founded by Freddie and Roger twenty years ago, that she did not love. Roger could never have imagined her relief when he assured her that what was begun for tax purposes—naming her president of the company with a fifty-one percent controlling interest—would not change with the divorce. Sheila knew it was because Media Gains was so unimportant to Roger, his ambitions far better served through the visibility and success of the network.

She began to thumb idly through some papers pertinent to the meeting when the telephone rang. There were three messages on her answering machine from people she had not felt like speaking with; she was letting the machine screen her calls.

"Hello, this is Derek Lang. I was wondering if—"

Sheila immediately clicked off the machine and took the call.

"Hello, this is Sheila Gainey. Roger's not here."

"Actually, it's you I wanted to speak with. I called your office and they said you were home. Have I caught you at a bad time?"

What in the world was Derek Lang calling *her* for? Sheila wondered. The head of Best for Less, BFL-TV, was Roger's strongest competitor in the home shopping network sweepstakes. Aside from seeing him at conventions or the occasional local Phoenix social or civic function, she and Roger had steered clear of Derek Lang, a business tycoon originally from New York who made his fortune buying up companies on the cheap, turning them around, and then selling them high. He had a reputation for being ahead of what was happening, for sniffing out trends, and when he had bought a cable station in Phoenix it was because he understood the future, and could see the gold mine Roger Gainey was excavating with PCE.

Lang was an iconoclastic loner, never married, a man with many different women, many different hotels he called home, no roots, no commitments seemingly to anything but money, the deal, profit. At forty-seven, he was a darling of magazines and newspapers as a prototype of the businessman as renegade. It was as if the Marlboro Man had been reclad in a suit; Derek was tall and broad-shouldered, and even if he hadn't been exceedingly wealthy, there would be no shortage of women hopeful that they could be the one among many to tame the cowboy. Sheila found the man rather intimidating; he was so much larger than life, it seemed. A hero to some, a villain to others, regardless of the role, Derek Lang always made it uniquely his own. All in all, not your average guy. Now what could such a man possibly want with her?

"What can I do for you, Derek?"

"Actually, it's what we can do for each other."

"I don't understand." Impossible that he would already know about the pending divorce. Impossible. Roger wouldn't have told anyone yet. And Freddie? She didn't think Freddie had ever spoken a word to Derek Lang in his life.

"I know about you and Roger and—"

"You do?"

"—and I was wondering if we could have lunch."

"Lunch? You and me?"

A short, dry laugh. "Is there someone else you'd like to bring along?"

"No, no, it's just that . . . I'm sorry, Derek, my world isn't exactly on an even keel right now. You did say you wanted to have lunch, didn't you?"

"I did. To talk."

"Talk?" she repeated idiotically.

"I think that with the change in your circumstances we might have some unexplored mutual interests."

"Mutual interests?" This was ridiculous. She felt like Lamp Chop with Derek Lang as her Shari Lewis. "I'm sorry, but I can't imagine what you and I could have to talk about. You're my husband's strongest competitor. What would I want—"

"Ex-husband."

"I beg your pardon?" But Sheila had heard the quietly spoken words, had heard them all too clearly.

"That should make a difference. Shouldn't it?"

Twenty years ago, she and Roger and Freddie Bickford had spent day and night together, fighting for the success of Media Gains, a success that eventually went far beyond anything they could have dreamed possible. Roger, one of several game show producers for a giant media corporation in Los Angeles, had been exhaustingly energetic, ambitious, with an idea a minute and the charm and style of a natural-born salesman. More of his game show ideas made it to test markets than those of any of the other young producers, but he wanted more. When he and Sheila got married, he had just formed Media Gains with Freddie, a young lawyer from the same corporation. They had decided to base their new venture outside Phoenix, where costs were cheaper, and almost from the beginning, everything the production company made was a hit.

In time, things had changed for Freddie. It seemed that they had for her, too, Sheila acknowledged now, only she hadn't been aware of it. She had always thought that in Roger she had a wonderful lover, a caring husband, a mentor and a friend; a partner. They had a good marriage, one of loyalty and respect and passion. None of that had changed. She was not a stupid woman, only a too trusting wife. She had believed that loyalty and respect and abiding passion were so much more than what most husbands and wives shared that it would be enough to carry Roger and her over the bumps. Obviously, she had been wrong.

She had to get a grip on herself. Whether she wanted to believe it or not, that part of her life was over. Which meant that, somehow, she had to move on. Somehow.

"Sheila?"

"Lunch would be lovely, Derek, just lovely."

Chapter Two

It was small for a hotel suite, but the California king-sized bed was big enough for the couple now pulling the sheets up over their nakedness, the air conditioner chilling the sweat on their bodies.

Derek Lang watched as the woman beside him went through her by now familiar postsex rituals: Running a hand ineffectually through her tousled mass of thick, wavy blond hair. Running a forefinger under her eyes to rub away any smudges of mascara. Reaching over to the night table for her cigarettes. Marilu Diamante was the Washington, D.C.–based head of the National Infomercial Marketing Association, a group not even ten years old, but an important one, functioning as a watchdog to the electronic retailing industry, an effort to ensure that organized crime kept its distance. Interstate shipping, product payola, warehousing offered all kinds of opportunities the Mob loved, and it was NIMA's responsibility to keep the industry respectable. A former

New York City and Chicago advertising executive, Marilu had been one of the first to understand the huge potential in electronic retailing, and in the years she had been running NIMA, she had done much to legitimize the business, from establishing an annual convention in Las Vegas, to creating the JW Greensheet, the infomercial equivalent of a Nielsen report for ratings—which increased the appeal of infomercials to manufacturers because it meant instantaneous market feedback on their wares.

Derek had known Marilu for four years now, had been sleeping with her for three. She looked good and kept her forty-four-year-old body fit; she was well connected; and she was intelligent. There was really nothing negative to say about Marilu Diamante, and he knew she dated other men who were willing, even eager, to marry her. Just as he knew that she was in love with him. As if that mattered.

Derek Lang understood that what he possessed was both a strength and a weakness, but his lack of emotional neediness—what his enemies and ex–female friends called his glacial remoteness from normal human feelings—did not bother him too often or too much. His parents had divorced when he was young, and he had time enough to observe a mother and one sister love wrongly and dangerously, another sister give up a promising career "for love." Derek had at a young age discovered an ability to lock away any extreme of emotion and simply move on with what was important. For Derek, what had always been important was freedom, and nothing provided freedom better than the unbeatable combination of money and power. Emotion created the prison known as ownership, and Derek Lang totally rejected that as a concept of living for himself. Instead, diversity and divestiture became his ethos; those who wished to go along for the ride, like Marilu Diamante, knew that was all he would give—a ride, not a journey. If there were moments when he wondered what he might be missing by his lack of emotional need, they passed quickly. He had *chosen* this way; it was neither defense nor protection; it was choice. Maybe that was why business rivals and women in love kept thinking they could change him; they didn't understand the difference between choice and design.

And so, although he had enjoyed sex with Marilu Diamante and had performed satisfactorily, his mind, before, during, and now were not on this woman or the pleasure given and received. No, Sheila Gainey and their upcoming lunch together interested him far more.

"I thought sex was supposed to be fun. You look like you're weighing the advantages of another corporate takeover. Why so serious?" Marilu asked. "Wasn't it good for you?"

Derek smiled. "It was great, as usual."

"You could have it whenever you wanted, you know."

"Lu—"

"Sorry. Let's erase that."

"I was thinking about divorce, actually."

"Is that why you won't get married? With prenuptials the way they are today, you wouldn't have to worry about me taking you to the cleaners," Marilu said dryly.

"Very amusing." Derek laughed. "I was thinking about what un-tapped opportunities exist once the emotional sores scab over."

"An unappetizing analogy but not an unapt one," she commented. "Are you referring to Sheila and Roger Gainey, by any chance?" She sat up in bed, pulling the top sheet over her and looking at him with a sly, knowing grin.

"You heard about it?"

She nodded. "Sheila called me. We've been friends for years. She's absolutely devastated by what he's done. The bastard."

Derek shrugged, disinterested in personalities except as they im-pacted the deal. "He never struck me as a bastard. Actually, Roger Gainey always impressed me as someone who knows his particular business very, very well. I like a man with expertise, makes for a more even match."

"Fine, be impressed. That doesn't explain why their divorce has you looking like a hyena circling a pack of lion cubs."

Derek's smile was wide and almost reached his coal black, keenly alert eyes. "An intriguing image, that," he said. "Lu, did you know that Sheila Gainey is president of Media Gains, PCE's production company, and that she not only has a fifty-one controlling interest, the company is not even a division of PCE, it's an entirely separate company?"

"Sure, I knew all that," Marilu told him. "Roger did that years ago for tax purposes."

"That's when PCE-TV was really beginning to take off, right?" Derek asked.

Marilu nodded. "Roger turned over the production company to Sheila, making sure Freddie Bickford was there as his eyes and ears."

"Meaning?"

"Meaning that it's Bickford who took care of the critical minutiae like fulfillment, warehousing, that kind of stuff." Her expression turned snide. "Roger's not interested in the vital details."

"So he made Media Gains a separate company, not a wholly owned subsidiary of PCE? Dumb move," Derek said.

"Knowing Roger, he probably didn't listen when the advice to do what you're saying was given to him by his lawyers, by Freddie, probably even by Sheila. He no doubt figured Media Gains was still his even if Sheila had the title—he's still running the show, so what did it matter? And he was right."

"Then, not now," Derek said pointedly. "Legally, he can't do a damn thing about the arrangement, which means that Media Gains remains under her control, divorce or no divorce."

"So?" Marilu was unable to see where Derek was going with this, but there was a gleam of excitement in his eyes that she knew wasn't inspired by her.

Derek took a robe that had been at the foot of the bed, slipped it on, and began to stride around the small room, as though his energy had been smothered by the constraint of the bed. "Follow me on this, Lu," he said. "Sheila Gainey owns fifty-one percent of a production company that has been exclusive to PCE. The divorce lets her keep Media Gains and, *and,* frees her from exclusivity to PCE. Don't you get it?" His voice practically rumbled with relish at the scenario in his mind, and his large, broad frame filled the small space with so much raw masculinity that Marilu felt her mouth go dry with longing.

"Derek, come on back to bed, honey, we—"

"In a minute. Just listen, okay," and he started to speak aloud the brilliant, exquisite reality that he had figured out the second his lawyer had learned what he had been instructed to learn about the Gaineys' financial arrangement.

"Media Gains no longer has to be exclusive to PCE," he explained. "Sheila can get a media buyer to buy time at any network—*any* one, QVC, mine, whatever, not just Roger's. The buyer would make sure to get her the best price for the best time slot—and Roger will have to be competitive because—and this is the beauty of what's happened—because if he isn't competitive, he not only loses the forty percent commission on all products sold from the spot which the network always makes, his forty-nine percent of Media Gains *stops making money!* Basically, he has to compete against himself in order to stay profitable. Dammit, I love it!"

Marilu was silent, taking in all the ramifications of what Derek was describing. At that moment, his sexual appeal for her was almost overwhelming. An electric current sizzled off him, the power of a mind so much quicker, more cunning than most.

"You're unbelievable," she breathed.

He went over and sat at the edge of the bed, twisting around to face Marilu.

"What's unbelievable is the shortsightedness of people. For all that Roger Gainey has been outstanding at the home shopping game, he and his lawyers don't have a clue about human nature, it seems. If they did, they'd know better than to try to be decent and nice when it comes to money."

"Not everyone's like that, Derek," Marilu tried.

"Honey, sooner or later no one is *not* like that. Cynical? Maybe, but I call it realistic. The point is that once Sheila Gainey realizes the high hand she's holding, do you really think for a minute she's not going to play it, out of some warped sense of loyalty to a marriage and to a man that no longer exist for her?"

"Sheila is not a vengeful kind of person, Derek," Marilu argued. "She's been knocked for a loop by Roger, sure, but she's not the type to strike back. She's a very decent woman."

"We'll see."

Again there was silence as Marilu appraised the man, the words.

"You're planning to be the one who enlightens her, aren't you?" she guessed.

Just a foxy smile as answer.

"Why?"

"Why?" Derek repeated with a short laugh. "Why not? I'll get access to one of the top producers in the business before anyone else. That means *my* network will have better goods, increased viewers, and increased profits from the viewers and the products sold. Marilu, Marilu, I'm surprised at you. That question is so naive, and we both know that's one word that couldn't be used to describe you."

"Forgive me." Her smile was small and tight. "I forgot myself for a moment. I was just thinking that Sheila is vulnerable right now, she's hurting. Why bother her with business at this time? Knowing you, though, you'll just say vulnerable and hurting are perfect when discussing business. That is what you would say, isn't it, Derek?"

For answer, he slipped out of his robe, threw the top sheet off Marilu, and straddled her. "Does she know about us?" he whispered as he lowered his head to a particularly sensitive spot below her right ear.

"Mmm, sort of. I think."

He brought his head up to look at her, and the lack of continued action made her open her eyes.

"What?" she asked, nonplussed.

"What does 'Sort of, I think' mean, Lu?"

"It means I told her about us when we first started, three years ago. Nothing since. I figured it was best since she might see a conflict of interest in the head of NIMA and a major cable network player sharing pillow talk."

"And she hasn't asked in all this time?"

"There *are* a few other men in my life, you know."

"Good." He grinned. "I'm glad to hear that."

"Unfortunately," she murmured before pulling his head back down to the crook of her neck, "you really *are* glad to hear that."

When Derek Lang left the hotel room forty-five minutes later, Marilu Diamante was far from his mind. She knew that. And she was disgusted with herself for knowing it and not being able to walk away.

But to a woman like Marilu Diamante, with no concern for her biological clock; with one divorce long, long behind her; and with a serious commitment to a career she loved, walking away from a maverick like Derek Lang was to concede defeat, and that she could not do. In a world full of men like Roger Gainey, basically good, basically decent, basically too dumb to deal with the hormonal imbalance when it hits them, a cold, emotionally unreachable man like Derek presented the ultimate challenge not only to the core of her femininity, but to Marilu's high regard for her own intelligence, wit, and superiority over other women.

She was not worried that Derek would approach Sheila in any romantic sense. That would be stupid, and Derek was never that. She cared about Sheila, genuinely liked her. Although her job kept her traveling, she never missed seeing Sheila whenever she was in Phoenix. She had been telling Derek the truth about not confiding in the other woman, though. She hadn't been worried that Sheila would think it a conflict of interest; what concerned her was that she could tell Roger, who might view that kind of information as potential ammunition, if ever needed. And there truly were enough other men who drifted in and out of Marilu's life so that not mentioning Derek would not arouse Sheila's suspicions, especially given the man's reputation with women, and his frequent appearances in magazines and newspapers with this one or that one—photographs that tore at Marilu's heart.

She took Derek Lang on his terms because to do otherwise would be to lose him entirely. Marilu believed that she was the one woman smart enough to get him, that by giving the cowboy enough rope, someday she'd lasso him in.

Marilu was even smart enough to know when she was bullshitting herself.

Chapter
Three

Word of the Gaineys' pending divorce spread with expected speed not only through the corridors of the PCE offices in downtown Phoenix and in the Media Gains studio in nearby Tempe, but through law firms, advertising agencies, and talent agents' offices from Manhattan to Chicago to Dallas to Los Angeles. Even the warehousing centers for the various home shopping networks, located everywhere in the southwest from Albuquerque to San Antonio, were abuzz with the news, since PCE and Media Gains affected so many people, and perhaps even more because Sheila and Roger were thought of as a unit. For all that Roger was a real pioneer in the home shopping business, Sheila was never dismissed as being merely Roger's wife. She was highly regarded for her ability to handle the constant pressures of being a producer, which often meant pleasing as many people as possible without financial mishap, as well as having a sharp eye for making a product, a set, and the entire shoot look good on a budget. These talents helped make her a favorite of manufacturers and celebrities, which, in turn, contributed significantly to PCE's success.

By the end of the first week following the announcement, Sheila was so drained that she decided to take herself off to Rancha La Puerta in Baja, California. She needed to get away from the telephone. The barrage of calls had left her numb. While most people expressed outrage at Roger's action, a few were only perfunctorily solicitous, more concerned about the security of their projects. Regardless, the result was the same: How many more times could she parrot reassurances she neither felt nor believed?

Roger was not having that much easier a time of it, rapidly being made all too aware just how well liked and well regarded Sheila was. Shit, he thought, as he sat in his office waiting for his next meeting, he liked her, too, didn't he? Even loved her, in his own way. Maybe he would regret what he was doing, but he had given it a lot of thought. A lot. He wanted something new. He didn't want to wake up every morning for the next twenty years the same way, and with the same partner he had had for the past twenty. Did wanting change make him a bad person? Men did it all the time, didn't they?

He was fifty-one years old, fifty-one! He shook his head, remembering how he used to make fun of anyone over thirty. Hell, he hadn't known anything then. Now he had money; he took care of himself; women of all ages seemed to like him; and he didn't attribute that entirely to his success and semi-celebrity. No, he had never really had difficulty getting women. Sheila was . . . well, dammit, Sheila was his *wife*. He knew her better than he knew anyone else. Maybe that was it—maybe he knew her *too* well. Or maybe it was that she knew *him* too well. He wanted to be able to surprise a woman again, be surprised by one. He and Sheila had been young together, and if he stayed with her, that meant he'd have to get old with her, and he just didn't want that. He wasn't ready to get old. Not yet. And he wouldn't, not if a little change could make it different.

All right, so maybe he was going through male menopause, so what? He was entitled, wasn't he? It wasn't as if he were leaving Sheila high and dry. They could still be friends, dammit. They *should* still be friends.

"Yes?" he snapped into the intercom that buzzed sharply, breaking his concentration. "Okay, send them in."

"Freddie," he greeted by way of a nod. "Alicia, it's good to see you." And he stepped from his desk to give her a slight hug and an air kiss. "Sit, sit," he said, gesturing to a chair as he went back to his desk.

"It's good to see you, too, Roger," said the woman known as the queen of infomercials, taking a seat. "I heard about you and Sheila. I'm sorry."

He nodded again at his lawyer and closest friend. "Freddie here has been telling me nonstop what an ass I'm being. If you have another word to describe me, I'd find it refreshing."

Alicia's smile was gentle. "I always thought you and Sheila just belonged together, that's all. It's a shame when things don't work out. And don't I know! Two divorces don't exactly qualify me as a marriage counselor."

"What can I say? Sheila's great, we were great together, and I'm an ass. So maybe being an ass makes me feel good," but there was no humor behind Roger's words, only a strident anger that was making his gray eyes smolder. He ran his hand through his thick hair and caught Freddie's almost imperceptible shake of his head, warning him to calm down, get control. He could always count on his level-headed lawyer for that. "Sorry," he said. Then he turned on a smile that so effortlessly beamed sincerity that it was immediately apparent a master salesman was operating here, the kind who could get you to fork over money for something you didn't want and say thank you to him in the process.

"How was Nashville, Alicia? Taping a new video, weren't you?" he asked.

"I was in Fargo, North Dakota, where it was fourteen below with the windchill," she corrected him, "and I was opening a new mall there."

The queen of infomercials stiffened, wondering if Roger's mistake hadn't been intentional. It wasn't usual for him to know what other jobs his hosts and hostesses were doing except when they were big enough to bring significant publicity to the network. At the same time, he might have known and was not so subtly telling her he was aware her career was not as glittering as it had been. This, in turn, gave him leverage she did not want him to have.

Alicia Devon, at fifty-six, was taking her second swing at success, having been a well-known country and western singer in the sixties and seventies. Her popularity had waned as her age increased. About five years ago, her manager, Nicholas Covey, who had known Roger when he had been a game show producer, suggested to his old friend that he try Alicia out on one of his infomercials. Until then, Roger himself had been doing a lot of the on-camera hawking—that or using either inexpensive, local talent or a representative of the product's manufacturer.

Roger decided to take a chance that Alicia's homespun wholesomeness would have the same appeal to the middle-American female blue-collar shopper that made up the largest slice of the demographic home shopping pie as did his smile and charm. The older viewers would remember her, and that familiarity, ideally, would translate into trust: They liked the slightly pudgy woman with her brown hair piled high and her trademark spit curls by each ear; they liked her husky laugh and her old-fashioned songs about bad men you can't help loving. So if they liked the singer and her music, and if she wanted them to buy a product, well, then, it had to be worth buying. Roger was banking on the fact that she had built-in celebrity, an asset as valuable as his own "sincere" charm. And this fame, albeit faded, would further create the illusion of the commercial as entertainment, which is where he believed infomercials were heading.

Alicia might also be right for the younger viewer, the other half of a two-income family too busy to shop, the woman who dreaded the monster malls and liked the privacy and convenience of home shopping. For them, Alicia Devon was exactly the kind of woman they could relate to—like a mother or an aunt. She was an entertainer who didn't pose a threat, neither too glamorous nor too sophisticated to frighten off a buyer. That elusive, unteachable quality of seeming to be special without being untouchable was a trait Roger possessed as well, and it had helped sell out everything from his very first shipment of Taiwanese steak knives. He had a feeling Alicia Devon possessed it, too.

And she did, in a major way. First it was acrylic nails, then a venetian-blind cleaner, followed by an outdoor grill, then a self-cleaning stove-top Dutch oven. The results were amazing. Although the life-span of a successful infomercial was usually four months, Alicia's spots never died before six to eight. When Sheila told Roger about an astrological self-improvement system someone had come to her about, wanting Media Gains to produce the infomercial, it marked the first time he aired something other than consumer goods.

AstroAge minted money. As did HandMagic, an instant handwriting analysis kit and video; as did HairSoFul, and a host of other products that aired up to three-hundred times a week nationwide at thirty minutes each time, and each one sold meant 40 percent of the gross to Roger's pockets, and 4 to 5 percent of the gross to all the cable operators PCE distributed to by satellite.

Viewers recognized Alicia, trusted her, bought from her. She became a member of each viewer's family. They would pick up their remote control and surf until they found her, making her outdraw Cher, Dionne Warwick, Linda Gray, Ali MacGraw—all of the old-timers whose careers were being resurrected through electronic retailing.

Alicia's old records began to sell again, and in time, she cut two new ones, complete with videos. She started performing again, in Reno and Lake Tahoe, Atlantic City, on TV specials. And she started to make money. Although she did not develop and manufacture her own product, as did Susan Powter or Connie Stevens, who took home 30 percent of the net on $50 million gross sales of her cosmetics, Alicia did well nevertheless, earning between 5 percent and 8 percent of the gross on every product sold. Manufacturers loved it when she hostessed their spot, because reaction from the home shopper was immediate: they would know right away whether they had a winner, one whose sales could increase sevenfold at the retail level, as past performances had shown. If one of the products she hyped failed to sell, it was the product's fault, not hers.

Life was treating Alicia well, and she wanted nothing to change it, which was why she was sitting here now with her heart racing with dread. Her manager had called her in Fargo to tell her that Roger had requested this meeting. When pressed, all Roger would say was that maybe Alicia was going through a period of overexposure—how else to explain the drop in sales on her products over the past several months? So he wanted to talk to her, see what changes might be made.

Neither Covey nor Alicia had liked the sound of that. As a boss, Roger was rather a benign dictator. If things were going fine, he never interfered; if they weren't, even by the merest indication, he interfered, totally. Could he be right about her? she wondered now as she had for the past three days since her manager's call. Was she overexposed? She had to admit that opening a mall in Fargo, North Dakota, was a far cry from the kind of star gig she used to be invited to only a few months ago.

"I understand Nick won't be joining us," Roger said.

Alicia nodded. "He's in Branson, Missouri, scouting talent. We didn't think he really needed to be here." The words were a question of hope, not a statement of fact.

"Well, no, no, I guess not. After all, Freddie can discuss the legal issues with him another time."

The heart racing with dread instantaneously became a lump of acid burning in her belly. It was fear of failure, a poison she simply could not swallow again. Not again. If Roger wanted her off-guard and insecure, he had achieved that just by setting up this meeting. Anything more was overkill; surely he knew her well enough to know that would be the effect of his words. The bastard.

"Sounds ominous," she said, adding a small, tinny laugh.

"Not ominous, Alicia," Roger answered, "but I do think we have to face reality. And that reality is going to involve some changes."

She nodded, not trusting herself to speak. She glanced at Freddie, whose face betrayed nothing.

"Relax, Alicia," Roger said. "You look as if you thought I was about to fire you."

"You're not?"

He shook his head. "Don't be silly. Whatever gave you that idea?"

You did, you prick. But of course she said nothing of the sort, admitting only, "Call it typical artist's insecurity," and this time her laugh was fuller, more real. "When Nick told me you were worried that I might be overexposed"—she shrugged—"well, I guess my imagination ran away with itself."

"I *am* worried that you're overexposed; no maybes about it."

"But you just said—"

"I said I wasn't firing you. I didn't say what I *am* going to do."

"Alicia, it's going to be okay." This from Freddie. "Try to relax and just listen, all right?"

She barely nodded, eyes burning, her left hand playing nervously with the spit curl by her left ear.

"A couple of weeks ago you yourself mentioned, Alicia, how disappointed you were that AutoRite, the teach-yourself-how-to-drive book and video, barely lasted three weeks," Roger began, gray eyes hard on her. "We paid over one hundred twenty-five thousand dollars to produce that spot because we had to rent so many cars."

"It was a stupid spot," Alicia countered halfheartedly.

"That's exactly what you said when I remarked how badly we did on PhenoRub, the spot remover, and on Superskin, the infomercial before that one." Roger leaned across his desk, the complete businessman now, no charm, no salesmanship, just Roger Gainey going about the business of being boss. "All of these products had everything going for them—easy to understand and use, solid testimonials, outstanding markup, and they test-marketed well." He sat back and shook his head. "I'm sorry, Alicia, but there've been too many failures where there should have been no problems, none at all. Unfortunately, it's left me with only one possible conclusion."

"That the fault is mine, right?" she practically squeaked.

"I'm afraid so. It's not that you're not still great, Alicia," he assured her, "still the queen of infomercials. You are, but I do think we've over-exposed you, and I'm as much to blame as anyone. You've made a lot of money over the years for PCE and the cable operators we distribute to. You've had a long run, longer than most. I guess I got greedy—figured you could keep going strong forever—I was wrong."

"But, Roger—"

He held up a hand to stop her. "Let me finish, okay? Audiences are getting younger, Alicia, and that's the truth. Believe me, I don't like it any more than you do, but there it is. They're getting younger; they want *new* faces—it's as simple as that. Cher is finished. Even Dionne Warwick is hanging on only by psychic intervention." He smiled, but no one else did. "The competition is fierce out there with more and more networks needing more and more products to fill the cable pipeline. And people like me and Derek Lang and Ralph and Brian Roberts of QVC can't afford to take risks out of sentiment. I'm sorry, but we can't. Every second means dollars, and if those seconds cost us money instead of make it for us, we're out of business and the next guy standing in line to fill that air time is in. Your last infomercials cost us a shitload of money, Alicia. I can't afford to keep going with you that way, I simply can't."

There was no real sound in the room, just the artificial hum from the central air-conditioning system. To Alicia, it was a sound as deafening as applause dying. Only the slightly accelerated rise and fall of her chest indicated she was even breathing, so still had she become. Not even her eyes were blinking.

"Alicia?" Freddie said, starting to reach out a hand to touch her.

"I'm fine, thank you," she said stiffly, not looking anywhere but straight ahead, at Roger, but really through him, past him to a future too frighteningly bleak to contemplate.

She forced herself to focus on the present, on this room, this man, his words, and to ignore the roaring in her ears, the sound of her soul screaming. "Exactly what did you have in mind?" she asked.

"A spree."

"No." The word came out in a breathless whisper of disbelief and denial.

"I'm sorry, Alicia, but—"

"You can't be serious. You're joking, I know you are. He's joking, isn't he, Freddie?" she implored the lawyer whose silence spoke an answer she did not want to hear. Being fired would be better than a spree. She knew that unlike an infomercial spokesperson, the host or hostess for a home shopping spree was heard but rarely seen, the product really being the entertainment. Since it had been proven that no viewer deliberately turned to a spree but rather searched the channels for either a particular product or celebrity, what Roger was proposing would effectively shut down her visibility and therefore end her career.

"When?"

"When?" Roger repeated.

"What shift—early morning, midday—when?" she wanted to know.

He could barely meet her eyes as he said, "Graveyard."

"Now this time I *know* you're joking," Alicia said, even managing to laugh.

"I'm not joking, Alicia. I'm considering you for a three-hour home shopping spree in the three to six A.M. graveyard shift," Roger stated firmly.

"I'm trying to remain calm, but you're making it rather difficult," the singer said. "Why don't you just fire me and be over with it? My career's as good as dead anyway if you do this. You know as well as I that only alcoholics and insomniacs tune in the graveyard shift, and then the next morning they cancel everything they've ordered."

"I agree it's a down time and that's why you might be just what we need."

"I'm sure you have a very logical explanation for that statement, but frankly, I'm not interested. If Nick were here, he'd be laughing in your face. You can't do this to me, Roger, you can't."

"First of all, Alicia, he can," Freddie said. "By contract, Roger can legally put you in any spot at any time he wants. You and Nick signed over all assignments to PCE."

"Secondly," Roger took over, "I haven't decided anything definitely yet."

"You haven't?" Another question weighted with hope.

Roger shook his head. "I'm thinking about it, that's all. If you are overexposed, as I believe is the case, hostessing the spree at that hour would certainly change that situation. In addition, there's a potential plus in having you do a graveyard spree and that is that you might pull in the fans who will miss you during regular hours. Maybe they'll tune in your shift and then maybe the orders will stick." He ran a hand through his hair. "Look, Alicia, I know this is tough. It's tough for me, too. You've been an important part of PCE's success and don't think I'm not grateful. I'm not deliberately setting out to hurt you or your career, but I have to think of business first."

Very quietly she asked: "Do I have any say in this matter?"

Roger shrugged. "Sure. I suppose you could buy yourself out of the remaining two years on your current contract, or you could always try to break the contract—"

"—and be sued for breach," Freddie supplied. "You wouldn't want to do that, believe me."

"In other words, I have no choice." She got to her feet. "When will you decide, Roger?"

"I don't know. Tomorrow? A month from now? Who knows? You've got that new spot beginning its second week, the one for the Grill Pro from Presto. They could be a major source for us. Let's see what the results look like and then we'll talk again."

She nodded and began to walk to the door. "Are any results in from the spot yet?"

"Nothing definitive," Roger told her.

"Meaning?" she pressed.

"Meaning not as clear a failure as AutoRite, but not an immediate success like in the old days."

She weighed his words, wondering if he were lying to her. Anyone connected with home shopping knew that a strong element of its appeal to manufacturers was its ability to give immediate audience response. The results from Grill Pro should already be apparent. She opened the door slightly, ready to leave, then closed it again, and looked from Freddie to Roger a moment before speaking. "Don't be cruel, Roger," she finally said. "It's not lucky to be cruel."

Roger's expression was bemused. "Is that a threat or a curse, Alicia?"

"Neither. Just some old down-home country wisdom. Don't be cruel to another person. Cruelty has a funny way of coming back and biting you on the butt."

There was no bemusement on Roger's face when he said, with un-brookable strength in his voice, "I'm not being cruel, Alicia. It's called being practical. Down-home country wisdom would be real wise to learn the difference."

She said nothing in response, just continued to look at him a long moment, then opened the door again, this time shutting it behind her as she left.

A few minutes of silence passed while both men shed the tension of the meeting. Finally, Roger said, "That was not fun."

"She's still got her job," Freddie pointed out.

"No, she's still got *a* job. And if I do decide to move her to a spree, she's right, her career will be dead."

"Isn't there any other shift you can put her on?"

"Of course there is, you know that. But what's the point? The other sprees are making money for us. I don't want to tamper with something that's working. At least with the graveyard, we have no place to go but up. And it's not necessarily permanent either," he went on, al-most as if he were convincing himself. "It could just be temporary, un-til she's missed."

"Nice try, but bullshit, pure and simple," Freddie said. "As was that business about Grill Pro's results."

Roger smiled sheepishly. "How much bad news could I lay on her at one time?"

"The truth is that the party's over for our singing saleslady," Freddie commented unemotionally. "Spree, graveyard shift, what does it mat-ter? She's finished here. I have a feeling, though, that she won't go without a good, old-fashioned, down-home country knuckles-and-guts kind of fight."

"No way," Roger argued. "She's not like that. Besides, we have her dead to rights legally, you made sure of that before the meeting."

"Yes, we have her legally, Roger, but desperation is knocking at her door and it's a sound she doesn't want to hear, hollow and empty as it is."

"She can't do a thing to me," Roger stated.

"Maybe not legally, no, but you don't need bad publicity. Your divorce is providing enough of that."

Roger grimaced. "I suppose."

"Just tread gently with Alicia, that's all I'm saying. For your own sake."

"Advice heard, counselor."

"Better it be advice taken."

Chapter
Four

Sheila was in no mood for lunch with Derek Lang, but she knew enough not to cancel; it would only postpone the inevitable, since he would make another date, and another until she saw him. Besides, she had already canceled once when she decided to take herself off to the spa.

Her two weeks there had helped, to a degree. Long, solitary walks equalized the ratio of time spent in tears versus anger, but there were still too many tears shed for the loss, not only of the marriage, but of her own trusting innocence. And the anger still weighed heavily, anger directed toward herself, for not thinking, not seeing, not sensing; for assuming that because she was happy and satisfied in her marriage, her husband had to be as well; for believing that the little disappointments and compromises that she accepted as part of a marriage could not mount up to the point of unacceptability.

At the spa, she shared fatless, flavorless lunches with other divorced women who assured her that the seesaw of emotions would eventually level out to a pure, even rage—at Roger. As humorously as this struck her, Sheila could not help hoping that these women were right—and that it would happen soon. She felt so emotionally powerless that not even work interested her.

Having lunch with Derek today struck her as symbolic in a way; it marked the first time in five weeks that she was truly venturing back out into the world she shared with her soon-to-be ex-husband. She was meeting Derek at Emilio's, an innocuous-looking restaurant in a nondescript strip mall near downtown Phoenix that had become a favorite of the infomercial crowd for its outstanding northern Italian cuisine in this southwest mecca of beef and jalapeño peppers. By agreeing to meet Derek there, where there would certainly be others from PCE and BFL, Sheila was, in effect, announcing her return to the land of the living. Now if only that were true, she thought, checking her hair in the rearview mirror before getting out of the car and turning over the keys to the parking valet.

Emilio, the owner and chef, greeted her as if she had been gone a year, not a few weeks. He personally escorted her through the restaurant to Derek's table, and if she weren't frozen with self-consciousness as she smiled to this one, nodded to that one, she might have been able to remember how attractive she had always found Derek Lang. He was at the table, waiting for her, and he stood up, all six feet two inches of him, offering his hand and a smile that immediately warmed her and cracked her iced-over facade.

"Sheila, thank you so much for joining me today," he greeted her. "Emilio, one look at Mrs. Gainey and we should go off to one of those spas."

"Mr. Lang, you would be bored within the first thirty minutes, and I would want to make over the kitchen." They all laughed appreciatively, then Emilio said, *"Buon appetito,"* and left.

"I hope I haven't kept you waiting," Sheila said after she sat down.

"But you have, almost three weeks." Derek smiled. "Fortunately, I'm a very patient guy."

"It's been a rather difficult time for me, as you know."

"I do know, Sheila, and that's why I really am glad you decided to keep this lunch date. Although whatever they did for you at the spa certainly agrees with you. You look wonderful."

Sheila suddenly felt as fragile and unsure as a teenager on a first date with the football hero. All her confidence as a woman, her sense of herself as an attractive, appealing female had splintered and crumbled that fateful evening five weeks ago. Anger at Roger would surely come quicker than the restoration of her self-confidence, she thought miserably.

"I'm sorry," Derek said. "I see I've embarrassed you."

"No, no—well, a little," she admitted with a small smile.

"Would you like something to drink?"

"Just an iced tea, please."

It was not until they were on their espressos that Derek revealed the purpose of the lunch. Until then, conversation had been casual, light, punctuated frequently by greetings from people who stopped by their table. Throughout, Sheila found herself nodding when it was appropriate, commenting on cue, even smiling occasionally, but there was nothing genuine about any of her responses. She was here, but apart, observing, not really participating. She even reacted to Derek with a certain remoteness. He truly was a remarkably good-looking man, she thought, her attention repeatedly drawn to the midnight black eyes and the wide mouth with their full lips and the way his hair kissed the top of his jacket collar. There was an almost mesmerizing capacity for stillness about him, too, that she found odd—oddly intriguing and oddly disquieting. She wished that she could feel some physical reaction to him, something that would reassure her she was still a functioning sexual being, but no, she was appreciating him as if he were a fine specimen and she an objective judge.

Gradually, the effort of maintaining a normal, civilized mask began to fatigue her. Her skin became itchy with the need to be alone. She had ventured out for too long, in too public a milieu; she was not prepared for the exhausting price of pretense.

"Sheila." There was a seriousness to Derek's tone that startled and relieved her; now, at last, he would get to the point and she could go home. "Sheila, do you remember I said that I wanted to discuss something with you that could be of mutual interest?"

"That's why I'm here, although what that could be, I haven't a clue. You're still Roger's stiffest competition, and whether he's an ex-husband or not, I just don't see how you and I could have anything to discuss."

"First of all, I'm only Roger's competition in the home shopping business *for now.*"

Sheila looked at him quizzically. "I don't understand."

"You know, of course, that BFL is hardly my only enterprise."

"Yes, but—"

"It interests me, as I said, for now. It's an exploding world, and a highly profitable one or I wouldn't bother with it. But eventually I'll decide it's time to move on—sell the business, find the next one. That's what I do, how I operate—diversity and divestiture."

"So I've heard."

"Which means that what your soon-to-be ex-husband has created as his entire universe is only a segment of mine. Understand, I don't plan for BFL not to be hugely successful, and I'll do whatever it takes to make that happen, but I'd call myself more of a nuisance to Roger than long-term competition."

Sheila's smile was knowing, her dark eyes gleamed with life as they hadn't for a while. "Why is it that the powerful always try to underplay their power? Or is it that you're merely underestimating my intelligence?"

Derek shook his head. "Neither, Sheila, believe me. All I'm saying is that *I* am the least of Roger Gainey's concerns."

"I'm afraid that I'm not following you at all, Derek, and frankly, I'm suddenly very tired. Lunch has been delightful, but I think it's time for me to go."

He put his hand on her forearm, but over her sweater, careful not to touch her skin. "Just a few more minutes, Sheila. I promise you it'll be worth it."

She hesitated, then nodded.

"I understand that for years you've been the president of Roger's production company, Media Gains." He had removed his hand, and an intensity glittered hard in his eyes, making her stiffen with anxiety, wondering where he was heading with this.

"That's right. It's a separate company, not a division or subsidiary of PCE," she told him.

He nodded. "I also understand how having one's own production company can be an outstanding source of revenue for a cable network. I decided against forming my own because I know nothing about production and what I don't know at least a little something about— enough to make me dangerous," he added with a grin, "I don't get into."

That brought a similar smile to Sheila's face. "You mean you knew something about home shopping when you started BFL?"

"No, far from it," he admitted, "but I do own two local television stations and four local radio stations in a few states, and that helped convince me I might be able to do something with cable. The home shopping part I learned by studying Roger and Barry Diller when he was running QVC."

"Fascinating, Derek, but what exactly does all this have to do with me and you?"

"Forgive me for being impertinent, but do you get to keep Media Gains in the divorce?"

"Yes," she answered promptly, giving him the answer he already knew. "And thank goodness for that, too, because I love producing the spots."

"And you're terrific at it," he said, meaning it. "I suppose that if I could have you producing spots for BFL, I'd start up my own production division as well."

Sheila's eyebrows went up. "Are you offering to buy Media Gains from Roger?"

"Why would I offer to buy it from him?"

"But, then, what—"

"You're the president of the company, Sheila. *You* determine what happens with Media Gains, not Roger. If I were looking to buy it, I'd negotiate with you."

She laughed. "I'm afraid it doesn't work that way, Derek. The company is still Roger's."

"Who owns the majority stock?" he asked, again knowing the answer.

"Well, I do, but what difference does that make? This is Roger's company. He made me the titular head for tax purposes and he's letting me hold on to it, although I'm sure his lawyers aren't too thrilled about that," she added ruefully.

Derek Lang sat back and stared at her a long, disconcerting moment, his entire body motionless, his hands still, only his black-as-danger eyes alive.

When he spoke again, the purpose that gave his voice strength earlier had been replaced by a deep, slow, almost seductive whisperlike tone that was even more daunting. "You don't get it, Sheila Gainey, but you will. You can do anything you want with Media Gains and your ex-husband can't do a damned thing about it."

"That's absolutely ridiculous," she said dismissively.

"Is it? Don't you understand? You don't have to produce spots for him and only him anymore. He gets a Media Gains infomercial when and if he is competitive with his price and his times—competitive with me and any of the other cable players *you* invite to bid for your spot. In other words, you do not have to be exclusive to PCE anymore. And believe me, Sheila, BFL is prepared to be far more appreciative of your abilities than PCE can ever be."

Sheila was quick with her rebuttal. "What you're saying may be true in terms of the law, but as far as I'm concerned, Derek, it's Roger's company to do with as he wishes. I just don't see how it could be any other way." But there was the merest hint of doubt in her voice, and Derek heard it.

Patiently and clearly he then told her about the opportunities that now existed for her as an independent production company, a company that could develop its own media placement department or contract it out; a company that could solicit accounts, personalities, products, and not worry about presell because of her knowledge of the market; a company that could attract major businesses because air time was not dictated by one single cable owner, as it was now with Roger and PCE. In other words, Derek explained, in order for Roger, her soon-to-be ex-husband to have access to Media Gains, he would have to be competitive with himself—or lose his share of the profits Media Gains generated.

"Oh my goodness," was Sheila's breathless comment when Derek finished.

"Now do you understand why I said there was something of mutual interest for us to discuss?"

"And what's in it for you, Derek?" Sheila had the presence of mind to ask.

His smile was broad. "Why, access to the best-produced infomercials available, of course—providing I pay competitively in time and price."

Sheila was silent for a moment, then she slowly shook her head. "No, Derek, no."

"No?"

"I could never do that to him."

"I'm sorry, I don't think I heard you correctly."

"I know everyone thinks what Roger has done to me is awful, but sell a spot to anyone but him? No, I couldn't do it, Derek, I just couldn't. It would be . . . well, this sounds truly lame, but it just wouldn't be very ethical."

"Ethical?" Derek repeated, dumbfounded. "You're worried about ethics with this man who—"

"I know exactly what he's done," she stopped him, "and maybe he was wrong and, yes, I've been hurt, but two wrongs don't make a right. His reasons for leaving me seem very clear and logical to him, even to me at times. But to deliberately undermine him in business?" She shook her head, rejecting the prospect absolutely. "No, I could never do that."

"What exactly is unethical about taking the business of which you're president, of which you have the majority share, to other home shopping channels? It's not as if you're cutting Roger out of the bidding. You're simply making him *one* of the players instead of *the only* player. That's not unethical, Sheila, that's good business."

"I wouldn't expect you to understand," she said gently. "You've never been married, so you don't realize that after twenty years of that kind of intimacy, old loyalties die hard. Roger may have turned my world upside down, but Media Gains is his no matter what the papers may claim legally. I'm not a vengeful person, Derek, and to make him fight for what is rightfully his seems just that, vengeful."

Derek was losing his patience, evident by his rigid body language. "First of all, Sheila, Media Gains is no longer his, period, the end, and the sooner you realize and accept that, the better for you. Secondly, I don't consider this vengeance." He paused, leaning closer to her. "It's getting back your own, Sheila. Do you have any idea the satisfaction to be had from getting back what you deserve?" He sighed and straightened away from her, his voice more conversational. "Obviously, you're not as angry as I thought most women would be at this kind of treatment. Either that, or just not interested enough in having a future without Roger leading the way."

She glanced at him sharply. "No, Derek, I guess I'm not." She put her napkin on the table, and stood up. Derek did as well, giving her a long, hard, assessing look.

"Call me if you ever do get that angry. Or that independent," he said.

"I will," she replied, not for a second meaning it.

Sheila drove more slowly than usual, eyes burning from a blinding sun and unshed tears. For the briefest of moments back there in the restaurant, Derek had been describing a vision of the future that set her heart pumping with exhilaration. She had never undervalued herself to Roger, and she believed he was well aware of how much she contributed to his success, and how competently she ran Media Gains, but to do it without PCE? To function totally independently of him? Not only did that frighten her, but how could she stab Roger in the back that way? Divorce was one thing, getting even something else entirely. It was tempting, though, sorely tempting, and it made her wonder if the unshed tears this time were for not being tough enough or angry enough or smart enough to welcome temptation with a broad smile and open arms.

Derek Lang was not disappointed by how lunch had gone. He had not really expected her to be ready to fight, not yet. But he had planted the seed, a vitally important first step. Time and temperament would do the necessary watering.

"Lang, how're you doing?"

The words broke into Derek's contemplative thoughts. He was waiting for the parking valet to get his car, and Roger Gainey had just arrived at Emilio's.

"Roger, hello, how are you?"

"Fine, fine, yourself?"

"Never better."

"Good lunch?"

"The best," Derek said, barely containing a smile.

"Yeah, Emilio's is great. Well, better run, I'm already fifteen minutes late. Good to see you."

"Sorry to hear about you and Sheila," Derek could not resist tossing out.

"Yeah, yeah, well, those things happen, right?" Roger said. "The point is, just move on and make the best of it, right?"

"Oh, absolutely, absolutely. Move on and make the best of it, my philosophy about everything."

"Well, see ya, Lang."

"Goodbye, Roger."

Move on and make the best of it. Exactly what he was planning to do, Derek thought as he generously tipped the valet and drove away, a smile glinting off his eyes, the kind adversaries had quickly learned to dread.

Chapter
Five

Know who I saw today leaving Emilio's at lunch?"

"Derek Lang."

Roger looked at Freddie with open surprise. "How'd you know that? You weren't even there."

Freddie, which he thought should have been shortened to Fred back in high school, but which no one ever called him, allowed a small smile of satisfaction to appear on his face.

"I think I must have gotten a good half-dozen calls about his being there."

Roger was puzzled. "*You* did? Why? I didn't think you even knew the guy."

"I don't, I mean, not more than a nod of recognition at a convention or what have you. It was Lang's lunch companion that had Emilio's buzzing. I'm surprised you still don't know. Even more surprised you didn't see her."

"Don't drag this out, Freddie," Roger bristled.

"Sheila."

"What about—" Roger's gray eyes widened with comprehension, and he leaned across his desk, staring at his lawyer as if the man had spoken in tongues. "No." An emphatic word of absolute denial.

"Yes."

"I don't believe it." There was just enough doubt in his voice to belie his conviction. "Why in hell would Sheila be having lunch with *him?*" He began to talk as if Freddie weren't in the room, asking questions to which he clearly expected no reply. "You don't think she'd date that slimeball, do you? No, never happen. He's not her type, not at all. For Christ's sake, the woman's been married for twenty years, what would she know about the likes of a Derek Lang? No, no, it must have been a friendly kind of lunch—people are coming out of the damn woodwork in support of her, like I did something really malicious to her. Shit, you'd think divorce was a crime. But Derek Lang? Since when is he her buddy? He's too slick, he must want something from her, that's got to be it, but that doesn't make sense either. What does Sheila have that Lang could use? Shit, Freddie," Roger concluded, now wanting a reply, "what the hell is going on?"

Freddie was sitting in Roger's spacious office, listening and observing, and the more Roger went on, the more his usually somber, saturnine features relaxed until a wide grin creased his face and merriment lighted his smallish dark eyes behind their black-rimmed glasses. Younger than Roger by six months, Freddie nonetheless seemed considerably older. His fleshy physique, his thin, almost stern mouth, the deep crevices that ran from nose to mouth, his baby-fine brown hair, which had thinned to baldness even before he was thirty—all these features factored together gave the impression of someone who was old and tired and dull. In fact, Freddie Bickford was a highly intelligent man with an old-fashioned sense of right and wrong, a conscientious lawyer whose code of justice was to play fair, never underestimate your opponent, and always give as good as you got. Twice married and divorced, with one son who lived in San Diego and had become his favorite golf partner, Freddie did not possess Roger's charm, personality, trim physique, and certainly none of his celebrity. Nevertheless, the lawyer did not have difficulty attracting women, especially in Scottsdale where there was a surfeit of women, widowed or divorced, "of a certain age" who could see the value in a bright, successful lawyer, minimum sex appeal notwithstanding.

"What's so damn funny?" Roger demanded.

"You are."

"*I* am not amused that my wife had lunch with my competition."

"First of all, she's not your wife, or won't be soon enough—though I hasten to remind you, *yet again,* that your dumb decision can still be reversed. Secondly, calling Derek Lang a slimeball is kind of like"—he shrugged and looked up at the ceiling for inspiration—"oh, I don't know, kind of like calling me dashing and debonair. I'm lots of things, Roger, but not dashing and never debonair, and Derek Lang may be many things, but a slimeball"—he shook his head—"uh-huh, I don't think so."

"Fine, fine, so what was my soon-to-be ex-wife doing with that paragon of virtue and sophistication?" Roger ran a hand through his hair in his telltale gesture of tension. "What the hell am I asking *you* for? I'll just call Sheila." And he reached for the phone.

"Roger, Brickell is due here in minutes," Freddie reminded him.

"Let him wait. I want to find out what's going on."

"It's none of your business."

That brought Roger up short. "It's not," Freddie repeated. "You don't have that right anymore," he added softly. "Unless, of course," he could not resist adding, "you change your mind about this ridiculous divorce."

"I still care about her, dammit," Roger argued, but his hand fell away from the phone. "It matters to me that she's okay, doesn't make a fool of herself with some man who—" He foundered, seeking the right words, and began to fiddle with a crystal paperweight in the shape of a dollar sign.

"A man who," Freddie finished for him, "is rich, good-looking, smart—and I hesitate only slightly to add—younger than you." Freddie's smile was so irrepressible and impish that twenty years seemed to vanish from his face.

"You bastard." But then Roger smiled, too, and continued to handle the paperweight. "Remember when Sheila gave me this?"

"Sure. To commemorate the first time your reported income to the IRS reached a million dollars."

"'To Roger. My million dollar man. Love, Sheila.'" He read the words etched on the underside of the paperweight, a bittersweet smile of remembrance on his face.

"There's something else you should keep in mind."

"About Sheila and Lang?"

Freddie nodded. "You've left her Media Gains."

"Yeah, what about it?"

"Nothing, except she owns the majority share, so what's to stop her from doing business with another network . . . say, like BFL?"

"Are you out of your fucking mind?" Roger laughed dismissively and put the paperweight back on the desktop. "That's the dumbest thing you've ever said. She can't run Media Gains by herself."

"She's been doing it for years."

"Sure, with PCE, with *me* as a guaranteed outlet. Besides, Sheila would never trust anyone but me, even with the divorce. Sheila in business with Lang? Never happen, never. I know this woman, Freddie, I lived with her for twenty years. Shit, if I don't know her, who does, and I'm telling you that she won't be able to handle Media Gains without me."

Freddie said nothing, just stared steadfastly at his friend and colleague, secretly wondering if he himself had the same vast capacity for self-delusion.

"This meeting with Brickell should be fun," was how he finally changed the subject.

Roger grimaced. "And to think I used to find the guy funny. What a pathetic loser he's turned out to be."

"What'd you expect from a compulsive gambler?"

"Perfect timing that his contract is up within the year or I'd have to fire him and pay off what was left on it. Talk about adding insult to in-jury."

The sound of his secretary's laughter could be heard through his closed door, a signal to Roger that Scott Brickell had arrived.

"Well, here goes," Roger mumbled to Freddie as his office door opened and Scott walked in.

"Brick, thanks for stopping by," Roger said, standing up to shake the comic's outstretched hand.

"Rog, good to see you, and hey, you've got the big guns here, too, I see," Scott said, nodding to Freddie. "How're you doin', Freddie?"

"I'm fine, Scott, just fine."

The comic sat down in the other available chair facing Roger's desk. "Hey, you guys, you missed one helluva time in Vegas last weekend. I knocked them dead, I swear it. There was this producer from Fox in the audience, came backstage afterward. Looks like your buddy Scott here just might be getting his own sitcom. Hell, every other *new* stand-up comedian has one, why not a real pro like me." His laugh died as his eyes darted from Roger to Freddie, back to Roger.

"So? Say something, you guys. Pretty all right, don't you think?" he pressed.

"What do I think?" Roger pretended to consider the question, his eyes meeting Freddie's for a fractional moment. "I don't know, Scott. I don't know what to think. I mean, these other stand-ups with their sit-coms, they host infomercials like you do?"

"They sure as shit don't," Scott bragged, his smile broad.

"Maybe that's because they don't have gambling debts to pay off and careers down the toilet," Roger crackled, eyes steel cold and hard.

The smile vanished from Scott's face, and he began to chew on the cuticle of his thumb, his eyes again doing their hyper dance from the lawyer to Roger, then to the gnawed skin of his thumb.

Though thirty-six, the comic had the kind of boyish looks that had gone basically unchanged since he was fourteen, except for an almost visible layering of cloud over eyes that had been a far brighter and clearer blue before he discovered that being successful meant having more money to lose betting on every college and professional sport—

including lacrosse, track and field, and wrestling—to craps, high-stakes poker, and the horses.

Scott Brickell had happened fast and hard on the entertainment A-list when he was just twenty-four, a rather short but well-muscled young man from suburban Chicago with the wholesome appeal of a Tom Cruise, but the barbed, salacious wit of a George Carlin. Scott's particular object of derision was family; he used it as the linchpin for scathingly funny riffs on everything from Girl Scout cookies to baptisms, bar mitzvahs, and burials. By the time he was thirty, he was earning seven million dollars a picture and had three hits behind him, as well as a Grammy Award–winning hit comedy record, four of his own TV variety specials, two dinners at the White House, two ex-wives, and one palimony suit. By the time he was thirty, he had also acquired a growing reputation as a catastrophe waiting to happen.

Scott had always enjoyed the rush of betting. Even when he was in high school, he'd bet with his pals on the outcome of a football or basketball game, penny-ante stuff, nothing major, but the "thrill of the spill," as he took to calling betting—the "spill" being how the both literal and figurative dice could fall—already gripped him, only he didn't know yet how obsessively.

When he started to gain a local reputation in Chicago comedy clubs, he didn't make much money, but there was always enough to bet, win, bet again, lose. Trips to the Bahamas, Vegas, Atlantic City were his idea of vacation paradise; he spent no time on the beaches and every hour in the casinos or private games. Back then, he looked upon gambling as something to relax him, take his mind off the pressures of trying to make it as a comic. Even now he could not admit he had a sickness, insisting that gambling was just a passion that occasionally got out of hand, nothing serious, joking that sex could be far more addictive.

Not for Scott Brickell, though. Nothing made him feel as strong and hot and hard and invincible as putting money on anything, anything at all, and betting that *he* and Luck had a special understanding that could not and would not fail him. And because nothing else gave him this feeling, and because Luck was both fickle and faithless, he soon

enough found himself having to do too many shows in second-rate lo-
cales to pay off debts. His career didn't exactly nosedive as much as it
sailed south, not unlike a paper airplane that drifts down to stillness.
He had met Roger a few times over the years at high-stakes poker
games in Tahoe and Vegas, and two years ago, when Scott was deep in
debt with no immediate performance to bail him out, he approached
the network owner about giving him an infomercial to host, figuring
that with his audience appeal, he'd sell out the merchandise one-two-
three, and be out of debt and back on top in no time.

Roger never hesitated, even made Scott's percentage more generous than it had to be, and Scott went on to host spots for a man's re-
ducing belt, a desktop publishing computer program, a line of men's
grooming aids. He did, indeed, make enough money to pay off his
debts. And incur new ones. Very big debts to some very big people
who did not like to be kept waiting for their money. And given the sim-
ilarity in nature of the public and Luck, both fickle and faithless,
Scott's career remained earth-bound, audiences seeking newer faces,
fresher material, ever quick to forget the idols they themselves created. To make matters worse, Scott hated doing infomercials. And to
make matters even worse than that, viewers smelled that on him as if
it were body odor. His looks might be wholesome and boyish, his patter pitch-perfectly homespun, but middle America could read the disdain in his blue eyes and they could sense the falseness in his smile
and they could hear the ridicule in his voice. Middle America couldn't
quite get themselves to trust this man they once had found so hysterically funny, and when middle America didn't trust, they didn't buy, or
if they did, it was for a test drive only, quick to return the goods. Low
sales, high returns were an infomercial host's sign-off, of the permanent variety.

He now took a deep breath, and forced his left hand to still his right
hand in his lap so he wouldn't further diminish himself by chewing on
his cuticle.

"I'm getting things under control, Roger," he said with almost pathetic pride. "And my career will be fine again, you're wrong about
that, really wrong."

"Am I?" Roger asked with terrible gentleness.

Scott nodded his head vigorously, his strawberry blond hair bobbing, and he leaned forward in his chair in a pose of enthusiasm.

"That's why I was so glad you asked for this meeting. Like they say," he flashed his ready grin in Freddie's direction, "timing is everything."

"Isn't it though?" the lawyer commented.

"I was actually going to call you, Roger, but you beat me to it," the comic went on, ignoring or not hearing the irony in the lawyer's tone. "You see, I need just a little bit of help again, Rog," he began, keeping his blue eyes wide and what the gambler was betting seemed guileless. "After this, I swear to you, I swear on my lucky chip, it'll be the last time. Not another bet, ever, I promise you." He sat back, confident that Roger would come through for him, as he always had. The lucky chip he referred to had to clinch it for Roger, who knew it was Scott's most cherished possession. It was an eighteen-carat-gold five-thousand-dollar chip from the casino in Cannes—he had won it in a game of chemin de fer during the film festival and the gorgeous starlet he had been with had convinced him to have it covered in gold—after she had found some highly inventive erotic uses for it.

"You know how the tables can be," he went on. "When they're hot, they're hot. And when they're not . . ." he shrugged and spread his arms wide in a gesture of helplessness. "But hey"—he manufactured brightness—"between the Fox deal and your help, I'll be out of the hole in no time and back raking in millions for my movies and stuff."

"How much?"

The comic jerked his head in Freddie's direction. He stared, silent.

"I think the man asked you how much, Scott."

Scott swiveled his attention back to Roger. "Not that much," he answered on a tight, small, grating laugh. "It's been worse."

"How much?" Roger insisted.

"Thirty."

"Thirty?" Roger echoed. "Thirty what, Scott? Thirty dollars? You need my help for a gambling debt of thirty dollars?" His patently false incredulity contributed to the insult of the exchange.

"Thirty thousand. Thirty. Thousand. Dollars." The words were individually enunciated, bullets of shame that left a residue of resentment burning in Scott's belly.

"Thirty thousand dollars," Roger repeated, a sound almost like awe in his voice, though the chill in his smile was a more honest expression of how he felt. "Freddie, did you hear that? Thirty thousand dollars our boy owes. Pretty impressive."

"Impressive," was Freddie's dry agreement.

"Roger, Freddie, this is the last time, I swear it," Scott rushed in. "I swear it on my lucky chip and you know I would never do that if I didn't mean it. I'm a man of my word, guys."

"What happened to Gamblers Anonymous?"

"What?" Scott looked at Freddie.

"I believe he's referring to your promise the last time this happened that you'd go to Gamblers Anonymous," Roger reminded him.

"Yeah, well, I guess I lapsed." Another shrug, followed again by that lightninglike brightness. "But this time I mean it, you'll see. I know I've just been fooling myself with this crap about being able to stop whenever I want. I can't, I accept that now. So once I'm over this latest—"

His words faded as he watched Roger pick up the crystal dollar-sign paperweight and drop it from one hand to the other, his eyes unblinkingly riveted on the comic with that horribly humorless smile fixed in place. Like most addictive personalities, Scott Brickell had the tendency to be both self-absorbed and self-delusionary. How else to be convinced that he alone was Luck's favorite? And so, as happened too often when Scott gambled, he was surprised to discover that he had lost again.

"You're not going to loan me the money, are you, Roger?"

Roger shook his head, continuing with the paperweight and the smile.

"But there's more, isn't there?"

This time Roger nodded, placed the dollar sign back on his desk and relaxed his face into the honest disgust he was feeling.

"You have three months left on your contract, Brickell. There'll be no renewal."

"What? What did you say?"

"You're out. O.U.T. from PCE. Finished. Done. Gone."

"You can't do that!" Scott half-rose from the chair, his face flushing an unattractive pink.

"I can't?" Roger repeated with acid amusement. "Scott, Scott, no wonder you're in such deep shit, you don't have a clue what a loser you really are."

Scott Brickell breathed deeply, his eyes almost popping as he glared at Roger with utter disbelief. "If you don't renew my contract, you'll be making a big mistake, Roger, a big one. I'm loved by all those stupid overweight women out there in middle America with hair growing on their chins and Twinkie crumbs between their teeth. They'll destroy you if you don't keep me on the air for them." He sat back, so completely convinced in his vision that the initial shock of Roger's words was already fading into history.

Roger was calm as he said, "I think you overvalue yourself, Scott: as a gambler, most definitely; as a comic, regrettably; and as an infomercial host?" He shook his head in mock sorrow. "Well, as an infomercial host, you overvalue yourself totally. The truth is, as a host for all those fat, hairy women you have no use for, you suck, big time."

Scott gazed at Roger for several moments, swallowing hard, his hand almost involuntarily coming up to his mouth, the skin by his thumb gnawed at until he could regain some semblance of composure.

At last he said, "I don't know why you're doing this, Roger, why you're making up such lies, but—"

"Lies? Freddie here just happens to have with him the record of sales and returns on your shows, Scott. Freddie, show him what the truth looks like."

"I don't need to see anything." Scott waved Freddie back to his chair. "I don't give a shit what the accounts say, I know I'm good and I know those women out there love me. If returns are up, take a look at the product, or the scripts or the time slots. Take a look at the mistakes *you* make, Gainey, and stop blaming me." His hand was away from his mouth, and anger was slowly seeping through him, fueling him with an energy that Roger had almost stolen from him.

"So that's what you think, that your lousy numbers are my fault?"

Scott got to his feet. "Yeah, Gainey, that's what I think. And I'm gonna prove I'm right, too."

"Oh? And how are you planning to do that?"

"You're not the only horse at the gate, Gainey, not by a long shot. You're gonna wish you still had me on your stupid channel, just wait and see."

Roger stared at the younger man a long, heavy minute. "Of course I'm not the only horse at the gate, Scott," he agreed too nicely. "But I'm the only one who'd risk you on a ride. The only one. You're such a big-time gambling man, Brick, why don't you bet against that?"

Scott walked toward the door, then turned. "The only bet I want to make right now, Gainey, is on when your luck is gonna change. I'm gonna bet big, really big that it's gonna be much sooner than you could possibly imagine."

Chapter
Six

"Freedom. There's nothing like it, nothing. No one telling you when to do things you don't want to do. No one telling you not to do things you do want to do. You know those 'quiet lives of desperation' you're always hearin' about? Maybe even thought you've been livin' yourself? Well, they can be gone, over, just so much rubbish in the trash heap of disappointments.

"Twenty-two, just twenty-two little steps and your financial slavery is over, the ball and chain of working for anyone but yourself ended forever, leaving you economically, psychically, and emotionally master of your own universe.

"Peck's *Ladder to Liberty* has just twenty-two short, little steps, but they can be the most important steps you've ever taken. They lead to change and freedom and the kind of life you never dared dream could be yours. But dare to dream—because that kind of life *can* be yours! It happened to me and now I want to share what I've learned so it can happen to you."

You're good, boy. You are damned good." Keeping his arm around the naked blond woman on his right, Abraham Lincoln Peck, née Jack Rangel, remoted off the television and his number one selling infomercial. Peck's *Ladder to Liberty* was currently in its sixteenth month with not a sign of it lessening in popularity, and with Peck never tiring of watching himself. No one except Anthony Robbins came close to him for moneymaking charisma. And balls, he often thought. Like any good con artist, Rangel had sniffed around, smelled a weakness, and reinvented himself to take advantage of that weakness. The result became the number one selling infomercial, a bestselling book, a best-selling book on tape, a bestselling video, sold-out weekend seminars at $2,500 a person, without room or board, television appearances, invitations to talk everywhere from Bangkok to Boston, first class all the way. He was a star, *the* star of PCE, if not of all cable airwaves.

"How about some more wine?"

"Sure, Linc," came in stereo, since there was also a naked redhead curled in the circle of his left arm.

He loved it. He just never got tired of being catered to, sucked up to, accommodated, *pleased,* just as he never got tired of watching his infomercial. He eased his arms away from both women, giving each of them an affectionate caress on their rears as they got out of the bed. The blonde had the kind of body that was enjoying its moment of perfection when everything was so physically harmonious that it could not possibly be sustained for longer than a year or two. She was at that point of pure ripeness now, probably no more than nineteen, and magnificent. The redhead, on the other hand, had a few more circles around the tree trunk; she must be at least twenty-seven, twenty-eight, he figured, but the few extra years certainly served to prove the old saying that practice made perfect. She was a particularly adept oral expert, and Jack Rangel was a particularly ardent oral enthusiast.

To them, he was Linc. He had tried out Abe for a while but the weighty associations that came with that name made him uncomfortable, so he became Linc. To no one was he Jack Rangel. That guy dropped out of existence the day the metal gates of Joliet State Penitentiary in Illinois opened for him after three years inside. But it took another six hard years for Abraham Lincoln Peck to be born. In the intervening years, he tried to go legit, but scam was as much a part of him as his pale, Christ-blue eyes or the slight cleft in his chin, or the thick, straight, India ink dark hair that was still plentiful, a genetic blessing from his black Irish father. He could no more get rid of any of this than he could stop being a con man. From the time he was four-teen and charming his teachers into better grades than he deserved, to now, twenty years later, he understood and respected the awesome power in the art of persuasion, and the equally impressive willingness of most people to let themselves be persuaded. A slow, sleepy smile and a midwestern twang deliberately tinged with a touch of sugar for that good ol' boy effect; a tall, rangy body that made men think of cow-boy and women stop thinking straight at all; a facility to read instantly what a person needed and a wholesome sincerity that tricked people into believing he could supply it—all this made Jack Rangel one very good scammer.

For a while he was so good at it that he got sloppy, underestimating his marks, and so he landed in Joliet when some old folks, animal lovers all, discovered they had not been contributing to a fund headed by Dr. Rangel, eminent veterinarian, for research into increased longevity for Fido and Muffin, but rather into a very private and per-sonal fund known as Jack Rangel's pockets. In the course of the inves-tigation, the prosecution uncovered offenses from pyramid schemes to kiting checks. Jack knew he had been lucky to get off with only three years inside, and the day he walked out a free man, he vowed two things: to never underestimate anyone again, no matter how tempting it was to do so; and to figure out a better way for himself, even if it meant going legit. And for a while he got by, but getting by wasn't what Jack wanted for himself. It was the advent of home shopping and in-fomercials that set his always opportunistic wheels spinning, and a lady named Sheila Gainey who took the gamble that turned his life around.

Like most good con artists, Jack considered himself a gentleman thief. As such, he adhered to a code of honor that dictated no one he scammed ever be physically hurt; that fools are fair game; and that loy-alty should be rewarded, whenever possible. In his lifetime, he had damaged people's pride and bank accounts, never their person, and he had met and used a lot of fools; only Doobie, his shepherd-collie mongrel, had been worthy of his loyalty, and he had died when Jack was seventeen. His contract to Roger Gainey was tighter than his prison-cell lock, but his loyalty was to the man's ex-wife, and in the few months since the divorce, Jack had made sure everyone knew exactly how he felt.

On impulse, he picked up the portable telephone from his night table, and punched in Sheila's number.

"Here's your wine, Linc, honey," the blonde said, coming back into the bedroom.

"Thanks, babe. Why don't you two head into the Jacuzzi or maybe the shower, huh? I'll join you just as soon as I finish this call."

"A call now, Linc? I thought we're here to party," the redhead pouted.

"Hello?" came a sleepy voice.

"Sheila?" Jack waved the two women away, and when the blonde ignored him and started to put her head under the sheet from the foot of the bed, Jack kicked off the sheet angrily. "Out. Now," he whispered harshly, with a fiercer wave of his hand. The two young women looked at each other, shrugged, and then flounced off, hips rocking provocatively.

"Linc? Is that you?"

"Hey, Sheila, how're you doing?"

"Linc, it's two o'clock in the morning."

"Is it? Hey, what the hell, probably somewhere it's eight in the evening." He laughed. "Sheila?" His voice now was serious. "I'm sorry if I woke you, but I worry about you, that's all. I guess I wasn't thinking about the time."

"I guess you weren't thinking, period," she said, but kindly. "Having one of your little parties?"

"Yeah. You know what I always say, why be—"

"I know, I know—why be civilized when you can make a real pig of yourself." She laughed. "I'm flattered that at such a time, you thought of me."

"I care about you, Sheila, and I want to make sure you're okay."

"Thank you, Linc, I appreciate your concern, but I'm fine. I'll be especially fine when I get back to sleep."

"I really wish I could do something besides let everyone, including Roger, know what a dumb schmuck I think he is."

"Oh, Linc, stop saying things like that. Ever since it happened, you seem to think you can only like one of us, and you've chosen me because—"

"Because you went to the mat for me, Sheila," Linc broke in. "Because you and only you saw the potential in me, in my video, which Roger could not, and it was you who convinced him to give me a chance. You understood what I was doing and Roger didn't—he couldn't get that the time was right, that the public was looking for a quick fix that combined money and morality. It was the perfect infomercial and you sensed that. Come on, Sheila, if it weren't for you there'd be no *Ladder to Liberty*. Hell, if it weren't for you, there wouldn't even be a damn PCE!"

Linc heard the quick intake of breath on the other end. "Sheila, honey? I'm sorry, I didn't mean to upset you."

"I'm fine, Linc, honest."

"You sure?"

"I'm sure."

"Sheil? There's something else. I've been meaning to ask you about this for a while, but it seemed a little crass and selfish."

This brought a smile to Sheila's voice. "That's never stopped you before."

"I guess I just wanted to wait until some time had gone by."

"I'm not in mourning, Linc, I'm just trying to put my life back together. It's been three months. You can be crass and selfish with me if you want," she teased.

"Roger told me you'll still be producing my spots. I just wanted to make sure that was true. I'm working on something new and I—"

"Continuing in the fine tradition of exploitation by inspiration, no doubt?"

"Of course." Linc was taken aback slightly by Sheila's uncharacteristic cynicism. "So will you be handling it for me?"

There was enough hesitation at the other end for Linc to frown with puzzlement.

"Not necessarily," was what he soon heard.

"Not necessarily?" Linc repeated. "I don't understand. Roger said that Media Gains is still his production company, that nothing had changed as far as that was concerned."

"Roger is wrong," Sheila stated. "Media Gains is mine, not his. He has a large percentage, of course, but I'm the president, I have the majority stock, I run it, although," she added with a dry laugh, "not as well as I should have these past few months. Be that as it may, Roger is in no position, legally or otherwise, to determine what infomercials Media Gains will and will not be producing in the future."

Linc could not believe what he was hearing. "You can't be serious, Sheil," he said quietly.

This time her laugh was fuller. "Probably not, Linc, probably not. It's just that someone pointed out to me recently that I don't have to be exclusive to PCE anymore and I—"

"Someone who?"

"That's not important. What is important is that I can now choose what spots I want to produce and where they get sold, I can even go after my own manufacturers and celebrities if I want. You, unfortunately, are under contract to PCE, so you have no choice. I, on the other hand, do."

"I can't believe you'd really take your business anywhere else. Roger's a shit, true, Sheila, but he's also got the best home shopping operation going. Besides, it's *me* we're talking about here, not some stranger."

An audible sigh, then, "It was just a thought, Linc. Don't pay any attention to what I'm saying, okay? It's late and I'm half asleep. Ignore my gibberish."

"I don't know—"

"Good night, Linc. And thanks for the kind thoughts."

"Sheila, I—"

"Good night, Linc." And the line went dead.

For a few minutes, Linc remained where he was, considering what Sheila Gainey had said to him. He didn't really think she would venture out on her own. She was bright and quick, but also very sheltered. He could not imagine her working with people she didn't know at QVC or BFL. She might have been knocked for a loop by Roger the husband, but Roger the businessman was someone she could trust. Hell, even *he* trusted Roger professionally. No doubt one of her friends had been muttering in her ear about striking out on her own, and she was tasting the concept as if it were a new, exotic food. She'd get over it.

But because Jack Rangel could read people well, he also knew when they were lying, to him or to themselves. So as he got out of bed now to join the women in the Jacuzzi, he recognized he was guilty of the latter. He wanted Sheila to produce his spots, but there was no guarantee, there never was with anything, and so there was no percentage in telling himself what he wanted instead of what might be.

He looked around at his huge circular bedroom, with its wall of glass, its five-hundred-square-foot walk-in, hell, *live*-in closet, its state-of-the-art media entertainment system. He could push a button and the ceiling of his bedroom, one immense skylight, could open to the Arizona stars. Outside were his pool and Jacuzzi and even a nine-hole putting green. All this was part of an empire that he wouldn't put at risk for anybody, not even a friend. He wanted Sheila to produce him, but if she didn't, so be it. His contract was with PCE, and so, ultimately, it was Roger who had to be pleased, Roger who determined when spots aired, Roger who could make or break him.

Friendship? Loyalty? Nice in theory, but not terribly practical.

Sheila was unable to go back to sleep right away. Something Linc had said kept playing itself over and over in her mind, something that was an exaggeration, to be sure, but not without its elements of truth.

Twelve years ago, Freddie Bickford's then brother-in-law, who had been in the storage business in the Southwest, found himself with property donated to him by the owners since all their money would be tied up in federal legal matters for years to come. The brother-in-law hadn't known what to do with the cases of steak knives from Taiwan, portable radios from Malaysia, "brass" kitchen canister sets from Sri Lanka that had all "fallen off" trucks and landed in his warehouse. Would Freddie, a lawyer, please figure out a way to unload the stuff?

He did. The goods were used as premiums on some of the game shows Media Gains was producing. The sideline proved so successful that Freddie was soon seeking out overseas manufacturers who would sell them goods in bulk. The money poured in. Roger then had the idea to try a commercial-only show—a commercial that would be entertaining, that would be the entertainment. It was from that point on that Sheila's influence marked so many key events. It was she who believed they should try out the concept on cable, since so many American homes were subscribing to cable access. It was she who persuaded a local cable station manager that he'd be getting in on the ground floor of a gold mine if he'd let them have fifteen minutes of airtime as cheaply as possible. It was Sheila who convinced Roger that he needed a demonstrator for his products, and who better than himself, a natural salesman?

From there it was just a matter of years before Roger offered to buy out Freddie's share of Media Gains, and use the money to form PCE. And from there, Sheila now thought ironically, it was just a matter of a few years before Roger divorced her.

Linc had said that if it weren't for her, there'd be no *Ladder to Liberty*. And he was right. Just as there would have been no AstroAge for Alicia Devon, marking the advent of the nonconsumer good infomercial that made millions of dollars for PCE. But what was playing itself over and over in her mind, keeping her awake, was what else Linc had said. About there not even being a PCE if it weren't for her.

An exaggeration, but not without its truth. What Roger had achieved, he had not done alone. There was Freddie, of course, but much had been her vision and her keen understanding of her husband's strengths.

She might not be ready to take Derek Lang seriously and go off on her own, she thought as she turned off the light, but even voicing the possibility to Linc tonight had signaled a major step forward. Now if she could just get some of that nice, healthy anger to kick in, she'd know she really was beginning to heal.

Chapter
Seven

Sheila did not immediately leave her car. She briefly shut, then re-opened her eyes, and swallowed hard. She was not yet ready to take those few steps into the PCE offices. This afternoon would be the first time in four months that she would be attending a PCE product development meeting. The first time since Roger left, in fact, that she would be entering these offices.

Throughout the intervening months, Roger would call periodically, their conversations a stilted mixture of personal and business. After the first few times, at Sheila's insistence, he called her at the Media Gains office. As she explained, speaking to him at home was still too intimate not to hurt. And because her social life consisted of an occasional lunch, and her evenings always home, always alone, she had been able to avoid almost total face-to-face contact with him during this time.

She wasn't even sure anymore if she loved Roger. Her emotions were gradually evolving from pain at the breakup of her marriage and the loss of a man she had believed was her partner, to a dull ache over what he had done to her. Though anger toward him had not truly ignited yet, there remained only vestiges of self-recrimination and a simmering resentment that felt much better than the dull ache. What she did not need right now was a business meeting with the man.

About a month ago, he had started asking her to come back to PCE's weekly product development meeting, telling her, with truly awesome arrogance, she had thought at the time, that their divorce should not stand in the way of a terrific team in business. A flash of anger like heat lightning would course through her, but she would just say no, she wasn't comfortable being with all those PCE people yet. This week he had insisted, and she had called Freddie to find out why her presence was so important to Roger this time. Media Gains would produce whatever he wanted them to produce, everyone knew that. Well, no, she supposed that wasn't precisely true, given the legal arrangement, but of course she would produce whatever he wanted. No matter what the arrangement, or for that matter, what Derek Lang said, she couldn't shake the notion that Media Gains belonged to Roger. If he wanted her to produce a spot on magic egg rolls, she would, which is why his pushing her to attend today's meeting made no sense.

"Because he's bored," Freddie had explained.

"Oh, has he discovered that putting together an infomercial requires actual work?" Sheila had remarked.

"He doesn't even know the right questions to ask anymore," Freddie had gone on. "He's been so busy lining up celebrities and buying up cable time and—"

"And getting divorced."

". . . that all he keeps grumbling is 'Sheila knows about that,' or 'Ask Sheila.' You know how much he hates the details."

"You mean what you and I do for a living?"

"He needs you, Sheila." Freddie's voice softened.

"No, I don't think so. Besides, it's good for him to learn a little humility," she said with more animation, to dispel the suddenly somber tone.

"Let him remember what his roots are, how he got to be Mr. Infomercial."

"He needs you for that now, too. He's got a major celebrity and needs focus on the product."

"Who?"

"Come to the meeting, Sheila," Freddie hedged.

"Ah, Freddie, I can't."

"Come to the meeting, Sheil. It's time."

What had she said to Linc Peck—that she wasn't in mourning? But of course she was, for all that had been familiar and was now so chillingly strange. It was called life, she thought with a small, ironic smile as she gathered up her purse and briefcase, and it was time to get on with hers.

As she walked briskly toward the conference room, she was grateful she didn't see too many people, not sure she could handle the saccharinely sympathetic expressions she knew she would find in their eyes, their tentative smiles, and her responsibility to ease their burden by mouthing vacuous assurances that she was "fine, never better." She was about to turn the corner into the conference room, when down the hall she saw Alicia Devon exit Roger's office, then stride past Leila, his secretary, as if she did not exist.

Sheila had not seen Alicia for a long while, but she had heard, of course, what Roger's plans for her were if sales did not improve, just as she had heard that Scott Brickell was finished at PCE. Sheila had been so wrapped up in her own world that she hadn't really bothered with anyone else, but now, at the sight of Alicia, a woman she had always enjoyed, and to whom she would always be more than a little grateful for helping turn Media Gains and PCE into the megasuccess they became, she felt her pulse quicken with a genuine interest to find out how someone else was faring. Sheila just then realized how terribly selfish divorce made a person.

"Alicia, hi, how great to see you," Sheila warmly approached the other woman, arms outstretched for a hug. The expression on Alicia's face left Sheila's warmth stillborn. "Alicia? What is it? What on earth is wrong?"

The country singer looked at Sheila, but saw only someone closely linked to Roger. What Sheila observed was someone visibly filling with rage, her body, her lips, her chin quivering as it spread through her, only her blue eyes glassy and bright, but not with anger, with pain.

"He'll never get away with it," she hissed. "I told him not to do it. I warned him. Now he'll pay, I swear it."

"Alicia—" Sheila reached out a hand, but the singer twisted away.

"What did *you* do to get dumped by him—did your ratings slip in the matrimonial bed?" Alicia's laugh was as brittle as breaking glass.

"Oh, Alicia, I'm so sorry," Sheila tried, ignoring the sting of her remark. "I had heard that—"

"You had heard? That's a good one." Suddenly the singer looked hard at Sheila, eyes narrowing as she assessed a possibility. "How do I know *you* didn't encourage it?"

"What? What are you talking about? I—"

"Sure, you could have done that. Dumped yourself, you just want to make sure others go down with you. But I'll tell you something, just like I told your husband. Alicia Devon does not get treated like some ignorant, backwater know-nothing. I was a big, big country music star and then I became the Queen of Infomercials. Now what does that tell you?"

"It tells me—"

"It says that Alicia Devon has what it takes to be a winner no matter what." She stood up straighter, her floral scarf, her bracelets, her dangling earrings—everything in motion except her helmet of hair. "I won't let anyone take away what I've worked hard for and what I deserve, and that's to be on top. You and your husband better not forget one thing about me. I'm a fighter. I fought my way out of Alabama's dirt roads and I fought my way to the top of the charts and then I fought my way to the throne of this new world of infomercials. Don't you and your damned husband ever, ever forget that when you try to hurt Alicia Devon, you're up against a fighter who knows how to win, and who'll play dirty if necessary in order to keep on winning."

"Alicia, you don't—" But Sheila's few words were already falling on Alicia's back as the woman stormed off. In the old days, Sheila would have gone into Roger's office to discuss this dreadful conversation with him. But this was supposed to be a new day for her, and what he did with Alicia Devon was not her concern. The truth was, though, that Roger was not a deliberately mean individual. He would not move Alicia to a spree on a second-rate shift unless he had a very good reason for it. Even when she had been more closely involved with PCE, she had seen for herself that Alicia's spots were not claiming their old audience share. Still, the truth did not make change any easier to take, nor did understanding make the ugly confrontation she had just endured any less discomfiting.

"Well, that was charming. You okay?"

"Oh, hi, Leila," Sheila said, still reeling and unaware that Roger's secretary had come up to her. "I'm fine, but poor Alicia." Sheila had always liked Leila, a woman of about forty whose ambition was simple: keep her family happy, and if working helped do that, so be it. She didn't want to rule the world. She and her husband, a riding instructor at a local dude ranch, would rather have a life than a living.

"Forget Alicia. What about you? I've missed you."

Sheila smiled her appreciation. "Thanks. I'm fine. At least, I'm getting better. How's that?"

"Honest. You here for the product development meeting?" Sheila nodded. "Good," Leila went on. "It's nice to have you back where you belong." She glanced at Roger's closed door and screwed up her face. "The big idiot."

They walked the few steps to the conference room, Sheila making polite chitchat until Leila turned and went down another corridor. Then Sheila was alone with the closed conference room door facing her. She was thankful that at least Roger wouldn't be there yet.

But there was Freddie, who quickly came up to hug her, and two men from finance, several people from marketing and merchandising, regional sales managers to represent the cable stations and what they were likely to do well with, a whole contingent of opinions who helped determine whether Media Gains would produce, and PCE would air a product. Everyone came over to welcome her.

"Hey, you guys, I'm here for this one meeting only," she said, laughing, when she was able to come up for air. "This isn't a permanent thing again."

"We'll see about that."

The buzz immediately ceased at the sound of the boss's voice. There were a few tentative "Hello, Rogers" as seats were taken, eyes fixed on the couple.

"Hello, Sheila, it's good to see you," and Sheila, aware that she was being watched with the kind of rapt attention usually reserved for an auto accident, said, "Roger," and then smoothly stepped away just as he was about to lean in for a kiss. She took her usual seat, because everyone had left it vacant for her, the one at the opposite end of the table from Roger. She gnawed gently at the inside of her lower lip, dreading the next few hours.

"I'm glad you could make it," he said when he had settled in.

What choice did you give me? she wanted to say, but merely nodded. Then, "Freddie mentioned something about needing a product for a key celebrity. Why don't we get right to it?"

"Did you tell her everything?" Roger asked. Sheila immediately noticed his displeasure when he looked at the lawyer.

"Freddie told me nothing," she quickly interjected. She wished her heartbeat would slow down just enough so that she could hear herself speak, and she wished her tongue didn't feel as if it were scraping sandpaper. She was a nervous wreck, jittery and tense, and so on edge that she was sure she would not be able to maintain a public balance for the entire time this meeting would last. And then Sheila let herself remember that Roger had humiliated her once, enough to last a lifetime. She'd be damned if she ever gave him a chance to do it a second time.

"Okay, everybody," Roger began, "this is big news, which is why I'm glad Sheila is here." He smiled down the length of the table at her, but the face that looked back at him was expressionless. "Freddie knows about this, of course"—a nod to his lawyer—"and Rick Lovell," he added—another nod to his head of marketing—"but that's it." He leaned forward, gray eyes alive, such a familiar warmth in them that

Sheila's breath quickened. "We've got a chance, people, to snare George Hamilton for an infomercial."

He sat back, looked around the room and Sheila followed his gaze, noting, as did he, the total absence of expected excitement.

"What's wrong with you people?" he barked. "I'm talking Gorgeous George Hamilton, for Christ's sake!"

"What's the big deal?" commented Dina, a very hip, aggressive, ambitious woman from marketing. "He's old hat, Roger."

"Need I remind you that so is everyone who does an infomercial, that's the whole point." His look beseeched Sheila to help him, but she remained stone-faced.

Dina shrugged with disinterest. "I thought we were trying to trend up, get products or people that would attract younger, hipper audiences."

"We're trying to do both," her boss, Rick Lovell, said. "Roger, snaring Hamilton would be great, as I told you when you first mentioned the possibility. The key is the product. We need something that won't be taken either as a joke or as condescending. We've had that problem too many times with Brickell and we can't take that chance with George Hamilton."

"I agree totally," Roger said. "And that's the purpose of this meeting. Hamilton's agent has made it very clear to me, as I'm sure he has to BFL, QVC, all of us, that where his client goes is dependent on the product. He figures, rightly, that we'll all give him the deal he wants. Hamilton needs to keep up his public exposure since his talk show with his ex-wife failed, and that commercial for cream cheese didn't do much for his image either. But give him the right infomercial, and we all profit."

"So what are the possibilities?" asked Vince Palmer, the regional sales manager for the mid-Atlantic states. "Hamilton doesn't play the same in Delaware as he does in . . . say, Florida, with all those old farts. We need something if not as hip as Dina here would like, then something better than cream cheese."

Nate MacKensie was in charge of the vendors, and for the next forty minutes he put on a show-and-tell of products and product possibilities that ranged from a candy maker to a robotic lawn mower to a computer travel system. Since 1984, when the FCC lifted its limit of twelve commercial minutes for every one hour of programming on television, and the modern infomercial was born, certain categories evolved as top sellers. Health and fitness, beauty and personal care, recreation and leisure, automobile care, self-improvement, crafts, household and kitchen appliances ranked high, and when any one of these was combined with the right celebrity, everybody got rich. That was why the weekly product development meeting was so crucial, and why this particular one more crucial than most.

"The exercise system for men over fifty. The line of men's grooming products. The home tanning system—absolutely a natural for Hamilton. And the expert on phrenology and physiognomy," Roger finally declared.

Sheila, who had remained silent throughout Nate's presentation, burst out laughing. "You're joking!"

The room thrummed with the delicious tension that erupted whenever the personal and the professional went head to head.

"Why is that so funny?" Roger asked, too quietly.

"You need to ask? What's next, Roger, the numerology hotline, a handwriting analyst?" She turned her attention to Nate. "Is there an actual expert on this phrenology stuff?"

"Well, no."

"A tape? A book? Anything?"

"Uh, no."

"So there's no product per se, is that right?"

"I'm afraid not."

"Which means there are no testimonials in place." This was not a question, and Sheila looked back to Roger. "No product, no expert, no testimonials. Are they or are they not the three major no-nos to proceeding with a concept?"

"They are, but so what?" Roger shot back. "With Hamilton, we'll make the video, write the book, find the expert. The rules change for someone like him."

Sheila nodded as if in accord. "I still don't think it's right for the man known as Gorgeous George, a man whose skull and face are so perfect that his credibility is immediately diminished. And the home tanning system is no better. Talk about the obvious," she moaned.

Roger seemed to consider that. "You may have a point," he conceded.

Sheila's heart was still beating rapid-fire, but there wasn't a scintilla of nervous tension driving her. Now there was the exhilarating rush of doing what she loved to do and was so good at—asking the questions, seeing the possibilities, understanding the business of infomercials. Freddie had said it. This was the part of the job Roger had lost interest in a long time ago, the details that made the difference between a successful spot and a failure.

"Sheila's right," Vince Palmer dared. "It makes no sense to allocate money to produce and test-market a product that has absolutely nothing going for it but a high concept. Even someone with audience appeal like Hamilton can't make magic, not with audiences getting more and more sophisticated about what they spend their money on. The product has to match the celebrity."

"What about the grooming products?" Roger asked.

"What about them?" Nate responded.

"Is there a product? Is there a credible name attached? Are there testimonials? What does it cost to manufacture? How high can our markup be? Can it be mass-produced easily? Will it ship easily?" Sheila ticked off the key questions, barely coming up for air. When she was finished, she felt herself swell at the sea of faces smiling at her with approval. Her own lips twitched slightly when she caught Freddie's wink.

Before Roger could utter a word, Nate began to answer Sheila's questions. "Three of six products exist. Two Beverly Hills dermatologists are in partnership for the line. They've done the video already. I've got it in my office."

"Retail price?" Wayne Frisch, the finance chief, wanted to know.

"Under a hundred dollars with some freebies thrown in."

"Possible," Sheila muttered, "possible." She looked over to Roger. "What do you think?"

"Does it matter?" It was said as a joke, and everyone tittered, except Sheila. "To tell you the truth," he went on, "aside from the fact that so much of it is in place, I don't really like this one anymore. It's not as obvious as the tanning system, but it's still exactly the kind of product people would expect Hamilton to push."

"Is that so bad?" Dina asked.

Sheila understood immediately. "Yes, it is. One of the reasons Dionne Warwick's Psychic Network has been so huge is because no one could believe someone who sang Burt Bacharach would have anything to do with crystal balls and other weird stuff. It's sweetness and light versus the so-called 'dark side' and that contradiction has made it work." Her smile was crooked as she said, "Roger's right. We need something suitable to Hamilton's image, but not that obvious."

"Thanks, Sheila," Roger said, his tone brisk. "I told everyone how important it was for you to be here for this and that's been made extremely obvious. All right, let's move on with this. Nate, give us more on the exercise system."

"It's called Push Power," Nate described. "It's strictly for men, and for men over fifty."

Roger liked what he was hearing. "Good, good. Target market, the best kind. Find the niche and sell into it."

"Okay, let's get to the details," Sheila said. "Is it in existence?"

"Yes. The manufacturer is from Minnesota, has merched it for about a year now, great response. We have endorsements and testimonials up the wazoo, from users who talk about how effective it is and how easy to assemble, from doctors, personal trainers, the whole nine yards, but no video."

"How much?" Vince Palmer asked.

"You're not going to like the answer," Nate admitted. "It's been retailing for three hundred sixty-five dollars."

"Forget it," the regional manager stated. "No way our consumer will go for that, no matter what part of the country she's from. And don't forget it will be a *she* who buys it. For a price like that she's gonna want something for herself, not her aging hubby."

"Don't forget to factor in the cost of producing the video," Rick reminded them, "plus wouldn't you need a fitness expert to actually work the machine?"

"Not necessarily," Sheila said consideringly. "Hamilton's in good shape. Why not use *him* to show how effective the system is for men pushing past fifty, which he certainly is and then some. You save the cost of a fitness expert, plus you increase the credibility factor."

"But the cost, Sheila," Palmer objected. "We've got to get it down to under three hundred."

"We can do that," she assured him.

"No way, Sheila, forget it," Roger said. "What else do you have, Nate? We've got to find—"

"I think we can do it." Sheila plowed ahead. "As a come-on, we offer Push Power for an under three hundred price and it'll be for a limited time only, so the idea is a bargain and a unique opportunity, two solid sales hooks. Then, assuming the spot takes off, we up the price and figure out some other kind of hook to keep sales going, maybe some kind of freebie, or a three-minute free call to Hamilton himself. I don't know, we'll worry about it when the spot takes off." Her eyes narrowed as she weighed the possibilities.

The room went quiet again, this time because they knew they had heard something that could definitely work.

"I'll look into offshore manufacturers," Freddie said, "and then we'll run some financials, as usual. When you factor in Hamilton's percentage and his insurance, I still don't know if this is doable, but we'll take a look," he added with sobering practicality.

"What do you figure the production would cost, Sheila?" Roger asked. "The usual?"

Sheila thought about that. "At least one hundred thousand dollars to produce it, another thirty thousand to fifty thousand to test-market."

"And then we're looking at fifty thousand dollars a week for airtime," Wayne Frisch reminded them. "Let's not forget that only one in eight of these gets beyond the test run, so let's ask ourselves if we're willing to make the investment on this one."

Roger didn't hesitate. "I sure as hell don't want even George Hamilton's failure to go to BFL or QVC. Let's move on it. Sheila? What do you think?"

She put her pad and pen in her briefcase, snapped it shut, sat back, and stared at him, all the while not speaking. Finally, she said, "I think it may be viable because we're not dealing with pure concept. You've given Rick something to look at in terms of past performance and Freddie has a product and manufacturing prices to help in his negotiations. You've given Media Gains something to work with so we don't have to invent a valid spot. All these points are pluses. I'm not pleased that we have to create the video, and I do think the price is high, but my idea may mitigate that. In the end, though, it's your call, Roger. Isn't it?" There was just enough tartness in the way she said his name that the room again stilled, anxious about the anticipated showdown that had not yet happened.

Sheila got to her feet and started toward the door; Roger was immediately on his way to her. She stilled him with an outstretched palm. "I know the way out. It was good seeing you all." And before anyone, especially Roger, could say or do another thing, she was out of the room, striding purposefully down the hall, not taking a really full, calm breath until she was in the car.

Once home, she immediately poured herself a glass of chardonnay, and greedily downed two gulps that helped loosen the tightness in her neck and shoulders. How she loved the business! she thought, taking her wine into the living room, staring out through her sliding glass door that exposed the wondrously changing colors of an Arizona sunset, pinks and oranges and yellows and purples too vivid and unique for any palette but Nature's to create. She had not appreciated the sunset for too many months. But she was able to do it this evening. And she was actually tasting the dry, white chill of the wine, instead of drinking it for emotional numbness.

Today had not been easy, being with those people and, of course, with Roger, almost as if nothing had happened, nothing had changed, when everything in her world had altered. But the exuberant feeling of being back where she belonged could not be ignored. For months now she had been going to her office at Media Gains, but she had been mechanical, uninspired. Today, she felt the stirrings of her old enthusiasm, that indescribable satisfaction that came from liking what you were doing and knowing you did it well. She did know how to produce an infomercial. And she did know how to make producers happy and manufacturers comfortable. And she did know all the little dotted i's and crossed t's it took to get a spot working, a product successful, a celebrity communicating. She respected the details and because she did, she knew what questions to ask and what answers were correct. Roger's talents were his charm, his instinct about audiences, his natural salesmanship. Together, they had been outstanding. Today, for the first time, she realized that even alone, she could be a force to be reckoned with.

She took another taste of her wine, sat back and smiled into her empty room, feeling vibrantly alive and whole, almost as much as she used to before Roger's decision. He had insisted she attend his product development meeting to help him. She had dreaded going, but she had done it. And then, what had started out as an ordeal, a performance, had become healing therapy. Sheila was smiling expansively now, not because she felt so much better, but because Roger would be so very, very surprised what asking for her help would end up costing him.

Chapter
Eight

It took another two weeks before Sheila Gainey allowed herself to really swing open the doors to the next phase of feeling. Finally the realization settled in that no matter what, he was never coming back. Her marriage with Roger was over, for good. Accepting that totally truly freed her, so that as the ladies at the spa had promised, self-doubt and self-recrimination were finally able to blossom into a kind of rippling anger that was like a shot of adrenaline. She was hot and eager to show Roger Gainey exactly what he had given up.

So when the doorbell rang on this evening two weeks into the fifth month following Roger's desertion, she startled Marilu Diamante with the radiance of her beauty.

"Sheila?" came the question and its accompanying wide-eyed surprise.

"Oh, Lu, I'm so glad you're in town. I don't know what's happened to me, but—"

"Whatever it is, I want some."

Sheila grinned, poured Marilu her usual Finlandia vodka on the rocks with a twist of lemon, and said, "Let's go into the kitchen so I can keep an eye on the chicken."

Marilu's surprise deepened. "You're cooking?"

Sheila nodded. "If that's okay?" she hurried to ask. "I thought it would be nice to just hang out at home, but if you want to go out—?"

"No, no, this is fine. I'm surprised, that's all. When I was in town last month, you were still such a basket case that *eating* seemed a major effort for you. Now you're cooking and looking gorgeous." She lifted her glass to Sheila's wine. "Here's to healing," she toasted.

"Now fess up," Marilu asked when they had settled in around the kitchen table for a casual dinner. "This new Sheila has to be due to a man, right?"

Sheila smiled slyly. "Of course."

"You sneaky devil, you. Who is he?"

"Roger."

"Roger? You and Roger are back together?" Marilu was dumbfounded.

Sheila laughed, then quickly became serious. "No, Roger and I are not getting back together. To tell you the truth, I don't think I even want that anymore."

Marilu looked appraisingly at her friend. "I stopped playing twenty questions when I was twelve, Sheila. Now what's going on?"

"You asked if I'm feeling this way because of a man, and I told you the truth, Lu. Roger is why I'm beginning to regain control of my life, and he is nothing if not a man. If he hadn't walked out on me, if he hadn't started me on this roller-coaster ride of feelings I didn't even know existed in me, I'd never be experiencing this incredible *anger.* I've got to tell you, Marilu, I like it. It's more liberating than guilt and blame, that's for damn sure!"

"So you're happy about this?" Marilu asked with open skepticism.

"No, not happy—don't be silly. But I feel an energy to act instead of react, and that's so different from what I've been going through that I'm still just getting used to the change. Do you have any idea what I'm talking about?" Marilu shook her head, and Sheila smiled. "No, of course not, why should you when *I'm* confused? All I can say is that I'm finally taking some of the anger I've been feeling toward myself and directing it toward Roger."

"Why be angry with yourself, Sheila? You didn't do anything wrong—he did."

Sheila hesitated. "Because his leaving made me feel as if I had failed," she admitted in a thick whisper.

"Oh, Sheil, I'm so sorry, I had no idea, not really. I mean, I knew you were devastated, but I thought it was more from surprise."

"There was plenty of that, believe me," Sheila confirmed, shaking off the momentary teariness. "But when the surprise wore off there was all this blame and faultfinding, directed one hundred percent at yours truly."

"How awful for you."

"It has been awful. Even with the divorce, I turned over so much of myself, so much *power* to another person that I felt I had only myself to blame when that other person wanted change. Before you say it, I will—yes, I am smarter than that and yes, I should know better, but intelligence has absolutely nothing to do with feelings."

Marilu nodded. "Ain't that the truth."

"But my brains have reactivated," Sheila continued, grinning. "The result is that I am furious with Roger Gainey for being so stupid as to think he could ever do better than me!"

"Amen!" Marilu declared, clapping her hands. "You know, Roger isn't a bad guy as guys go—he's just typical. Hit a certain age and instead of getting plastic surgery they get plastic values. As with everything in this crazy world, men and women are destined to disagree about anything important."

Sheila got up to check on the lemon chicken, and made them both another drink. "You know, for a long while I honestly believed he'd change his mind," she said. "He'd scratch his itch and be done with it, come on home where he belonged. But you know what's happened?" she asked rhetorically, serving the chicken. "I don't want him to be done with it, and I don't really think I want him back, not the way it was, at least." She sat down at the table again. "What he did has made me reevaluate a whole bunch of things, including the very cavalier way I approached marriage, the assumption of equality when it was never actually that. My pain over what he did and over what mistakes I made and over what I turned over of myself to Roger will never completely go away, but I know I'm not going to be dragged down by it anymore. That's a huge difference, Lu, and a tremendous freeing. For the first time in five months, I really feel I can get on with my life instead of just going through the motions of doing so."

Marilu stared hard at her friend a long, long moment, then said gently, "I don't think I realized before the toll this has taken. I guess maybe I've never loved anyone that much."

Sheila's sigh was audible, her smile too tight, too sad. "This isn't about love, Marilu. It's about safety."

"Safety?"

"When there are surprises almost daily in your work life, the one place you want to feel safe is at home, with the people you trust totally. Roger stole my safety, and I don't think I can ever forgive him for that, ever. And now I'm letting myself be angry at him for doing that to me."

Marilu was thoughtful. "You know, I value a certain kind of safety, too, although I don't think I ever realized that's what it was until just now."

"What do you mean?" Sheila asked.

"I grew up with two parents who hated each other," Marilu explained. "I mean, a mismatch if ever there was one, but my mother could never leave my father because she was totally dependent on him financially. And so I decided at a very, *very* young age that that would never be me. My safety has been work and career, with human relationships coming in a poor second."

"Do you ever feel you've missed out on certain things?"

Marilu shrugged. "You only feel you're missing something if it's something you want and don't have. I've met exactly one man in my life I've wanted enough to sacrifice my definition of safety for."

Sheila's eyebrows went up. "Oh? And who might that be?"

Marilu's smile was swift. "That is none of your business."

"Marilu! I spill my guts and you don't tell me a thing. Now, come on, who was he?"

"It was a long time ago," Marilu dissembled.

"Knowing most of the guys you've been involved with," Sheila was thinking aloud, "I'd say the only one worthy of sacrifice would be Derek Lang."

Marilu's expression grew sharp and watchful. "What makes you say that?"

"Well, he's rich, successful, good-looking. What more could a woman want?"

"I told you, we were a brief and long-ago item."

"Fine, then maybe I'll have a shot at him." She laughed at Marilu's surprise. "Just kidding. Believe me, the last thing on my mind is sex."

"That'll change."

Sheila grimaced. "I doubt it."

"So how do you plan to get on with your life?" Marilu asked, anxious to change the subject.

"Oh, I don't know, I guess just not feel so miserable anymore. Is there anything else I should be doing?"

Marilu nodded, grinning. "I've discovered that to make anger truly worthwhile you have to make it work for you. And there are only two things anger is good for. One is a really spectacular fight. The other is revenge."

"Revenge?" Sheila echoed. "Against Roger?"

"No, against me, silly. Of course, against Roger."

"But how? What could I do? He's richer, more powerful, better connected." She shook her head. "Besides, that's not my style."

"A knockdown, screaming fight is?" Marilu rejoined. She saw Sheila's scowl. "I thought not. That leaves getting back at him. Just think for a minute before saying no. I'm not talking some evil scheme, Sheila. I'm talking about Roger having some vulnerability that you can exploit, some weakness to use against him." She grinned devilishly as she watched Sheila's expression shift from rejection to cautious attention.

"Well, he does feel unbeatable when it comes to his charm," Sheila allowed. "You know, his ability to charm the top names—celebrities, manufacturers, what have you—to PCE."

"And if you happened to outsmart him, or rather, outcharm him," Marilu pressed, "what do you think would happen?"

"You're assuming I could do that."

"You're assuming you can't. Mistake number one."

Sheila tasted the idea, her eyes beginning to sparkle as one vivid fantasy began to take shape, an idea that had been dismissed out of hand just a few short months ago.

"I wouldn't know where to begin." But the broad smile shining on her face revealed the words for the fib they were.

Chapter
Nine

Y ou can't do this to me! Freddie, tell her she can't do this! Sheila,
   you can't do this!"

"But I can. Can't I, Freddie?"

"You can. She can, Roger."

"I don't fucking believe this! Bickford, what the hell do I pay you for!
Make her stop!"

Sheila looked at the phone and grinned with satisfaction. She had
expected some reaction from Roger, but not this tirade. She could just
picture him and Freddie in Roger's office, the speakerphone on so that
they could have this three-way conversation. She could imagine Roger
sitting there, eyes stormy, and Freddie calm and self-possessed, and
impotent to stop her.

A few days after her dinner with Marilu, Sheila did some careful
reading of the papers that spelled out the arrangement between Media

Gains and PCE. She hired a lawyer to do the same, and then offered to put him on retainer as Media Gains' chief counsel, which he accepted. Once secure in the knowledge that she did indeed have full, legal control over Media Gains, Sheila finally accepted the irrefutable fact that she could, indeed, do anything she wished with the company, even sell it if she so desired. And the first thing she did was call in the phalanx of Media Gains lawyers, accountants, business managers, and other backroom operations personnel—each and every one chosen and hired by Freddie and Roger. She instructed them to have their resignations on her desk by noon that same day, and to be off the premises one hour after that. She might need a lawyer or two, an accountant or two, but she didn't need an army of them, especially not an army loyal to Roger. Besides, this action made a statement that could be interpreted only one way: *she* was running Media Gains, independent of Roger and PCE. Which was why he was frothing now.

"Freddie, tell Roger he can't do anything. How do you like that sense of helpless surprise, Roger? It's kind of devastating, isn't it, being sneaked up on and then blindsided."

"Sheila, this isn't like you. You're not a vindictive woman."

"You're absolutely right. I'm not vindictive, I'm just doing what I am completely entitled to. Stupid me, I kept thinking I owed you something. The truth is, I owe myself a lot more, which is why I've accepted the resignations of—"

"Accepted the resignations! Hell, you fired over twenty of my people!"

There was a pause, and then Sheila said softly, "Freddie, did he or did he not make *my* point?"

"Roger, I told you how many times?" Freddie said. "Your divorce lawyer warned you. Don't ignore Media Gains. But you wouldn't listen, you couldn't be bothered. Well, now you shouldn't be so surprised it's come to this."

"But I only gave Media Gains to Sheila to help me with taxes. Freddie, tell her I never meant for her to really run it without me or PCE. Dammit, Freddie, tell her!"

"Sheila, he—"

"Thank you, Freddie, I heard him quite well. Roger, it's not all bad news," she continued too sweetly.

"What? Now you'll tell me you're not cutting me out, I'll just have to play like the competition."

"You *are* smart."

"You can't be serious! Sheila, this is absolutely unacceptable. You can't, I won't let you!"

"Freddie—" Sheila prompted with patent boredom.

The lawyer's sigh was audible. "All right, Sheila, Roger. Let's cut this out right now. By law, Roger does not have a majority position in Media Gains, that's true. But we all know that he never meant to lose control of the company."

"Exactly," Roger asserted.

"Then it should have been part of the divorce arrangements," Sheila stated.

"I didn't think it would come to this," from Roger.

"You didn't think it would come to this?" Sheila echoed, incredulous. "Did you really believe we could go on as before, that I would ever be able to work with you again in the same way? Did you truly believe that, Roger?"

"Well, yes," he admitted.

"Arrogant *and* insensitive—a lethal combination. Wonder why I never noticed before," she muttered tartly. Then, more forcefully, "Media Gains is a producer of commercials, and we don't need to add to our overhead with *your* attorneys et al. I'm sorry these people suddenly find themselves without work, but downsizing has become the American way."

"What was that about not being vindictive?" Roger groused.

"I'm not finished. I admit I may make some mistakes; after all, without PCE as a sure thing, it's a whole new ball game for me. I don't know if I'm tough enough or talented enough or smart enough, but—"

"You are."

"Excuse me?"

"I said you are." Roger spoke the words more clearly and deliberately as if, Sheila thought with a smile, he might otherwise choke on them.

"Thank you," she whispered.

"Sheila?"

"Yes, Freddie?"

"Good luck. And if you ever need anything—"

"Shut up, Freddie!" Roger commanded.

"Thanks, Freddie. And thank you, too, Roger. Neither of us might really understand this yet, but I'm beginning to think divorce was one of your more brilliant ideas," and before he could respond, she gently hung up the phone.

As self-empowered as Sheila was learning to feel, the next several weeks were as filled with anxiety as they were with exhilaration. Each day that she took another step closer to giving her ex-husband a dose of his own medicine by startling him with a loss that would leave him reeling from humiliation and surprise, as he had done to her, was a day that also had her riddled with self-doubt, not only about whether she could succeed, but whether she really wanted to.

Roger had taught Sheila that the single most important factor in making PCE such a huge success so quickly was his ability to woo the celebrity names who would most appeal to the home shopper. In most cases, he had been able to convince even the most recalcitrant of former stars that infomercials were not only not beneath them, but could actually do them a lot of good. He had a gift for treating them as if they still commanded the best roles, sold the most albums, drew the biggest live crowds, and he did it all with a believable sincerity that made him, and PCE, their first choice when it became embarrassingly apparent that their careers were in serious need of resuscitation. The one star he wanted desperately and whom he had not been able to get yet was Gayle Crockett, an exquisitely beautiful black performer who had made it big as both a singer and an actress in the sixties and seventies and whose career extended well into the eighties when she had an ongoing role in an enormously popular prime time soap opera. But when that show was canceled, it effectively marked the beginning of the end of her career. She was out of sync with the times, her singing style strictly cabaret, her aging looks too fabricated, too old Hollywood glamorous. She still enjoyed a certain popularity in Europe and could be counted on for the occasional made for cable, or straight-to-video film. Otherwise, for her, it was over.

Roger was convinced she could sell the life out of a product for one of his infomercials, her dusky beauty appealing to both blacks and whites. But he needed the right product. Gayle had told him that if she ever did decide to do an infomercial, she would do it for him, but she had to believe in the product she'd be selling. Meanwhile, she wasn't ready yet for home shopping burial. For the past three years, Roger had not been able to come up with a product he thought she would like enough to take the infomercial plunge. He had considered, and rejected, everything, from a line of clothes—evening wear only—to wigs, luggage, an electronic backgammon game (because he knew she loved to play), skin-care products, makeup—the list was endless. Every time he saw her, he pitched and wooed, but offered nothing because *he* had decided what she would and would not find acceptable.

That oversight gave Sheila her opportunity.

She called. She made a date. And she flew out to Los Angeles to meet with Gayle Crockett. . . .

Sheila tried to be as unobtrusive as possible, standing at the rear of the set drinking a cup of coffee and watching, fascinated, as Gayle Crockett blithely lied to a smitten police detective about her connection with the dead man found in her office suite. For all that home shopping appeared on television, it had as little to do with genuine entertainment as comic books did with reading, and so observing an actual cable movie being made thrilled Sheila no less than it would any other fan.

"Sheila, hi!" the actress greeted, calling out and waving as she left the set.

"You look ravishing!" Sheila exclaimed, embracing the actress with genuine affection, then holding her at arm's length; even heavily made up and more mature than today's criteria allowed as beautiful, she was truly lovely. "Gayle, you must have made a pact with the devil himself to constantly look better and better while the rest of us mere mortals deteriorate with age."

Gayle beamed, gratified. "You're sweet, Sheila, and blind. Speaking of looking well, obviously divorce agrees with you."

"A recent development, believe me."

"I understand it was rather unexpected?"

"That's one way of putting it. But, Gayle, I know how busy you are and I don't want to waste your time talking about my divorce. I really can't begin to thank you for agreeing to see me."

The actress put her hand on Sheila's arm. "We've known each other a long time, why wouldn't I see you? What's one lousy made-for-cable movie anyway? Just a way to pay off two ex-husbands and a mortgage." She laughed. "Besides, what you told me on the phone sounded intriguing. I always told your husband—sorry, *ex*-husband—that if he came up with the right product, I'd listen. I'm still willing to listen, but he's never come up with anything."

"He was trying to find something worthy of you," Sheila explained.

"Worthy of me? Screw that. All I wanted was a product I believed in and that seemed right for me to be selling—not like some rip-off psychic network, if you know what I mean."

"I think Roger just wanted it to be extra-special."

"Look, Sheila, I've been approached by the others—that can't come as a surprise to you—but I meant what I told Roger, that if and when I decided to do a spot, it would be for him. But truth to tell, I'm ready now and it's getting hard to keep the others at bay. I need to do an infomercial, and I'd like it to be sooner, not later. When you called and said you had the right product for me, I figured I wasn't really breaking my promise to Roger." She grinned slyly. "After all, *you*'re still a Gainey, so I'm keeping it in the family. Sort of."

Sheila smiled her appreciation. "Sort of."

"I have to go back on the set now. Why not come over for dinner tonight and we can discuss everything over ice-cold margaritas and char-broiled steaks. I know how politically incorrect that is, but hell, I've always been more Vegas than Beverly Hills."

"Sounds great. Where's Mitch?" Sheila asked, referring to Gayle's third husband.

"In London," Gayle answered, and an almost adolescent softness crept into her face. "He's lining up a couple of concerts for me in Europe, where, thankfully, they still appreciate age in their cheese, wine, and women. See you later," she said, and left.

Sheila was so used to the colors and vista of the desert that she tended to forget there were other landscapes, different yet equally breathtaking. Gayle Crockett's ranch-style house, high in the Hollywood Hills above Mulholland Drive, afforded such a view.

"Pretty spectacular, isn't it?" Gayle said, coming up behind her, a margarita in each hand. "To seeing you again," she toasted, handing Sheila her drink. "Let's sit down over here," she said, gesturing to the lounge chairs. "Mako, our Hawaiian angel, will be barbecuing out here soon, but for now he's in the kitchen doing the salad, and I love the view at this hour if there's no pollution to hide it, like this evening. So, now, tell me about this product you think is right for me."

"Before I do that, Gayle, I want to make sure we're clear about two very important issues," Sheila said, suddenly all business.

"And they are?"

"One, that Roger has no idea that I've approached you. And two, that he and PCE may not necessarily get your spot, should you decide to do one."

Gayle understood in a flash exactly what Sheila was saying and what she was leaving out. "Anything else?"

"In case you were worried, I *do* know what I'm doing."

"I never doubted that."

Sheila needed to explain. "I'm not just some vengeful wife out to punish my husband. I've been involved in Roger's business from the beginning, and while I'm not claiming to have his expertise or to understand all the nuances of the business of cable shopping, I *am* a terrific producer and a very astute judge of what kind of product can work." She leaned toward the actress, animated, energized, loving what she was doing, which, she was not surprised to discover, had more to do with being in total control of what she enjoyed and was good at than with any blueprint for revenge.

"What I'm trying to say, Gayle, is that I can produce a spot for you that will make you money and give you increased visibility in the right way. In this new world, the celebrity is the product, the commercial itself is the entertainment. What you sell is important, no question about that, but so is who is doing the selling. And I'm convinced you're the right kind of celebrity to sell big."

"Not exactly a compliment, is it?" Gayle commented. "After all, it's the next-to-last stop before entertainment oblivion, and let's not pretend otherwise."

Sheila could not argue with that assessment. "It's a way to make money and keep you alive in the public's consciousness. Is that so bad?"

"Tell me about the product."

It was such a natural that Sheila was almost embarrassed about it, especially since it had come across her desk sixteen months before, but when she had shown it to Roger, it landed in his "not good enough for Gayle" pile. It was a line of skin-care products and cosmetics for the "tawny" skinned woman. Roger had dismissed it as too downmarket for Gayle, whose appeal was not necessarily to Afro-Americans or Hispanics, but to white women—pudding-bodied, middle-aged middle Americans who were glamour wannabes, as he had described them. He said the black/Hispanic market was wide open, and he wanted very much to get into it, but he needed the right product and the right personality, and this product and Gayle Crockett were neither. Sheila would press him for some kind of description of what would be the right product, since the skin-care and cosmetics line, if not suitable for Gayle, struck her as being good for at least the black/Hispanic market in which he was seeking entree. But Roger had claimed the product was too "obvious" and could be insulting to the audience. Sheila hadn't understood what could be insulting to a woman of any color about having beautiful skin and looking good.

Neither did Gayle Crockett after Sheila finished describing the line, taking out samples, giving the history of the company—founded by a female black doctor who had created the products and had been selling them for three years through mail order only from dermatologists' recommendations. There were testimonials and endorsements from doctors and customers, and everything was legit. Sheila had the manufacturer's guarantee that Gayle would receive 6 percent of every product sold plus a onetime fee of $150,000. It was top dollar, top product, and the top producer, Sheila concluded with uncharacteristic immodesty.

"Don't forget a top celebrity," Gayle supplied, grinning.

Sheila tilted her head, expression expectant. "Does that mean—?"

"Yes. I'll do it."

"You're serious?"

"Totally. I trust you, Sheila. I trust Roger, too, but you're here, and he's not. In this cockeyed world of entertainment, timing is everything, you know that. And the right timing for me to do this happens to be now. So"— she shrugged, smiling that wily smile again—"so screw Roger."

Sheila laughed and lifted her glass in another toast. "Oh yes. Screw Roger!"

Chapter
Ten

Derek, Derek, my man, you're a hard guy to pin down. I've been trying to get to you for weeks now; you're never available. I was beginning to think maybe you didn't want to see your old pal Scotty Brickell, that you were deliberately avoiding me, but I knew that wasn't possible."

"I've been on the road. After all, I've got businesses all over the country, not just in Phoenix."

"Yeah, I know, but you could have called." There was such petulance in the comic's voice that he himself was embarrassed. "Sorry, it's just that things are a little tough right now and I've kinda been counting on you and that promise you made me."

"Promise?"

"Well, yeah, you know. How you always told me that anytime I was ready to leave PCE, BFL would be my new home. So, Derek, old pal,

I'm ready." His laugh stung with acidity. "Hell, talk about an under-statement."

"I heard about your troubles with Roger Gainey. I'm sorry." If there was true regret in Derek's voice; if there was the presence of any emotion at all, the comic was unable to detect it.

This time Scott's laugh relayed all the mirth of a dagger slice. "The fucking bastard! Can you believe what he did to me! I could kill him, I swear I could." Suddenly, he checked himself and presented a less malignant posture. "But we'll show him, won't we, Derek? You and me. We'll show that asshole and his two-bit network what real pros can do. Right?" A crooked smile and fingers dancing on the armrest of the chair in Derek's office revealed anxiety that a cocky tone of voice could not hide.

"So what did you have in mind, Scott?" Derek asked with deceptive blandness.

"What did I have in mind?" Scott repeated. "Isn't that your department? I mean, we're talking a Scott Brickell infomercial. What's the big deal, my man?"

"It has to be the right product, Scott, you know that."

"I don't know squat!" the comic exploded. "I need money and I need a gig. You told me anytime I wanted, you'd have a place for me. So I'm telling you now, Derek, I need a job."

"I appreciate your predicament, Scott," Derek continued, unmoved by the comic's obvious desperation. "But first and foremost I'm a businessman."

"Meaning?"

"Meaning, that if you and the product are not a good mix, then neither you nor BFL would benefit. And we don't want that, do we, Scott? After all, I can't very well hire you to fail, can I?"

Scott Brickell's deal was over at PCE; his agent had tried QVC and been turned down. There was no money coming in, a lot going out, a lot more slated to go out. In truth, he didn't care whether his next infomercial was a failure or not; all he wanted was money, enough to buy himself some breathing room from the Las Vegas IOUs. But all he said was, "I understand, Derek."

"I knew you would." Derek then produced the kind of manufactured smile that made Scott's stomach knot. It held exactly the same kind of iciness Scott saw often enough on a pit boss's face whenever he okayed Scott's markers. The dealer knew he had Scott, one way or the other. Derek Lang had the same look now.

"You know what bothers me about you, Scott?" he asked, not waiting for the comic to respond. "I don't know if I can trust you. You—"

"Hey, wait a minute—" Scott stopped in mid-sentence as Derek's hand came up and his smile grew chillier.

"Let me finish, please. You see, I know you were shopping yourself to QVC, to me, even to some of the local stations the whole time you were with Roger. You needed money and having an exclusive contract with PCE didn't matter to you. That troubles me, Scott."

Scott shook his head, and his fingers stopped dancing. "Come on, Derek, you're making a big deal out of nothing. You know all entertainers, especially when they're hot properties like me, have to keep their options open, talk to interested parties at any time. Keeps everybody honest so no one takes the talent for granted. Sure I was talking to other people, but Roger didn't care, he knew it didn't mean anything."

"I'm glad to hear that, Scott, because I'd hate for you to come to BFL and then go behind my back trying to sell yourself to a competitor for more money. I don't tolerate disloyalty, you might as well know that."

"I'd never do that, not me, man, never."

"I find it interesting that you call yourself a hot property, Scott." Derek's smile was suddenly gone, and the frigid contempt in his voice brought the comic to full alert. "I've had my people do their homework, and do you know what they learned?"

All Scott could do was shake his head and gnaw nervously on a cuticle, his eyes large and fixed on Derek. He crossed his legs, and his knees began to bob as if pulled by a puppet string. His fingertips were jitterbugging again on the armrests.

"They confirmed what I had feared—that you have no drawing power. You can imagine how that worries me, Scott. After all, how can I hire someone who—"

"Dammit, you've been talking to Roger Gainey, haven't you?" Scott shouted. "That lying bastard sabotaged my entire career on PCE. He gave me a product from hell in a time slot from hell, then blamed me for not having audience drawing power. Shit, Derek, you can't really believe I don't know how to pull in an audience."

"My people studied all your products at all your time slots," Derek went on, relentless now, going for the kill, "and nothing seems to have clicked. Why do you think that's so?"

Scott willed his tapping knees to still, and he folded his arms across his chest. "What are you telling me, Derek?" he asked in a strangled whisper. "Are you blowing me off, is that it? Telling Scotty Brickell he's not good enough for you and BFL? Is that what this is all about?"

Derek took so long in answering that Scott would forever after wonder at his self-control, how he was able to sit there and wait, instead of punching the patronizing bastard black and blue the way he wanted. He stared at Lang and hated him with every fiber of his being, hated him even more than he hated Roger Gainey. He hated Derek Lang because he had power, and that power gave him control, and Scott needed him because he had both. He stared at Lang, tall and handsome and impeccably groomed and blindingly successful, and he hated him so strongly, so deeply that he could feel his cheeks burn from the fire of the hatred. Trembling inside, he managed to get to his feet and move to the door, no longer interested in anything Derek Lang had to say.

"You know, Lang, you've been on a long, long winning streak. But one thing you learn in this world is that it can come to an end at any time. That's the mysterious beauty of Luck." His smile was so thin with effort it was almost painful to observe. "It changes when you least expect it, least want it to. Be careful, Derek. Your luck might be changing and you don't even know it."

Scott barely made it to the men's room. Mercifully, it was empty and so no one saw him drop to his knees and lay his flaming cheeks against the cold floor tiles. He was close to hyperventilating, he could feel that gray fuzz of dizziness in front of his eyes, filling his head, sense the strange weakness in his upper thighs and that horribly frightening shortness of breath. He got into a sitting position, lowered his head and forced himself to breathe slowly, deeply, getting oxygen back into his brain. When the veil began to lift, he held on to a washbasin and tottered to his feet, splashed water on his face, soaked a paper towel and placed it at the back of his neck. Gradually, he could feel the return of calm, and with it, a return of that consuming hatred that had been born in Derek Lang's office. But now the feeling was not just for Lang, but for Roger Gainey and Freddie Bickford and for the people at QVC, for his agent, for anyone and everyone who made him weak, who made him want, who made him ask, who made him scared. Who made him lose.

He had been doing pretty well, too, until Roger told him he was finished. Not even a snort of the white stuff for five, six months, but then he had that damn losing streak and the only way to recoup his losses was to play and he had needed cocaine confidence to go back to the tables. Shit, he owed his drug dealer, too, he just remembered, but he could wait. He only broke bones, he didn't kill.

Scott was scheduled to perform in Tahoe next week—a gig his agent had somehow managed to arrange. It wasn't the main room, but who the hell cared, it was a gig and it paid. Which meant he could lay off a healthy bet on the welterweight fight being held there. Of course, he'd need a couple of grams for the weekend, which meant that the boys in Vegas would have to wait. Again. How long could he keep putting them off? He was already performing in Vegas for free these days, just to get his markers down, but that was barely making a dent in his debt. Besides, nonpaying gigs were a loser's way, and Scott Brickell was a winner, dammit, he was a winner on a bad streak, that's all, nothing more!

There had to be a way to get an infusion of money fast, someone out there he could tap who still believed Scott Brickell had the goods, or if not that, he thought as the light of hope slowly came back into his eyes, someone like him, shunted aside, demeaned, humiliated, eager for revenge.

The smile of boyish charm reappeared on Scott Brickell's face. Luck. He knew it hadn't run out on him.

• • •

"I'm sorry, Scott, I just don't have anything suitable. Besides, you do have an image problem. If you would only try to—"

"Sheila, this is me, Scott Brickell. Find something for me, Sheila. I'll change, I promise. Just find something for me, please. I need it bad."

"I'm sorry, Scott, I can't. It's not like it was with Roger. I'm on my own now. It's not a matter of just going out and getting you a product with guaranteed air time. If I could help you, I would. But frankly, you've got to help yourself first."

"Sheila, please—"

"If it's money—"

"Don't patronize me, bitch! I'm not looking for handouts, I want work. Scott Brickell earns his way, dammit!"

"Listen, Scott, I—"

"Fuck you. Fuck you and fuck your ex-husband!"

Sheila heard the deadness in the phone, and replaced the receiver, only mildly saddened by the comic's predicament.

Chapter
Eleven

Alicia Devon straightened and got to her feet. She did not have to pat down her hair or refresh her makeup, except for her lipstick, of course. That was one of the, no, the *only* positive thing to be said about a blow job.

"Thank you, Alicia, that was mighty fine."

"Cut the country corn, Peck. I lived up to my part of the bargain, now it's your turn."

A. L. Peck smiled a smile that could raise gooseflesh. "Honey, you're good, but I've had better, and I didn't have to help them get jobs."

"But you said—"

"What I said, Alicia, is that you have a very kissable mouth. I didn't ask you to give me any demonstration, sweetie, although I'll never turn one down. *You* assumed a *quid pro quo,* that I would help you out of your predicament with Roger." Peck shrugged, pulled up his shorts, and put an end to the conversation by getting up from the poolside lounge chair and diving into the water.

Starbursts of rage exploded in front of Alicia's eyes. Her reaction would have been even more extreme if she had known that Peck, not a particularly cruel or unfeeling man, merely a selfish one, had already forgotten the momentary pleasure she had given him. What Alicia would never be able to appreciate was that there was no reason why he should remember it, or her, or help her. She had never been more than perfunctorily courteous to him on his way up, and to think that she, on the way down, could enlist his help was on a level of selfishness equal to his. Of course, Alicia did not understand this, and so she stumbled out of his house, suffocating with anger.

Coming to Peck this afternoon had been an act of desperation, and to be further humiliated by someone not good enough to clean the filters in her air conditioners was unbearable! Damn Roger Gainey for putting her in this position, damn him to hell!

She was at her wit's end. Time was running out. Nick Covey hadn't had to check the contract to confirm that Roger could put her wherever the hell he pleased, selling anything from dishes to dishrags at any hour of the day. As he pointedly reminded her, it had been her idea not to play hardball with the negotiations since all she cared about was the money and the exposure to safeguard her against entertainment obscurity. What she had done was now putting her at risk of having that very fear realized—an irony that did not amuse her.

She had been to see Freddie Bickford, imploring him to get Roger to change his mind. For him, too, she had offered to perform certain "services." He had turned her down, with regrets, on both counts. The truth was, he had told her, there was no arguing with the dollars and their absence from her infomercials.

She had flown out to Westchester, Pennsylvania, to meet with the QVC people—against Nick's advice. They had done their homework, and had "a full roster of celebrity talent at present," they claimed. She had mistakenly believed that if she met with them in person, she could use her wholesome charm on them, but charm, or sex, she was beginning to realize, had no impact on smart business decisions.

She had sunk so low that she had even invited Scott Brickell to her home for dinner, a man she truly disliked and who had certainly never shown her any amicability. But she had assumed he was good friends with Roger and could intervene on her behalf. She had been prepared to do whatever was necessary . . . as she had been with Freddie, as she was with Peck this afternoon, but Brickell had saved her additional degradation by almost hysterically admitting that she was better off than he—at least she had a job, whereas Gainey had fired him!

She needed something, something incredible, something that combined a unique product with the kind of vibrant, country appeal that had made her a star—twice. And then she had to make sure the tape was seen by Derek Lang. She didn't dare disregard Nick's advice another time, and he had warned her that to see Lang on the basis of what she had done for Roger would get her exactly the same response QVC had given her. She needed something new that would make Lang sit up and take notice. But because she had been hoping that she would not need Derek Lang, that someone close to Roger could somehow help her, convince him that a home shopping spree on the graveyard shift was not fair to the woman who had done so much for PCE and the whole world of cable advertising, she had telephoned A. L. Peck, a man she had only contempt for, a man whose phoniness was as rancid a stench as a raccoon dead at the edge of a swamp on a hot August afternoon. But no one said no to Peck. Not even Gainey. Peck was the eight-hundred-pound gorilla, and that's what she needed on her side.

What she conveniently let herself forget was that eight-hundred-pound gorillas don't do favors for anyone unless there's something in it for themselves. Then again, it was a big, big mistake to think Alicia Devon was out of the game, she thought as she got into her car. A. L. Peck would be wise to remember that it was a climb to the top and a fall to the bottom, and life had a way of changing your position without notice.

Nevertheless, there was little choice left her now. She needed a new spot to convince Derek Lang that BFL and Alicia Devon were an unbeatable combination. And there was only one person to give her that kind of spot.

• • •

"Be the expert, Gayle. Look into the camera and keep the humor out of your eyes."

"Sheila, this is funny!"

"Pan the camera to the product line more often, Bill," Sheila instructed her key cameraman, ignoring Gayle Crockett's remark.

"Gayle, remember while the voice-over is doing the send-a-check address during the call to action, and some of the endorsements are airing, you have only twenty to thirty seconds of lag time."

"I can't even go to the bathroom that quickly," the actress complained.

"Live with it," Sheila told her. "Look, for a thirty-minute infomercial like yours, there are three calls to action and they don't start until you've done the introduction to the product line and Dr. Angela Wilbur, the dermatologist who created the line, discusses the benefits of the products. We'll have two or three women joining the two of you, but they're more for decoration. The real endorsements will be pre-taped, so the first eight minutes before we go to the first call to action are all you. You have to hook the audience, Gayle, so, please, be serious. Remember how much money you stand to make."

"I didn't realize how much work one of these things takes, how many rehearsals are necessary. There's me alone, then Dr. Wilbur, then the two of us, then the other women, then plugging in the taped part." The actress shook her head. "I should have charged a higher fee," she complained from the set, which had been made to look like an elegant yet cozy living room, with a line of makeup and skin products in their intriguing matte black glass bottles and jars arrayed on a round glass coffee table.

"You won't mind if it works," Sheila promised. She then turned to a young man who had been standing nearby. "Al, remember, the first call to action lasts forty-five seconds and the price has to be kept on the screen for thirty seconds. Don't put on the eight-hundred number or the send-a-check address until the price has been mentioned, and make sure the voice-over announcer states the eight-hundred number and the address twice during each call to action. Don't forget the limited-offer price, either, and the bonus gift, and let's see, what else? Oh yes, the shipping and handling have to be mentioned twice, too. Got all this?"

The young fellow nodded, not once looking up from the clipboard on which he had been frantically writing all of Sheila's instructions. Sheila smiled at her new assistant producer, a senior in communications at the University of Arizona who was working for her without salary as part of his senior thesis—the kind of help she could afford, she had told A. L. Peck last week when they had had lunch together. She missed seeing him as regularly as she had when she had been with Roger. Now they had to make actual dates to get together, since his career had him traveling weeks at a time, giving his seminars and making money wherever he went. Their lunch had been a delightful two hours of gossip and recollected good times that did not make Sheila's heart twist, not even when Peck described Roger's social life as a succession of one-night stands as if, Peck had said with insight that had surprised Sheila at the time, to see a woman twice would mean that she found something likable in him, and since he couldn't figure out what that might be, she couldn't be worth much herself. A strange mind-set for a man who had divorced a wonderful woman because he thought he was missing something in life!

"Sheila?"

Hearing her name brought Sheila out of her musings to find Alicia Devon at her side. Sheila wondered that she had been permitted on the set, then realized that no one would think to keep the queen of infomercials *off* the set.

"Al, I'll be in my office." She looked at Alicia. "I thought you had wiped me off your slate," she began, starting to walk. "The last time we met, you were hardly warm and welcoming," she reminded her.

Alicia patted her right spit curl with telltale nervousness. "I'm sorry about that, Sheila. I was striking out at everyone who was close to Roger. You happened to be at the wrong place at the right time."

Sheila indicated that Alicia should take a chair in her small office.

Nothing about Media Gains mirrored the opulence of the PCE offices. This was a working production office, with important space given over to the set, not offices.

"What brings you here, Alicia?" Sheila asked, all business. "As you could see, I'm in the middle of rehearsing a new infomercial for Gayle Crockett."

"Quite a coup. Congratulations."

"I still have to get the spot sold, so save your congratulations. It's not like it was with Roger, you know. Nothing Media Gains does is an automatic PCE spot anymore."

"*Nothing* is automatic anymore, is it?" Alicia said. "Not jobs, not even marriages."

"Alicia—" Sheila did not bother to hide her impatience.

"Sorry," Alicia hastily apologized. She leaned forward, her body language speaking of tension and need, her face suddenly pasty, the usual animation in her eyes now flat, deadened by desperation.

Sheila was startled by the transformation. "What is it, Alicia? What can I do to help you?"

"Get me a fabulous product, Sheila, please, and produce a spot for me, something so spectacular that I can take it to Derek Lang over at BFL and have him buy Roger out of my contract."

The words tumbled out in a breathless rush. Then Alicia sat back, waiting warily for Sheila's response. The lengthening silence unnerved her. "I've got to get out of the contract, Sheila, I must. I can't let everything I've worked so hard for be destroyed and that's what will happen with what Roger has planned for me. I start next week, Sheila, next week! You've got to help me. Please."

"Have you spoken to Derek Lang?" Sheila asked the question gently.

"Not yet. Nick told me not to. I made a big mistake by not listening to him when I went up to see the QVC people." She grimaced. "I didn't exactly bowl them over. Nick said my only hope was to get a new spot and let it do the talking for me."

"I don't have anything, though, and even if I did, there's no guarantee that BFL would take you on."

"Of course they'll take me!" Alicia argued with impressive conviction. "Why shouldn't they? I'm not over the hill, Sheila. I may be overexposed; I'll accept that, but a little breather from the airwaves can change that, especially if I come back with something incredible. A little breather doesn't mean obscurity, which is exactly what I'll get from the graveyard shift. I'm still the best and Derek Lang will pay for the best, I know he will!"

She suddenly fumbled in her oversized purse and extracted a videotape.

"What's that?" Sheila asked.

"It's my tape from Magic Fingers, remember that one? I sold out the full shipment of one hundred thousand electric massagers the first two hours the infomercial was shown. Give me something like that, Sheila. Something new and exciting and—"

"But that was years ago, Alicia," Sheila reminded her. "When you *and* infomercials were new and exciting."

"I know that!" the singer snapped, plopping the tape on Sheila's desk. "I want you to watch it and bring me the same quality of freshness for today. I need a product that Alicia Devon and only Alicia Devon can sell, like Magic Fingers."

"It was timing, Alicia, not you or the product."

"It was the right product for me and I want you to find another one just like it!"

Sheila was shaking her head. "I don't know, Alicia. I just don't think I can help you."

"Does that mean you won't even try?"

Alicia unblinkingly met Sheila's probing, assessing stare, as if willing the producer to say the words she needed to hear.

"I'm not promising anything," Sheila hedged.

Alicia's smile spread from spit curl to spit curl. "Thank you, Sheila. I won't forget what you're doing for me."

Sheila nodded, then gave Alicia back her videotape. "Take that with you. I remember it well, and if I can't do better this time around, I'll be looking for another job, too."

Later that afternoon, Alicia called her manager and instructed him to do whatever was necessary to break the contract with Roger Gainey. There was no way she was doing the spree, no way she was doing a graveyard shift. No way. Buy him out, if that's what it took, there'd be more soon. When Nick pressed for details, she told him only to trust her. When he reminded her that until the ink was dry on both contract and check, a deal was no more real than a wish. She told him to stop being an old worrywart. She had a big surprise in store for him. She knew what she was doing, she had never felt more sure that she knew what she was doing.

"This will be the best, Nicky, you'll see," she purred. "I'm going to be bigger than ever, so big that Roger Gainey will come begging to get me back!"

> "Take it from me, Alicia Devon, *Starting Over* is the program no one can afford to be without. My life changed after just the first hour of practicing the exercises in Malcolm James's remarkable video, and you, too, can gain the strength, confidence, and optimism to take your life and start over, gaining the pride, satisfaction and financial rewards you deserve. *Starting Over* is the lifestyle program for all of us—and I do mean us—who have hit the midlife mark and want more, more, more!"

"Good, Alicia. Keep going, you know what to do," Sheila instructed off-camera.

Alicia smiled in the direction of a ponytailed man in a black turtleneck and tweed jacket sitting to her right. He was a man of indeterminate age, no less than forty and perhaps considerably past the midpoint of life.

> "You've all now had the pleasure of meeting and hearing Malcolm James, a foremost career counselor and author of the remarkable book and videotapes that until now have been available only to subscribers of his private newsletter."

She turned a hundred-watt country smile back to the camera.

> "Thank you, Malcolm James, is how I begin each day in this new phase of my life. And you will, too, with *Starting Over,* the program that gives you back the promise and the potential you thought were gone with your youth."

"Give me applause," Sheila called out. "Okay, the final call to action . . . let the address linger . . . linger . . . turn up the new Devon 'Starting Over' song . . . let it play . . . let it play . . . and cut!"

Alicia slowly removed the chest mike and shook Malcolm James's hand. She patted down her hair, her spit curls, and then got to her feet, grinning as the cued applause turned genuine, everyone on the set, including the midlife guru, clapping loudly for her.

"You were great, Alicia, just great," Sheila said enthusiastically. "Two takes and you had it down perfectly, you're such a pro. And how do you do sincerity so damn sincerely?" She laughed.

"It is a good spot, isn't it?" Alicia needed to hear it again. "Good product for me, too. It's got the mystery of the Peck program, but I give it a basis in reality the audiences can relate to."

Sheila sobered slightly. "Now comes the real work—getting it marketed."

"Derek Lang will love it. He'll buy it and give it prime time exposure."

"Alicia, you've got a one-in-eight chance to get beyond the test run, those are the known, proven odds. Malcolm James seeded me the money to produce the spot because his agent was looking for a tax write-off for his client. I need this infomercial to beat the odds as much as you do, but I certainly wouldn't take out any guarantees on Derek Lang."

"He'll want it," Alicia repeated confidently, believing her own words. Suddenly she laughed out loud. "He'll want it. 'Starting Over' will become a new gold record for me, and Roger Gainey will be eating his heart out for not having faith in a star. Nothing can go wrong this time, I just know it. Alicia Devon *is* a star—and stars may dim from time to time, but they never fade away!"

Chapter
Twelve

There's talk you're going to take on Brickell."

Derek Lang's laugh was vicious. "Are you kidding? Scott Brickell couldn't sell his way out of a bad joke anymore. If there's talk, he's the one generating it."

"That's what I thought. I couldn't imagine you accepting a PCE reject."

"I might—if I discovered that Gainey was at fault somehow for a celebrity not being able to move a product. That's highly unlikely, though, isn't it?" Derek sat back, his eyes suddenly hooded as he observed the visitor to his office. "I presume this isn't a social visit, so what do you have for me? You know I don't like you to be seen here, so I hope it's good."

"*You* don't like me to be seen here? Well, that's too damn bad. I told you long ago I'd never sneak around—besides, I think between us we could figure out one or two 'legitimate' reasons for my coming here.

But just keep one thing in mind, Derek, if liking had anything to do with our arrangement, I would have stopped a long, long time ago."

Derek continued to study the other person, wondering not for the first time in his professional career if the real reason for his success was not extraordinary business acumen but acute clarity of vision, so acute that there was little about another person—weakness or strength—that could remain hidden to him for long. This person sitting here now wouldn't care if Derek were the devil himself—maybe that's exactly what he did think Derek was. This person had a need that Derek was able to fill. And from such did profitable deals spring. Of course, it was always wise to offer a reminder as to the proper balance of their roles.

"I don't think so," he stated flatly.

"Don't think what?"

"I don't think you would have stopped long ago. I don't think you *can* stop. You need me and you need to do what you've been doing because it helps you live with yourself. I sensed that and realized we could be mutually beneficial. So, please, don't get either self-righteous or arrogant with me—both postures ill become you."

"You're such a prick."

"Yes. But a prick who has provided you with an excellent source of unreported income as well as a balm to your ego."

"In exchange for my providing you with some highly confidential information that has helped you make profitable deals and avoid costly mistakes," the visitor quickly said.

"Life is nothing without *quid pro quo*," Derek said softly.

The visitor smiled, a small, humorless expression. "Actually, life is probably everything without it—except that it wouldn't be the kind of life we'd enjoy."

Derek laughed. "Well put. Now, what do you have for me, since we have definitely established this isn't a social call?"

"Gayle Crockett."

Derek's brow creased with curiosity. "The entertainer?" A nod from the visitor. "What about her?"

"She's doing an infomercial."

"Impossible," Derek dismissed the words. "I would have heard about it."

"Do you always know what celebrity is going cable?" the visitor asked with amusement.

"Of course not, but Gayle Crockett and I are friends, we have a history together." Derek briefly recalled a highly pleasurable weekend with Gayle two years ago when they happened to be at Aspen at the same time. "She's told me, as recently as three, four months ago, in fact, that if she ever did decide to do a spot, it would be only for me and BFL. She would have consulted me first on the product, I'm sure of it."

"She's doing a spot, Derek. Trust me on this one."

"For whom? Hawking what? Who got to her? Dammit, who?"

The other person shrugged, then lied. "I don't know the details—sorry."

Derek's eyes darkened with interest. "So it's not a presold show?"

"I don't think so. That's why I'm here today. I figured you'd want the inside track on this one."

"You figured right. There'll be a bonus for you this afternoon—cash deposited before three, as usual."

The visitor got up. "Thank you." A pause, then: "You know I don't need the money."

Derek's smile was merciless. "I'm well aware of that, but getting it helps you pretend that you're not leaking information merely for the pleasure of revenge. And the sense of power it gives you." He picked up the phone, but did not immediately dial. "You know, you never have to pretend with me, but then again, the pretense isn't for me, is it?"

"You're arctic, you know that? Don't you have any mortal needs, any weakness, any feeling at all? Don't you ever wake up in the middle of the night with your mouth dry and your heart pounding from some unnamed fear—a fear that's real, not a nightmare, but real, like fear of ending up alone or failing or making some kind of mistake that means you're human? Aren't you ever scared, Lang?"

Derek did not speak, but his right eye twitched so lightly it could easily have been mistaken for a blink. "I'll be seeing you," he said, and the other person knew better than to linger.

As soon as he was alone, Derek replaced the phone in the cradle and leaned back in his leather chair, staring up at the ceiling of his office, reviewing, as he occasionally liked to do, the panorama that was his life. There were many closed doors along the corridor of his journey, and behind each was a memory of a person and a possibility that he had left unexplored. His visitor had asked if anything ever frightened him. The answer was yes. Emotional rejection scared him as nothing else could, and had since he was a young boy, when his parents had gotten a divorce, his love for both of them ignored as he was shipped to this school, that camp. That had been the beginning of his decision to not care about a person, and to focus only on what benefit he could derive from a relationship. Was he cold? Yes, and usually that coldness worked to his advantage. Eradicating emotional chance from his life meant no one could hurt him. That was also the harm of it. Maybe someday he would open one of those closed doors, to assure himself that he had not really missed anything. He doubted it, though. One of his first rules of business was never to take on what he couldn't do well. And every closed door along that corridor stood for what he couldn't do well: feel.

He came forward in his chair with a thud, the action, the sound effectively restoring Derek Lang's force of will. It took less than ninety minutes for his people to locate Gayle Crockett and get her on the phone for him.

"Bitch."

"Darling, please identify yourself. I'm afraid too many people call me that, especially men."

"It's Derek Lang. Remember me, *darling?*"

"Of course. How are you? What a wonderful surprise. Actually, I was hoping to hear from you."

"I'm sure you were."

"Don't be cocky, sweetie—it's purely business."

"So is why I'm calling."

"Oh?"

"I hear you've finally agreed to do an infomercial."

"That's right."

"I thought you and I had a special understanding, Gayle. Why should I have to hear about this from an outsider?"

"Sorry, darling, bad timing, I guess. On your part."

"Does BFL have a shot at it, at least?"

"I suppose. I don't bother with those details."

"Who does?"

Gayle then told him about Sheila Gainey, and about Tawny Temptress, the line of products she would be selling. "The infomercial is being edited now. As far as I know no network has been lined up. We did it on the come."

Derek was barely listening, his mind whirling with the implications of what she had told him. So, Sheila Gainey had finally come to her senses, he thought. Good girl. Smart, too, just as he had her figured from the start.

"What you're telling me," he then said, "is that she's using a media buyer to place your spot. Is that right?"

"I don't know the language, Derek, but she made a point of letting me know that she had no guarantees lined up. Her ex-husband and she didn't still have an automatic partnership."

"That's true."

"Which is good for you, isn't it, darling?"

"Mmm, it could be."

What was not good for Derek Lang, although if anyone warned him of the potential enmity he would have shrugged it off, was the acidlike anger eating away at the person who had left his office two hours ago, an anger that burned whenever he dealt with Derek.

Freddie Bickford's antipathy had almost as much to do with himself as it did with Derek Lang. He was a lawyer, yet for years now he had been willingly and willfully breaking the law by giving Derek Lang inside information and getting paid for it. He didn't even hate the person he originally blamed for his duplicity as much as he had come to loathe both Derek and himself.

Never had Freddie Bickford been happier than when he and Roger had first created Media Gains. They had been young, hot, fearless—at least Roger had been, and Freddie had been the back-office brains who made it all come together. Theirs was a perfect partnership, each balancing the other's strengths and weaknesses. He had assumed Roger viewed the relationship the same way, and that whatever they did, it would be done as partners. His shock when Roger had suggested buying him out in order to set up PCE had left Freddie paralyzed as if by emotional stroke. He never recovered. His wife at the time, the mother of his son, had been so impressed by Roger's generosity and the financial security she thought it represented, that she had encouraged Freddie to sell. Freddie hadn't really needed encouragement. He was too hurt, devastated, by Roger's treachery to do anything but numbly agree to the buyout.

Since his family was settled in Scottsdale, Freddie did not want to put down roots elsewhere, and so when Roger offered him the job—*offered him a job!*—as PCE's corporate counsel, Freddie accepted. From the ashes of his disappointment came a streak of vindictiveness Freddie had not known he possessed. And in time, even when he no longer had to stay in Arizona, he remained, needing proximity in order to regularly savor the bittersweet taste of revenge.

Roger's competitiveness toward Derek Lang, coupled with a rather strong personal dislike, provided Freddie with the perfect opportunity, and while the lawyer cared as little for Lang as he did for Roger, maybe even less, he was willing to take his money in exchange for certain privileged information that either cost Roger or thwarted Roger. Usually Roger was indifferent to his business rivals, but whether it was Lang's good looks, his incredible success with a variety of businesses, or his cold, calculating intelligence that made him first among equals, Freddie had never been able to ascertain, but he did know that Roger resented Lang as he did not others who entered the cable entertainment circus, and so feeding Lang information he obtained from Roger, information that gave Derek a favored position, satisfied Freddie even as it filled him with disgust.

Lately, though, he had begun to tire of the game. He had told the truth, he didn't need the money, and Derek's attitude of knowing contempt was becoming less and less tolerable. Today's conversation, for example, angered him greatly. Lang genuinely seemed convinced that Freddie could not stop, that betraying Roger was as essential to him as breathing, eating, that it allowed him a mistaken sense of control and power he had yielded when Roger bought him out. Control and power that Lang now had over him. It would be a terrible mistake on Derek Lang's part to underestimate him. That's what Roger had done, and look how long he had been getting away with stabbing him in the back. Freddie Bickford hated being underestimated. And now, with Sheila part of the equation, his little game promised to get much more interesting. Yes, Derek would be wise to show Freddie more respect. Saturnine, quiet, agreeable, *passive* Freddie Bickford really could not tolerate being underestimated.

Chapter

Thirteen

The Sheila Gainey who met Derek Lang for drinks was significantly different from the one of eight months ago. This Sheila wouldn't even have minded meeting him at Emilio's, but he had suggested the lounge at the Biltmore, an irony that pleased Sheila, since Roger was still living there.

Sheila had been about to give the go-ahead to the media buyer she had hired, Direct Time, to pitch the networks on Gayle Crockett's spot when she had gotten the call from Derek. She had decided that with this spot she would give up a piece of her own percentage of gross sales in exchange for the best time she could buy. This first solo effort had to make everyone take notice, make them realize that Sheila Gainey and Media Gains could do quite well with or without Roger Gainey and PCE. Success with Tawney Temptress could also help sell Alicia Devon's new infomercial. A lot was riding on Gayle and that was why, when Derek called, explaining that he was an old personal friend of the entertainer's and would love to discuss a BFL exclusive, Sheila had agreed to meet him and hold off going to Direct Time.

If there was one thing Sheila had learned from Roger, it was always to be prepared, which was why she rang Gayle as soon as her conversation with Derek had ended. She had a good idea what "personal friend" meant; she wanted to find out if there were any professional ramifications she should know about.

"So it was just that once?" Sheila asked.

"Darling, with me once can last a lifetime." Gayle laughed throatily.

"Spare me, Gayle," Sheila responded, but kindly. "Tell me something, though. Did you promise him an exclusive if you ever did an infomercial?"

"Promise him? Well, I might have told him I'd want his network to have a favored position, or some similarly meaningless thing."

"Like what you told Roger, isn't it?"

"I suppose. But, Sheila, sweetie, you know it's all just show-biz talk, and before you say another word, no, I never slept with Roger. I thought about it, but I didn't."

"You are a bitch, aren't you?"

"Yes, but an honest one."

Sheila laughed, short and dry. "Okay, okay. But you wouldn't have a problem if Derek did buy the spot, then?"

"Problem? Oh, sweetie, it would be a pleasure doing business with that man. You should try it yourself sometime," and with another throaty chuckle, she said her goodbyes and hung up.

"You should try it yourself sometime." The words began to echo in Sheila's brain with mocking insistence. If there were one facet of life she had been deliberately avoiding, it was sex. In her forty-odd years, she had been with exactly three men, and two of them had been before she was twenty-one, when sex was more discovery than sensation. Until the divorce, Sheila had never doubted herself as a sexual partner, and Roger had never given her any indication that he did not enjoy her and what they shared sexually. But she had been so wrong about the status of their marriage, about Roger's contentment, that her own sexuality now seemed questionable. She had taken so much for granted and been hurt. Months were wasted before she could find the courage to push forward professionally. She could not afford to risk herself in the sexual arena . . . yet. Still, it felt good to go out and buy a terrific aquamarine gabardine suit with short skirt and shawl collar that was just the littlest bit naughty. Even if she weren't actively doing anything sexual yet, she felt as if she had taken the important first step.

"You look spectacular," Derek greeted her, standing up to grasp both her hands in his as she approached the velveteen banquette in the Biltmore's lounge.

"Well, thank you." Sheila smiled. "I hope I haven't kept you waiting," she added, noticing the half-empty glass of bourbon.

"I usually try to get to appointments at least fifteen minutes early," he told her. "Gives me time to get my thoughts in order, shed the mood of whatever call or meeting came before, be more of a *tabula rasa,* I guess you could say."

She cocked her head with interest, then sat down, not next to him on the banquette, but across the small cocktail table, in a hard little chair. Next to him she placed her briefcase, a silent signal of how professional she intended to keep this meeting. Sheila knew all about Derek Lang's reputation. She was sure he viewed her as easy pickings, the vulnerable divorcée hungry for attention. Then again, she reminded herself, hadn't Derek Lang been the first to open her eyes to her own business independence?

"Why so pensive? You have a frown between those gorgeous eyes as if you're considering someone's fate. Surely deciding what to drink can't be that serious?"

"Sorry. I'll have a chardonnay."

Derek ordered, and when her drink arrived, he lifted his glass in a toast. "Here's to you. No, I take that back. Here's to Roger, who did a lot of people a favor by leaving you—not the least to you yourself."

Sheila's hand stopped in midair, startled by what Derek had said. She tasted the words as if they were the wine, and then she smiled, liking the flavor. "I'll drink to that," she declared.

"You've changed," Derek went on, studying her. "When we had

lunch, you were so tentative, so unsure." He shook his head, unable to take his eyes from her. "Roger truly is a jackass."

"I believe that's a compliment," she replied, smiling, "so thank you. And a belated apology for that lunch. I'm afraid I still thought divorce was the end of the world then."

"And now?"

She felt almost a physical impact from the warm admiration she saw reflected in his eyes. Suddenly, there seemed to be hot liquid running in her veins. Here was a man who openly wanted her. She was flattered and frightened, curious and cautious. Above all, she was giddy. The man who wanted her was her ex-husband's strongest rival! She loved it!

"Now," she answered, "I'm seeing it can be a beginning. It's like learning to walk all over again, this independence thing," she confessed, smiling. "I'm discovering aspects of myself I didn't know existed, didn't have to know since there were different parts involved as a couple. Am I making any sense? Probably not," she spoke for him.

"I understand what you're saying, Sheila. Believe me, you're making perfect sense."

His smile made the liquid that had replaced her blood bubble with heat. She laughed self-consciously. "I think we better start talking business or we both might regret it."

"Speak for yourself. I never do anything I regret, never."

She looked hard at him, read the challenge in his chiseled features, briefly wished she could possess the kind of implacable confidence that brooked no regret, even over a mistake, the kind of confidence that could throw down the sexual gauntlet and not be shaken if it were not picked up. This attitude struck her as vitally masculine, a quality that eluded even the most successful and accomplished of women.

"No, I don't imagine you do," she said quietly, "nor anything you feel guilty over either, I'd bet."

"Guilt?" Derek repeated quizzically, as if the word were in a foreign language. "If ever there was a feeling that should be forbidden, it's that. What a waste for all concerned."

"What *do* you feel?" she asked, grinning, meaning nothing by the words but seeing immediately, by the rapid disappearance of warmth in his expression, by how he sat back against the banquette, putting additional physical distance between them, that she had touched a nerve. It was time, she quickly decided, to steer the conversation back to its original purpose: business, strictly business.

"So, you heard Gayle Crockett's done an infomercial for me," she said, smoothly bridging the awkward moment. Sheila could have no idea how this impressed the man sitting across from her, a man used to seeing women, even highly sophisticated women, flutter and founder with discomfort and self-blame when they thought they might have displeased him. Sheila asked no questions, as other women might; did not stumble with apologies, as other women might; did not pout in silence. Instead, with quiet dignity that exuded a level of confidence and self-possession that probably would have amazed her, Sheila allowed them both the room and the rhythm needed to resume their professional roles.

"What can you tell me about it?" he asked.

"What have you heard?" she countered.

He shrugged. "Not much, even Gayle's not talking."

Sheila's eyebrows lifted. "You spoke to her?"

"As I told you, we are old friends," he said with clear innuendo.

"I presume she told you the product is Tawny Temptress?"

Derek signaled for another bourbon, eyed the question at Sheila who shook her head in the negative. "Yes. Makeup and skin care products for the dark-skinned woman—Afro-American, Hispanic—hell, even someone with a good tan. I'm surprised she's doing it with you. Sorry, but you're just starting out, Sheila, I'd think she'd want—"

"A pro?" Sheila supplied, her tone testy. "I'm just starting out on my own, Derek, but I've been producing infomercials for years. If Gayle Crockett wanted a pro, she's got one."

"I apologize. I just meant—"

But Sheila wouldn't let him off that easily. "You meant why go to me who has to then go out and sell the spot when she could go directly to

you—her 'old friend'—and have a sure thing? After all, with your con-
nections, you could get her to be spokeswoman for any number of
manufacturers clamoring for BFL air time. Right? Isn't that what you
really meant?"

Derek said nothing, and in that silence, Sheila felt her bravado fail,
felt herself retreating, chased by the old doubts, the old insecurities,
the old confusions. She had eventually forced herself to walk forward
alone, without their damaging, though familiar company. Now here
they were again, jeering at her for daring to think she had the where-
withal to do without them.

"Beautiful and smart I always knew you were. But this determination, this purpose—" Derek was shaking his head, his grin broad,
reaching his eyes again. "You're an incredibly exciting woman, Sheila
Gainey, and yes, that is exactly what I meant. Trust me, though, I'll
never make that mistake twice."

"And what mistake is that?"

"Undervaluing you. Only a fool would do that, and you'd have to
agree, I'm no fool."

Sheila considered his words, his expression, and decided that if he
were manipulating her by saying just the right thing, he was masterful,
because she believed him.

"I have the tape in my briefcase," she said, nodding toward the banquette. "Why don't you look at it on a two-day exclusive. If you want it,
I'll instruct Direct Time to negotiate for the Monday through Friday
ten A.M. slot."

"For fifteen instead of the usual twenty percent producer's fee,"
Derek proposed.

"Sixteen and a half," Sheila came back.

"Agreed." Derek beamed. "I can't remember when I've so enjoyed a
deal. Not only am I working with a beautiful and smart lady, but this
lady's ex-husband is going to end up making money because his ex-
wife is doing business with his archrival."

Sheila laughed. "The situation does have its appeal," she admitted.
She reached over for her briefcase, extracted the tape and gave it to

Derek, then got to her feet, her hand outstretched. Instead of shaking it, Derek held it in both of his, as he had when she first arrived, only this time the grasp lingered, long enough for the warmth to be felt.

"As I said, Roger Gainey is a jackass. He may have made two of the biggest mistakes of his life—walking away from you as a woman, and not thinking enough of you as a professional. Believe me, I'd never be so stupid."

Sheila's smile was tight and cold. "Believe me, unlike my ex-husband, you won't have the chance."

With the sound of Derek's appreciative chuckle ringing in her ears, Sheila floated out of the lounge. She was inordinately pleased with herself, and with her performance. She really was getting better, stronger, despite momentary lapses; strong enough to call another's bluff, strong enough to flirt. Maybe soon she'd even be strong enough to have sex, she thought with a giggle bubbling in her throat.

That laughter might have become audible had she known that driving up behind her as she took the keys from the valet and got into her own car was Roger. He was about to honk the horn to get her attention, but she drove off too quickly. Frowning with curiosity, he got out of the car, wondering what Sheila had been doing at the Biltmore Hotel. Before he took the elevator to his rooms, he poked his head into the lounge, but saw no one he recognized, no one who might have met with his wife. Curious. Could she have been here for some romantic assignation? he asked himself. No, impossible. *He* would have heard if Sheila were involved with anyone. They hadn't spoken much lately, of course . . . she was so damn busy with that Gayle Crockett spot she stole from him, so damn busy being a traitor by helping out the woman *he* put on the map, Alicia Devon. And he had to sit idly by, hoping she'd succeed so he could make money. He and his lawyers somehow had to figure out a way to buy Media Gains from her. This rooting for his enemies was killing him, it really was.

Which still didn't answer the question of what Sheila was doing here, and with whom, he sharply reminded himself.

The answer to that had been in the men's room when Roger peeked into the lounge, and was now waiting for his car. Sheila was lingering in Derek's senses like the aftertaste of a particularly fine meal. It had been a long time since he felt so attracted to a woman—beyond animal lust. Marilu was probably the last woman he felt drawn to after sexual hunger had been satisfied. And lately, he could smell need on her like a bad perfume, cloying and obvious.

No doubt, Marilu would deny any desire more ardent than lust, but Derek recognized the small signs of loving that women revealed even when they thought they were being most covert. Like looking through his wallet. His coat pockets. Like preparing an elaborate breakfast when he was in Washington last month, and had stayed at her apartment. Like discussing friends' relationships and how serious they were getting. Marilu was getting tired of waiting, and Derek couldn't really blame her; still, he had never promised more than what he could give. It was not his fault that she wanted the kind of commitment he could not make, not to her, not to anyone. And it was not his fault if she fell into that same old female trap of believing that she could be the one woman to change him. Marilu had been good for him, and had lasted longer than most. But Sheila Gainey? Well, Sheila Gainey just might be even better.

There was a loveliness to her that gave her a youthful glow denied other women her age. For all the pain of the divorce, and for all the single-minded purpose to succeed on her own, Sheila had somehow managed to hold on to a softness and feminine vulnerability that he found impossible to resist. What could Roger have been thinking to leave a woman like her?

Ultimately, of course, that's what made Sheila such an interesting object of seduction for Derek. Screwing Roger would be as pleasurable for both of them as screwing each other.

In due time, he would have to divest, as he did with every endeavor, but by then Sheila would have achieved her profits as well—of that he had no doubt.

Chapter
Fourteen

You can't be serious! I don't believe it, she wouldn't do this to me, never, not a chance." Roger picked up his crystal paperweight, hefting it from one hand to the other until Freddie reached over the desk and took it from him.

"You're making me nervous with that thing. I wouldn't want you to hurt yourself." But his grin indicated he was far from concerned.

"This isn't funny," Roger fumed. "I can't believe Sheila would do this to me. Media Gains isn't hers, doesn't she get that? Wait until my lawyers—"

"*Your* lawyers, I hasten to remind you, including this one right here, warned you this could happen, but oh no, you said not to worry, she was too honorable, too loyal, too devoted to ever think Media Gains really was hers even though *legally*, I again hasten to remind you, it is."

As Freddie spoke, he began to use the paperweight for emphasis until Roger, with a glare, snatched it away and put it back on his desk.

"It's bad enough that she gets the one celebrity spokesperson I've been after for years, but then to take the spot to Derek Lang of all people." Roger ran his hand through his hair, shaking his head in disbelief. This was Sheila, loyal, honorable Sheila, his wife of twenty years. He was genuinely devastated by what he perceived as the ultimate treachery, yet one look at Freddie told him that he was getting exactly what he deserved.

"What did I do that was so terrible?" he muttered, gray eyes clouding with confusion. "People get divorced all the time, don't they? You did it twice, Freddie, and no one treated you like Attila the Hun."

"I wasn't married to a woman like Sheila," the lawyer said. "When you have the best, why shop elsewhere?" he added softly. "It's not that people hate you, Roger, it's just that they can't understand what you've done, why you've divorced her. She's a very special woman."

Roger glanced appraisingly at his colleague and friend. "You obviously think so. And are you planning to be disloyal, too?"

"Meaning?"

"Are you going to go after her, Freddie? Are you going to try to sleep with my wife?" Roger was now bellowing, and the paperweight was again being angrily hefted from one hand to the other.

"I would if she'd have me," Freddie quickly assured him.

"You bastard."

"And she's your ex-wife now, kindly remember that."

"You're still a bastard." He put the crystal dollar sign back on the desk, and when he looked at Freddie, Roger's expression was absent of anger.

"I've been a jackass, haven't I?" he asked rhetorically. "I just took her for granted. Typical, right?" Freddie cocked his head and raised his eyebrows in a small gesture of accord. "I could always get her back." This time his lawyer's expression held unmistakable skepticism. "Okay, I could try. We had a great marriage, we were partners. Hell, that kind of closeness and communication doesn't stop with divorce, at least it doesn't have to, and it shouldn't, damn it!"

Freddie leaned forward on Roger's desk until their faces were inches apart. "I know you're not as idiotic as you sound. I also know you're not ignorant enough to actually believe what you're saying." Freddie's voice was atypically raspy, as if he were using every muscle, even in his throat, to control his anger. "You dumped a woman every man I ever met in this town wanted, and you expect her to continue to feel close to you? You think you can turn around after humiliating her, hurting her, upsetting her entire life, and say, 'Oops, honey, I goofed, let's pick up where we left off before I made that silly mistake.' Are you really that dumb!"

The two men glowered at each other; it was Roger who was the first to look away. "She's going to make a fortune with Crockett and Lang," he stated flatly.

Freddie nodded. "As will you," he reminded him.

"If ever I'll hate making money, it's from this."

Freddie sat back and timed his pause perfectly, waiting to see that Roger was more relaxed, the cloud lifted from his eyes, his posture less rigid. "I wonder if she's having an affair with him?" the lawyer questioned, his tone casual.

"What did you say?"

"I was just thinking aloud, Roger. You know, whether Sheila and Derek might be—"

"Fuck you, you bastard!" Roger barked, pounding his fist on the desk and getting to his feet. "Damn you, Bickford, that's a filthy, rotten, *disgusting* thing to say. Of course she would never do that! How could you even think such a thing of her! I can't believe what you said. I really can't. Get out of here. I can't bear to look at you right now. Sheila and Derek having an affair," he mumbled, sitting back down, not noticing Freddie's suppressed smile as he left the office. "Never. Not my Sheila. Never."

Sheila's heart thumped hard as she followed the hostess at Brandon's, a pleasant pub off Camelback Road, to the table where Roger was waiting for her. Despite the emotional progress she had made, when Roger called and invited her to lunch, the pain and the anger welled up in her as if brand-new. Although they spoke occasionally, she had not seen Roger for months. She had stopped going to PCE's development meetings when she fired Roger's hand-picked staff from Media Gains. So this lunch would mark the first time they had been together—and alone—in months. Mixing with the pain and anger, therefore, was a heaping helping of nerves. She knew he knew about Gayle Crockett and also about BFL. She assumed that the purpose of this lunch was to woo her into selling Media Gains back to him. What other reason could there be? She just hoped she could keep the anger in check and handle herself with cool, detached professionalism that left *her* in control, not him.

"Hello, Roger."

He got to his feet, a smile washing his face with almost boyish eagerness. He put out his arms to embrace her, leaned forward, lips puckered for a kiss. Instead, he got a switch from her hair and a rigidity that sent the hug reeling.

"You look fantastic," he said.

"Thank you." She frowned, studying him. "You don't."

He ran his hand through his hair, and laughed briefly, selfconsciously. "I guess it's the lack of home-cooked meals."

"Not funny."

"Sorry." He glanced up as the waiter approached for their drink order. "Spicy Bloody Mary for me and an iced tea, no lemon, for the lady."

"Chardonnay, please," she corrected him.

"Since when do you have a drink at lunch?" Roger asked.

"Since you gave up the right to order for me," she quickly came back.

"Ouch. Not undeserved, but ouch nevertheless."

Sheila smiled in spite of herself. There was that magnetic charm of his, that ability to defuse a potentially explosive situation with just the right balance of wit and grace.

The waiter arrived with their drinks, and Roger lifted his glass. "To seeing you again, Sheila."

She looked thoughtful. "I have a better toast. How about, to Gayle

Crockett and Derek Lang? After all, they *are* why we're here today, aren't they?"

"Whew!"

Her eyes narrowed. "Let's get to the point, Roger, please. I'm sure you find this as difficult as do I, and I'm also sure we both have better things to do with our time."

"I don't," he stated with charming simplicity. He then reached out to place his hand over hers on the table. She left it there a moment, staring at the hand, at the warmth in his eyes before coolly slipping her hand out from under his and shaking her head gently.

"Don't," she instructed.

"Why not? You can't still hate me."

"I never hated you, Roger. I hated myself, but never you."

"You mean you blamed yourself?" He understood her silence as an affirmative. "You didn't do a damn thing wrong, Sheil. It was me, all me."

"Roger, I really don't want to discuss this. Please." She was miserable. It would be so easy to let herself be won over by him again, to be seduced by comforting familiarity. But then what? She had fought so hard to stand on her own, and for what? To have him topple her again? No, no way, no.

"May I ask you just one personal question?" he asked. "Just one, I promise, and then it's strictly business. I think I've done you enough damage—I have no intention of ever hurting you again, believe me. I won't begin to apologize, that would be ridiculous. But I do want you to know that my selfishness had nothing to do with you, nothing. If anyone's to blame for screwing things up, it's me."

"I couldn't agree more," she rejoined. "Now that you've assuaged your conscience, you get one question. What is it?"

"Conscience, hell! I'm talking the truth, dammit!"

"One question, Roger, or I'm out of here, now."

He sighed, took a swallow of his drink, and looked measuringly at her. "Do you think the day can ever come when you and I can at least be friends?"

She shook her head, and smiled, in awe of his manipulative prowess. "That's your one question?" He nodded. "Well, I don't know."

This was obviously not the answer he had been expecting. "You don't know!" he balked. "How could you not know if we can be friends? Dammit, Sheila, are you really ready to walk away from twenty years of closeness, of—"

"You did."

"Oh, Sheil."

Sheila dared not speak. Her stomach was flip-flopping with emotions she had believed were gone, and now she could feel them returning as if the months of growth and change had never taken place, as if the discovery of herself as a woman of strength and determination and independence was the finding of fool's gold. But no, she *was* that woman of strength and determination. If her former husband still held appeal for her, why shouldn't he? He had not grown fangs and horns; he had not lost his charm or wit or looks. What he had lost, however, was his ability to be first in her life. And that loss made all the difference for her.

"We'll see," she stated.

"That's not an answer."

"It's the best I can do."

Roger pursed his lips, absorbing, accepting. He knew better than to pursue the subject further at this time. "So how did you steal Gayle Crockett out from under me?" he asked. "And why in the world did you take her to Derek Lang? I would have cut you a better deal, you know that."

"It's not signed, sealed, and delivered. Yet."

"You don't really expect me to bid for my own company's product produced by my own wife, do you?" he exploded.

Sheila smiled serenely. "Ex-wife. Ex-company."

"Dammit, Sheila, you can't—"

"Actually, the deal with Derek is just about done, but maybe next time."

"Derek, is it?"

"You and I have had dinner with the man, Roger. I've known him for years. I'm not about to start calling him Mr. Lang!"

Roger gauged her expression, told himself not to do it, but his self-control was running on empty. "Are you sleeping with him?" he blurted out.

"How dare you! How *dare* you!"

"I'm sorry, I'm sorry, it's just that . . . oh shit, Sheila."

Sheila might have enjoyed Roger's genuine discomfort if there wasn't a scintilla of guilt lurking in the corners of her conscience. Stupid it might be, given what he had done to her, but the twinges and pangs tweaked at her, demanding attention. The guilt was there, no doubt, because while she hadn't slept with Derek Lang, she had certainly thought about it—more vividly each time they met. And so, although her ex-husband deserved nothing more honorable than contempt from her, inwardly she cringed with culpability, as if caught in the actual act.

Roger took Sheila's silence as anger, but that wouldn't stop him. "I know you're ready to kill me, that you're thinking I gave up my right to advise you or question you, and maybe that's true, but I didn't give up my right to care about you, that didn't end just because I signed my name to a piece of paper. And I'm telling you to be careful, Sheil, please. Derek Lang is a cold man with regard for nothing but the deal and the profit he can make from it. He has no passion for anything but the deal, no real passion that is."

"We'll just have to see about that, won't we?" She got to her feet, her drink barely touched, and walked off before he could say another word. She had to get away from him. She felt horribly exposed, her loneliness of the past long months, her sexual interest in Derek Lang, her determined effort to make Roger regret what he had done to her—all of it, all the feelings, new and old were there for him to view, to pick at and savor, leaving her naked with vulnerability.

If Roger Gainey had been trying to convince his wife to steer clear of Derek Lang, he had succeeded as nothing else could in driving her directly into his bed. It wasn't that Sheila Gainey was determined to do the opposite of whatever Roger said. No, she was smarter than that, more mature. At the same time, though, Sheila was a woman divorced recently enough to remember the loss and self-doubt, and still occasionally feel insecure, unloved, unlovable. There was no way she was going to let her ex-husband leave her with those feelings, not a second time.

Chapter
Fifteen

The next few weeks would linger long in Sheila's memory as the
time when she truly passed to the other side of the bridge connect-
ing her past and her future. She took such steady and confident control of her life that it struck her as almost laughable that the pain of
less than a full year ago had been felt by the same woman she was today. Of course, she wasn't the same woman. She had tapped into the
stranger who was herself, and found she was wealthy beyond imagination, rich in strength and courage. She found a woman she liked. Her
creativity soared, unfettered by convention, bolstered by success.
There was a youthful fearlessness about her that freed her, daring her
to explore new, exciting areas of business, believing in her own power
to make them work. She suspected that tonight she would finally try
out her sexual freedom.

She and Derek had been seeing each other regularly for the past
three weeks. At first, they had both pretended business was the rea-

son, an excuse as transparent as gossamer. But business did not require her to take such pains with her clothes as she did each time she saw him. And he certainly had other things to do besides find time for her three and four nights a week.

She was not a fool. She had no doubt that part of his attraction to her was that her ex-husband couldn't stand him. Similarly, some of her appeal to Derek might be that she was Roger's former wife. Sheila didn't think the unspoken advantages to a liaison between them mattered. Theirs had swiftly become a friendship grounded in commonality. She liked him—*liked* him—and for the first time in her life, she fully understood what it meant to like herself, enough so that if having sex with him somehow spoiled the friendship, if for some reason he decided not to see her again, the pride and confidence she had been nurturing would not end with his departure. Once she realized that, the decision to have sex with him was easy.

Which didn't mean she wasn't nervous and jumpy and almost giggly with anticipation as she reapplied her lipstick and moved the vase of tulips a third time and patted down her sleek, dark cap of hair as if her head were a lucky amulet. It didn't mean she could stop the doubletake when the doorbell rang. And suddenly, she froze into a glacier of fear and doubt. *What if he didn't want her?* What if she were wrong and only *she* had been having extraordinarily erotic fantasies about them together? What if he wanted nothing more from her than a lucrative business arrangement?

It was with those devastating thoughts reeling in her brain that she opened the door. Then Derek was looking at her, relishing the sight of her, and she knew she had been worrying for nothing.

She smiled up at him. "Derek, hi. Come on in. I'll make us drinks and we can have them outside." She turned to lead him into her house, the first time he had been there.

She made the drinks, a bourbon on the rocks for him, a white wine for herself, and started to open the sliding glass doors to the patio. "Sheila?" She stopped, looked at him questioningly.

"It's time we took the drinks into the bedroom, Sheila."

There it was, out in the open. She said nothing, staring up at this exceptionally attractive man, with the kind of solidly masculine looks that would age with dignity and increased appeal. His eyes, dark and hard and star-bright with intelligence, revealed only what he wanted them to show. His mouth rarely relaxed with spontaneous amusement. Roger had warned her that the man had no passion, that only deal-making stirred him, making him sound frighteningly dangerous and soulless. Maybe that was part of his tremendous appeal for her. What woman could resist the challenge of being the one to ignite the fire in such a man?

"Sheila?"

Slowly, she nodded, and, walking past him, careful not to touch him, she led him into the bedroom, the room she had shared with her husband, the bed she had made love in with her husband. She hesitated, snared in that tricky web spun by guilt warring with want.

"Derek, I—"

"Ssh, I know. I'm the first, and I'm flattered. It's going to be fine, trust me. And you're not doing anything wrong, so stop feeling guilty."

She smiled her appreciation of his understanding. No man could calculate and manufacture that kind of sensitivity. Her instincts told her that going to bed with Derek Lang would add another building block to her sense of self-worth. She trusted him to treat her well; more than that she dared not ask.

He took both her hands in his and brought her close to him. With incredibly sensous gentleness, he began to caress her face, then her neck, her shoulders, her bare arms, not for a second taking his eyes off hers, letting her see his naked desire, be reassured by it.

Soon he cupped her face in his hands and brought his mouth down to hers in a kiss of such exquisite softness and slowness that Sheila thought she would explode with the erotic sweetness of it. The reality became far superior to every fantasy. . . .

As wonderful as sex with Roger had been for all their years together, nothing could have prepared Sheila for the insatiable lust Derek inspired in her. That night was the first time, but it was only the begin-

ning. In the days and weeks that followed, they met as often as their
busy schedules allowed. She thought about him constantly, vivid rec-
ollections of their lovemaking intruding in meetings, in negotiations,
in the shower, at the bank, the hairdresser, the dry cleaner. She was
fairly certain that she wasn't in love with Derek, but it didn't matter to
her. That alone told her how far she had grown in self-confidence since
the divorce. Never would she have believed herself capable of so much
passion if love were not present. She might not love Derek Lang, but
she certainly enjoyed him. To think that if Roger hadn't divorced her
she would have missed out on this. The next time she saw him, she
would have to thank him.

"That grin looks positively lecherous."

They were in her bedroom on a Sunday afternoon, where they had
been since the evening before. Derek was leaving that evening for a
week in New York.

"Oh, just thinking about how good you make me feel," she said.

"Give me five, no, at my age, make it ten minutes to catch my breath
and I'll make you feel even better," he teased. "Of course, if you came
with me to New York we wouldn't have to cram a week's worth of sex
into one day."

Sheila didn't respond. He had asked her to join him, but that would
have meant rearranging her business schedule, and she had no intention of doing that, not even for Derek. She wondered if he had a
woman in New York. And perhaps in Los Angeles. Washington. Paris.
London. Derek traveled all over the globe; she had to assume there
were others. She was well aware of his reputation, of course, but
wasn't it possible for even someone like Derek to find the one single
woman who eclipsed all others? She hated the route her mind was taking. Typically female, she thought, chastising herself for creating a
happy-ever-after scenario instead of being satisfied with the situation
as it existed. What was it about being a woman that required exclusivity as a symbol of honest emotion?

"Have you ever been in love?" she found herself asking.

Derek looked at her a moment, tenderly brushing away some hair
that had fallen across her cheek. "I'm afraid not."

"That's too bad."

He smiled. "I'm not complaining."

"It's a worthwhile experience, Derek, even when it fails."

"Loving comes with a price I find too high to pay."

Sheila heard in those words what she had been suspecting. There was a part of Derek Lang that was vulnerable and needy, like other mortals. For whatever reason, he had found the only safe way to deal with his own particular weakness was to pad it in thick layers of denial and avoidance until he could convince himself that it did not exist. Sheila did not have to know what caused his defensiveness; at their age, curiosity was a form of selfishness. She respected him too much to pry into the "why," satisfied, instead, with the knowledge that the diamond was not as hard and brittle as most people would believe.

"What if you found someone so right that you felt comfortable enough to let your guard down?"

His eyes caught and held hers, and he reached below the sheet for her hand. "What makes you think I deliberately guard against love? Isn't it possible that I simply don't believe in it, that a relationship built on good conversation, good sex, shared interests, a tablespoon or two of laughter is all we should expect? And that's not shabby."

"Put that way, not shabby at all," she agreed. "As a matter of fact"— she grinned playfully—"put that way, I'd call it love."

"Women!" Derek said with mock exasperation. Still gripping her hand, he threw off the sheet that had been covering them, and swung one leg over her body until he was on top of her. "Are you sure you won't come with me to New York?" he asked while planting tiny kisses on her neck and between her breasts.

"I really can't. I have to fly out to Boulder, to *your* warehouse, I might point out."

Derek stopped in mid-kiss, frowning. "Why are you going there? I thought everything was set for Gayle's infomercial to air next week."

"That's why I'm going to Boulder. I want to speak to your order operators, explain the product. Roger used to have me do that with a really important celebrity, and it helps. Besides, I've got a great premium for the upsell and I want to introduce it in person," she added, referring to a premium product the order operators sold to a customer that was not advertised on the air.

"What is it?"

"A three-piece tortoiseshell comb, brush, and mirror with a glass-and-tortoiseshell vanity tray. Freddie Bickford got me a great price."

"Bickford did? Isn't that conflict of interest?"

"Not really. He told me Roger had no use for it; besides, Freddie and I are old friends."

"One can never have enough of those," Derek remarked dryly, causing a sharp glance from Sheila.

"Freddie's very loyal to Roger, Derek. He's just doing me a favor for old times' sake. I needed an upsell premium quickly and inexpensively and he had this one. That's all."

"Okay, then fly to New York after Boulder," Derek smoothly went on.

"I really can't. I'm scheduled for San Francisco after Boulder. There's a designer there who specializes in clothing for the large woman, and she wants to do an infomercial that will go cable as well as on-line. That could mean a potential audience base of twenty-five million! I'm surprised a business genius like you hasn't thought of this up-and-coming trend," she twitted him.

"I have," he told her. "In fact, that's one of the reasons I'm going to New York—two of my guys in new business development have found a small on-line operation that would be perfect to buy and develop. There'll be many uses for it, including as an outlet for BFL. I'll be able to increase the fee to the manufacturer as well as up my percentage of gross sales. My kind of deal," he added, smiling.

Sheila dug her fingers into Derek's hair, losing herself in the dark heat of his eyes, no longer wanting to discuss deals and percentages, no longer wanting to talk about anything. She brought his face down to hers. "One week without this," she murmured against his lips, marveling as she did so often lately at the immense physical delight she took in this man. "I'm going to miss it."

He placed his hands at the sides of her head, stilling her, forcing her to open her eyes and look at him. "It's you I'll miss, Sheila. *You*." He spoke with a fierceness that left her breathless with pleasure, and this time it had absolutely nothing whatsoever to do with sex.

The forest green velvet brocade bedspread, initially folded neatly at the foot of the bed, now lay in a pile on the floor, upon which rested two bolsters that had been similarly kicked aside. Whatever was going on in this bed, Marilu thought, coming up for air from under the top sheet, it sure as hell wasn't the kind of sex she was used to with Derek.

"I'm sorry, sweetheart," she said, drinking thirstily from the glass of champagne on her night table. "Must be that presentation I have to give tomorrow that's preoccupying me. Give me a few minutes and we'll try again."

Derek shook his head and smiled gently at her. "You have nothing to apologize for, Lu, and you damn well know it."

She didn't answer, the brooding concentration on his face, the distance in his eyes, silencing her. Earlier, he had made love to her in a programmed, mechanical way that was hardly fulfilling; then followed her inability to arouse him orally, which always had been so effortless that it became a joke between them. She was deeply concerned. She had not seen him in almost two months; she had been in Mexico and Canada on NIMA business, unable to meet up with him until this quick trip to New York, which she had suggested after calling him and finding out he'd be in New York. His not calling to arrange things should have been her first clue that something—or, far more troubling, *someone*—threatened to spoil everything for her.

She pulled the top sheet off the bed and went to stand by one of the huge windows that overlooked Fifth Avenue from the bedroom of their two-room suite at the St. Regis Hotel. When she and Derek managed to be in Manhattan at the same time, they always stayed here, in this suite that also provided them with their own butler. The place was so special that it seemed their lovemaking, always exceptional, managed to go beyond even that when they were here. Until now.

She turned from the window, her flesh chilling with dread. "There's someone else, isn't there?"

"Lu, don't do this to yourself."

"Oh shit."

"Lu, please, come on now, don't—"

"Do I know her? Never mind, don't answer that. Oh shit, Derek, why? No, don't answer that either."

She walked over to the standing wine cooler and poured herself a fresh glass of champagne. She had always been aware that Derek had other women, but she had assumed they were as meaningless as her own occasional forays into other arms, an appetite slaked, nothing more. They were a good match, Derek and Marilu; they could go on for a long time, a long time, and then he would realize just how good it really was, and just how long it had been going on, and they would marry. This is what Marilu had assumed; this is what she had told herself over and over when sometimes it seemed that the patience and the waiting and the silence about her true feelings would choke her. Where had she slipped up? How could she be everything she thought he wanted and not be the one woman he wanted?

She went to sit by his side of the bed, holding onto her champagne glass with both hands to hide their trembling. She could do nothing about the throbbing in her voice. "Do you love her?"

"Oh, Marilu, honey, please don't do this to yourself."

"I thought we had something special together that we valued. We liked each other and we enjoyed each other, enjoyed the time we spent together." She would not whine. She would not cry. She would somehow try to make sense of this, so she could make things right again.

"That's true, Lu, you know it is. Christ, I've been with you longer than any other woman and—"

"But what we have isn't enough anymore, is it?" she said, breathing deeply. She watched as his dark eyes filled with regret, and when he reached out to stroke her cheek with more tenderness than he had ever before shown her, she had more answer than she wanted.

Slowly, she got up from the bed, squeezing her eyes shut, feeling the hot burn of tears behind her eyelids.

"Lu, I don't really know what's happening myself," she heard him say; she could not turn to look at him. "I have met someone, yes. I don't think I knew how important she was to me until now, being with you; otherwise I would have told you. I would not deliberately hurt you, Lu, not you." She faced him then, assessing his sincerity. "I may be a bastard," he went on, "but not to you. You've never given me cause."

"Maybe I should have," she offered tightly. "You still haven't answered my question, Derek. Are you in love with her?"

"I don't know. I'm feeling things I didn't know I was capable of feeling . . . no, that's not true . . . I'm feeling things I thought I had made myself immune to feeling. Is it love? Who the hell knows, Lu, but she's here in bed with us, that's the truth. I'm sorry, because you deserve better."

Marilu Diamante was not a woman to give up on what she wanted. All her life she had opened closed doors, and Derek Lang would be no exception. She loved him and wanted no substitute. She would wait while he went through this phase, be there for him when he grew tired of the no doubt young bimbo who had somehow captured his attention. And meanwhile, she would give him something to remember her by, a yardstick to measure his little slut against and find her wanting.

She took a deep, steadying breath and then dropped the sheet so that she was naked in front of him.

"Lu, don't. I'm not—"

She ignored him, got back into bed. Before he could protest again, she spread his legs swiftly and got on her knees between them. She took a gulp of champagne, which she did not swallow, bent over, and brought him deeply into her bubble-filled mouth. The shocked moan of surprise became gasps of pleasure as she bobbed wetly over him. When she came up to get another swig of champagne, his hand impatiently found her head, grabbing her hair to push her back down.

"Don't stop. Jesus Christ, don't stop!"

She had succeeded in arousing him again, but Marilu felt no triumph. This was a temporary, therefore hollow, victory, a respite from failure, not the relief of success.

• • •

Derek was feeling particularly testy when he returned to Scottsdale a day early to be with Sheila only to have her call him from San Francisco to say that she would be delayed up there another three or four days. By then, he would be in London.

Derek did not handle disappointment well, especially the unfamiliar personal kind. He needed to restore his sense of control over life. He did not want to be around people who were predictable, obvious in wanting something from him. He needed to have some fun, and Derek Lang derived the most fun from the challenge of dealing with a worthy player, someone clever, someone with an honest passion for money, not just a need. Someone who actually thought he could say no to Derek Lang instead of understanding that he was merely being allowed to think that. Someone who amused Derek with his arrogance, an act as fabricated as his name. Derek decided he wanted to spend time with the man who had reinvented himself as Abraham Lincoln Peck.

Chapter
Sixteen

J ack Rangel, aka A. L. Peck, liked nothing so much as walking tall to his reserved table at a restaurant, always the best table, the best being the one all incoming traffic could not miss. Not since Barry Goldwater had there been a celebrity in Arizona as beloved or recognizable as Peck, and he ate up every last second of it. Success was sweet to Jack, since he was smart enough to know how fleeting it could be. So he enjoyed himself often and fully now, while he could.

He nodded to his left, his right, called out a "Hi there" to this one, pecked the cheek of that one, his grin broad, his pale blue eyes darting, brightly evaluating the room as if it were one of his seminar audiences. Tonight he was dining at Martinis & More, a currently "hot" restaurant known for its politically incorrect triple-sized drinks. At his table, a banquette against the wall in full view of the room and the room in full view of the table, his Rebel Yell 101 proof sour mash on the rocks was already waiting for him.

Twice a year for the past four years he had had dinner with Derek Lang. Tonight was one of those occasions. Rangel enjoyed Lang to an extent that went beyond the pleasure of being pursued by a top business mogul. What Rangel liked was being one of two top con artists working on each other.

Within six months of the infomercial's launch, Derek had been trying to get Peck's *Ladder to Liberty* over to BFL, and regardless of how Derek sweetened the deal, Jack was never tempted to leave PCE. For whatever Roger was, he was a man who could be trusted, and Derek Lang was not. Jack dealt with Derek from the vantage point of like recognizing like; he knew that Lang had about as much authentic feeling as a department store Santa Claus. He danced the dance, sang the songs, smiled the smile, kissed the kiss, but the man was distanced from ordinary human considerations. Life and, therefore, people were a matter of purpose served. There was not a doubt in Jack's mind that Lang trafficked in weakness like any good con, and he didn't fault him for that. No, he didn't fault him, but he certainly would never trust him.

He wondered, not for the first time since Derek had started to woo him, if Lang would be as enthusiastic if he knew who Peck really was and how he came into existence. But of course no one knew a thing about him except what he had carefully chosen to tell them, and so no one had the remotest idea that an ex-convict had become a world-class player. Jack had left the past so far behind that sometimes he himself forgot who he really was.

Since a good con was not just smart but opportunistic, Jack had taken the pulse of the times—people seeking salvation for their sins, trying to become better persons, who liked themselves more—increasing their self-esteem, by increasing their wealth. He watched the televangelists build theme parks to themselves from donations, their congregations eager to give up thousands of their hard-earned dollars to the saviors of their souls. He observed how certain books climbed the bestseller lists, and how some of these new things called infomercials spoke about wealth and freedom through real estate or franchises or five golden rules of time management. Jack quickly assessed that the promoters were all cons, so what would happen if the best con of them all played their game? He'd win, of course, and so he did, because what was the point of playing in the first place if not to win?

He felt sure that Derek Lang approached his various businesses the same way: patiently measuring the market, studying the competition, putting together a little of this, a pinch of that until he had the winning combination. Although "Best for Less" was not number one in the cable network race, it was still a major force—Derek didn't do anything in a minor way. And by pursuing Peck, he figured to beat his prime competition, Roger Gainey.

But Peck wasn't playing. Lang could sell BFL tomorrow and never look back, that was his style. PCE was Roger Gainey's life, which meant a kind of loyalty that a man like Derek Lang could never understand. Jack didn't like Roger more than he liked Lang, but Gainey *cared* about PCE, and that difference, that element of feeling, was the reason Jack would not switch networks. It was also the reason why he would soon take to Roger an idea that was so on target he couldn't believe no one had yet thought of it. He was just about finished working out all the details, and planned to talk to Roger about it next week. Lang would shit a brick when he found out, Jack thought with smug delight.

"You're looking pleased with yourself."

"Derek, good to see you." Peck shook his hand as the maître d' brought him to the table. "And one triple Rebel Yell makes me pleased with the world."

"I'll have the same," Derek said to the maître d', who passed on the order to a hovering waiter.

After the drinks were served and casual small talk was exchanged, Derek said, "I checked—you're still the number one infomercial."

Peck laughed. "I can't tell from your tone, but were you hoping I wouldn't be?"

"Yes and no. Yes, because then you might not be so valuable to Gainey, and no, because then you wouldn't be as valuable to me."

Jack knew about Derek and Sheila and had given some thought to bringing up the subject with him tonight. He had only bad, real bad feelings about the whole thing, yet he didn't dare mention them to Sheila, who had been through enough with Roger.

"So how are you and Sheila Gainey?" he plunged in.

Derek frowned, hesitating, and Jack knew it was because the man was not used to having his actions questioned. "I like her, a lot," he finally said. "She's a very special person. But you ought to know that, you've worked with her."

"Exactly. Which is why the idea of you and her together makes me very nervous. She's been through a lot, Derek. What she doesn't need is to be hurt again, especially by somebody like you."

Derek met Jack's combative stare with one of his own. "What the hell is that supposed to mean?"

"You're a cold, tough bastard who goes through women the way a test driver goes through cars—you ride them for a while and then discard them for a shinier model. Come on, Derek, she deserves better than what you can give her."

Derek took a sip of his drink before answering, and when he did it was with a seriousness that surprised Jack. "She's different, and I feel differently about her. That's as much as you're going to get from me, Peck, so if you don't like it, that's too damn bad. Now shut up and order, I'm starving."

Jack considered the other man, and with a small smile, he buried his face in the oversized menu. Be careful, Sheila, he telepathically spoke to her. Just be careful. A caring Derek Lang might be even more dangerous than a cold Derek Lang.

The evening progressed as in the past: offer made, offer refused, the rest just good food and drink and conversation. Jack was feeling particularly mellow after three triple bourbons and two Napoleon brandies V.S.O.P. Too mellow.

"Derek, old pal," he began, leaning closer to the other man, "I gotta tell you something. I shouldn't, but I gotta." His words were getting sloppy, drenched by alcohol; he could hear it, but he couldn't stop himself. The liquor had soaked his common sense as well.

"And what might that be?" Derek gave no indication that he was not as sober as when he sat down three hours earlier. Not even too much alcohol could fully relax his guard.

"I've come up with an idea . . . it's so damned brilliant I can't believe guys like you and Gainey haven't already thought of it."

"Maybe we have. I won't know unless you tell."

"I can't. Wish I could, but it wouldn't be fair to Roger."

"Okay. You were the one who said you had something to tell me. It's your call."

Jack Rangel, for all his cleverness, his respect for timing in life, his astuteness about people, became, as do many men when they've had too much to drink, not just ordinary, but so ordinary that they need to seem special in any way possible.

"I want to tell you, Derek, I mean, Christ, you're gonna flip when you hear, but I owe it to Roger, you know . . ."

"Look, Peck, if there's one thing I hate it's having my curiosity unsatisfied—kind of like sex without coming. Now are you going to tell me or is it going to cost me another brandy to get it out of you?"

Jack's smile was loose, his blue eyes too bright and glassy. "I'll tell you, I'll tell you, what can it hurt, but another brandy wouldn't hurt either."

"No, I imagine not," Derek muttered under his breath, nodding at the attentive waiter stationed a discreet distance from the table.

"A home shopping credit card," Jack blurted.

"Explain," Derek dictated, suddenly all business, the effects of a heavy dinner and a great deal of alcohol vanished. And because Jack Rangel was filled with self-importance, magnified by spending the evening being courted as well as by too much reality-dulling liquor, he explained it all.

"I've done the research and it can't miss. The network, PCE, of course, will issue its own card like department stores do, and PCE will pay the manufacturer whose goods have been bought, getting a fee for usage plus a percentage of any finance charge that might accrue. It's a potential gold mine—fees for air time, fees from a credit card, fees for producing, give me another coupla months and I'll come up with a way to charge for just turning on the television set!"

"We already have that," Derek reminded him.

Jack looked confused, then nodded. "Oh, right, right, sure, that's what makes it cable. So what do you think, Derek? Damn clever, wouldn't you say?"

Derek smiled dutifully, and so Jack had no indication of the excitement churning within the businessman at the scope of Peck's idea. Jack also had no idea that he had provided Derek Lang with inside information just for the price of a dinner. He had sold himself far too cheaply. But Derek's smile told Jack none of this.

"Be right back," Peck said, sliding out to go to the men's room. Derek gestured for the bill, which he handled while Peck was gone, his mind spinning with ideas. It was funny how opportunities to screw Roger Gainey kept coming his way, one way or another.

When Jack returned, Derek was on his feet, indicating that it was time to leave. "Can I drop you off?" he offered.

"No, thanks. I'm okay."

"You sure? I wouldn't want anything to happen to you—one of these days you *will* work for me, so I want you in one piece."

"Well, until then, these dinners are always pleasant. Thanks, Derek, I enjoyed it."

They walked outside to wait for the valet to bring their cars. As they stood there, Jack turned to Derek with a sheepish awkwardness. "Derek, uh, listen, you know what I told you back there was . . . well, hell, it was the booze talking. I haven't told Roger yet, like I said. I'd like you to forget it, okay, just chalk it up to the one that got away. What do you say?"

The air, thick with humidity and desert breeze, suddenly grew still. A smile crept along Derek's mouth, dying before it could reach his eyes. "The one that got away. Interesting concept. Unusual for me, but interesting."

Then the valet was bringing Jack's car to a screeching halt, and Jack was shaking Derek's hand. "Thanks again for dinner, Derek, and for the offer, and for being more of a gentleman than I gave you credit for. And Derek? Remember—go easy with Sheila."

"You have my word."

If the irony of that was lost on Jack, so was the rest of the sentence as he got into his car and drove away.

"You have my word, Jack Rangel," was what Derek Lang actually said.

That night Derek Lang found himself missing Sheila Gainey fiercely, so strongly that he almost hated her for causing him this discomfort. She had given her word that she would call him tonight, but there had been no message waiting for him, and the phone had been silent throughout the night. It was then he realized, as never before, that it was the weight of disappointment that could tip the scale between hope and hate. And balance was a terrible thing to lose. A terrible thing.

Chapter
Seventeen

There is only so much a person can take. Most people who experience hate or pain or rage or regret or disappointment rely on time to mellow the emotion. They move on with their lives, away from the cause of the disruption.

Occasionally, however, a limit of psychological endurance is reached—often provoked by nothing particularly exceptional from what has occurred in the past; but the corrosive effect of perceived misdeeds repeated and unpunished has finally taken its toll. When this happens, it becomes impossible to move on until action is taken, something done to retrieve control, self-respect. It is not that the person has made a sudden decision to climb out of the hole of victimization. Rather, it is an extreme negative feeling that requires, desperately, an outlet.

• • •

"What are you doing here? Whatever you want, couldn't it have waited?"

"No, I've waited long enough."

"I don't appreciate you coming here uninvited. So will you please turn around and leave. Now."

"No."

"No?"

"No."

"This is absurd. I want you out. Whatever is troubling you can be discussed at a more convenient time."

"This is convenient. For me. And frankly, I don't really care whether it's convenient for you. You see, the truth is that what you want no longer is going to matter much to anyone, least of all to you."

"Are you drunk?"

"Never more sober. I don't need false courage for what I'm about to do."

"What are you talking about?"

"I'm talking about putting an end to your arrogance, to your humiliation of me, to your absolute refusal to listen to me and to hear me. I am talking about—" A hand shot forward, snapping sharp into visibility like a switchblade. In the hand was a hard object that smacked against the other person's head, stunning him.

"Wha—"

Another hard blow to the side of the head and the person tottered. Another, fiercer, blow, and the person collapsed to his knees.

"Stop. We'll talk. Just stop this madness before you do something you'll regret."

"I did something I regret. That's why I'm here now."

The hard object was dropped to the carpet. The hand retreated to a pocket and emerged with something far deadlier.

"It's time. I decided it's finally time."

"You can't be serious."

"Never more serious in my life. Or yours."

The six shots from the .32-caliber gun riddled Derek Lang's body.

The hard object, sticky with blood and hair, was then strategically placed by Derek's head.

It was definitely a case of overkill, an irony the murderer appreciated.

PART

TWO

Chapter
Eighteen

Sheila was numb. In the past few days since Derek's murder, she had experienced a range of emotions she had previously believed were the concoctions of a novelist's overwrought imagination. Shock and grief, rage and helplessness, fear, despair, as well as the varying levels of each as they flowed toward and away until the next feeling claimed dominance.

And now, with the cruelly bright Phoenix sun beating down on the parched dark earth of Derek's grave, she felt nothing. She stared straight ahead into the limitless horizon, heard the murmured platitudes of the minister, and felt nothing. Even her grief had frozen into something so hard it no longer hurt.

It had been Linc who had called her with the news. She remembered how eagerly she had answered the phone's ring, hoping it was Derek. They had quarreled the night before, a stupid disagreement, she had thought, hoping he would think so, too, and was calling to mend fences. But that would never be. No more calls. No more exquisite nights of passion with a man who had breathed new life into her. No more fantasies formed, then fulfilled. Not even any more foolish arguments.

Murdered, Linc had told her. It made the eleven o'clock news, but Sheila had been reading, the television off. If Linc had not called, she might have awakened to learn about her lover's death on the front page of the morning newspaper—like a stranger. Linc had offered to come by, but she preferred to be by herself, needing to be alone to absorb the incredible finiteness of what had occurred. Freddie had called; Roger, too, and many people from her office who were aware of her relationship with Derek. She remained calm during each conversation, so calm that she never cried. Still had not. When the shock ebbed, all those other feelings flooded in, and there seemed to be no room left for the tears.

As she stood graveside now, a night two weeks ago came to mind. She and Derek had been in bed, making plans for a romantic weekend at L'Auberge in Sedona. Then they had made remarkably sweet and tender love, the kind of unhurried sensuality that lingers in all the senses long afterward.

She would never again experience that with him. Nor he with her, she reminded herself. She did not know if they had loved each other, but now they would never know. Both of them had been cheated by this senseless act of violence.

It was, she realized, the never knowing what might have been that hurt the most.

As the last of the dirt was shoveled over the grave, Sheila noticed the mourners forming a line to pay their last respects. She did not want to stand in line behind others, did not want to wait to tell the man who had become so meaningful to her in such a short time how badly she would miss him. She had to leave. She would come back another time, alone. Maybe then, when it was just the two of them, she'd be able to cry for what they each had lost.

Walking out of the cemetery toward her car, Sheila wondered, not for the first time since learning of how he had died, what had happened. Instinctively, she did not believe it had been a random act of violence, a defensive action by an intruder who had not expected Derek to be in his hotel suite. Someone had deliberately set out to put an end to Derek Lang's life. Why? What had Derek done to provoke someone to take such drastic measures? She did not think she harbored any illusions about Derek. As a businessman, he held nothing more sacred than his own desires. But she knew a caring, supportive, funny, generous Derek, a man made frightened by feelings, a man with vulnerabilities. Could this man have committed an act of such ruthlessness against another that only murder existed as a solution? She was unwilling to accept that possibility; to do so would diminish—no, destroy—what she was convinced they had shared.

Sheila wanted Derek's killer found quickly. Death has a way of making memories selective, always erring in favor of the deceased. If Derek had been capable of making someone angry enough to kill, she needed to know this about him so that she could move forward in life without regret for the fantasy of what might have been weighing her down.

Chapter
Nineteen

Detective Michael Raintree of the Phoenix Police Department, Homicide Division, hated funerals. He hated them because they meant that someone no longer could taste the sand on his tongue or feel its grit in his nostrils when a fierce sandstorm blew in across the desert. Could no longer stare in wonder at a desert rose amid the cacti. Could never again watch the sun set and a ball of moon appear. He hated funerals because they meant that some poor soul was eternally relegated to being beneath the Arizona earth he cherished.

Despite his line of work, Detective Raintree attended few funerals, usually only when they might help solve a case. Which, technically, was not true with today's services for Derek Lang. The suspect could have been picked up four days ago when the chambermaid first discovered Lang's body in his permanent suite at the Scottsdale Princess Hotel. There had been enough crime-scene evidence to give a new definition of open-and-shut. Which is what bothered him. Which is why, on the basis of an outstanding seventeen-year career and a solved-case record of 93 percent, Michael was able to convince his lieutenant to let him dig a little deeper for a few days—on his own. Michael knew better than to discount the obvious, but the stench of frame was all over this one. No killer could be stupid enough to leave his damn name lying around.

Once Detective Raintree's lieutenant had given him the go-ahead, Michael determined not to question his prime suspect until all other possibilities—assuming there were others—had been looked into. And so now he was at this funeral, in support of his theory that crimes like this were usually committed by someone close to the victim, someone who had reached the end of his emotional tether with the victim.

He had been studying the various worlds of Derek Lang for the past several days and nights. The man's reach had been far, but Michael was concentrating on Lang's Phoenix life, the world of infomercials and home shopping that Raintree's wife had recently discovered to be even more fascinating than soap operas. He recognized a few of the people standing graveside and had begun to delve into their personal histories in order to unearth the various psychologies at play. At forty, Michael had the kind of wisdom only very old or very saddened people possess. He was able to hear pain or anger, disappointment, frustration, and discern the almost imperceptible nuance that told him the pain or anger, disappointment, frustration went far deeper, and was thus more dangerous, than was being claimed as the truth.

That was why he chose to leave his prime suspect for last. He wanted time to discover if anyone else had motive to murder, since even without the physical evidence found by Lang's body, Roger Gainey would definitely lead off a suspect list, his former wife a close second, given that same physical evidence. Michael had already learned that the victim had been Gainey's toughest rival in business, and he had also been up close and personal with his ex-wife. Then again, Michael had not learned this through any official channels; his own wife had turned out to be a source of gossip or valuable information—further investigation would determine which.

Motive. Means. Opportunity. On the surface, Roger Gainey seemed to have plenty of motive. The means was locked away in the station's evidence room. No doubt, he'd find the man had had opportunity.

Too pat. Just too damned pat.

Michael made a short list of local suspects, aware but unconvinced in his gut that it could have been someone from out of town or a total stranger.

The list was unscientifically put together by his own particular method of referencing and cross-referencing. At the outset of any investigation, when a name came up anywhere more than once, it made his short list. That gave him a place to start. He also liked to begin with the least likely candidate, as a warm-up exercise. So he began with Gayle Crockett.

"Yes, I had an affair with the man, but that was years ago, we've remained friends. I try to remain friends with my lovers, don't you, Detective?"

Michael ignored the taunt. He was not particularly uncomfortable interviewing the glamorous entertainer, but he knew it would be all too easy to succumb to her charm and forget the reason he was in her hotel suite now, asking her questions about her relationship to a dead man. She was still a magnificent-looking female, more dynamic and exciting than women half her age. He didn't know what she was selling as an infomercial, but he didn't have a doubt it would be a huge success.

"Ms. Crockett, I apologize for having to question you like this, and frankly, I have no doubt of your innocence, but because you were once close to the victim and do know some others who also had dealings with him, I was hoping you might shed light on certain issues."

"I'm not really a suspect?"

Michael smiled briefly. "Really not. I checked out your phone bill from your room here at the Biltmore the night of Lang's death. You were on the phone a lot, Ms. Crockett, a lot. And then there was room service. No, I'd say you're in the clear. But you did know the deceased and you have an infomercial slated to run on his network. The connection seemed worthy of further investigation, that's all."

"I don't see how I can help. I met Derek Lang on vacation quite some time ago, and we had a brief fling. At the time, I didn't know a thing about home shopping or infomercials. In fact, I think Derek was just starting out in the business then—he had made millions in a variety of businesses, you know."

Michael nodded. "I'm aware of that, but since Phoenix is where he was killed and Phoenix is where he had his infomercial network, I'm making a big leap of faith that his killer might have had something to do with that business."

"I still don't see how I can help you, Detective. I've only just completed my first infomercial—Sheila Gainey produced it for me and Derek Lang bought it for his network."

Raintree consulted a notepad. "Sheila Gainey—weren't she and Mr. Lang involved?"

"Involved?" the actress repeated with a sly smile. "As in, were they sleeping together? Yes, Detective, I believe they were."

"Did they have a falling out?"

"How would I know? Sheila and I don't exchange girl talk on a regular basis, Detective. We're both professional women with a lot on our plates. Besides, if you think breaking up with Derek would be a motive for murder, you don't know Sheila. If she didn't kill her ex-husband, then she can't kill anyone."

The detective pretended to consult his notes. "That would be about a year ago that he left her, right?"

"Something like that."

"Another woman?"

"I wouldn't know. Why don't you ask him?"

"I intend to, Ms. Crockett, count on it." He waited a beat, then: "Do you know Roger Gainey, Ms. Crockett?"

She nodded. "Yes, for a long time. I met Sheila through him, in fact. Roger had been after me to do an infomercial for his network—Derek, too, for that matter. I had been resisting—sort of the end of the line for a performer," she admitted with a rueful shrug.

"Obviously you changed your mind."

"Obviously I thought I better."

"Sorry, I didn't mean—"

"Never mind, Detective, I'm just a little sensitive about the whole thing, that's all. And yes, I changed my mind. When Sheila approached me, the timing seemed right. I didn't care who aired the infomercial—that was Sheila's business. But she came to me at the right time with a product I could live with, which neither Roger nor Derek did. And no, before you even ask it, I did not have an affair with Roger Gainey, Detective."

Raintree's lips twitched. "I assume Gainey and Lang knew each other?"

"That I wouldn't know, but I would assume so, too. After all, they're both in Phoenix and they both are in this crazy new business."

"Ever see them together?"

"Never."

"Never?"

"Detective," Gayle said with some asperity, "I told you, I'm new to infomercials, and I've been to Phoenix maybe six, seven times in my life. I just happened to be here when one of the few people I know in this town got murdered. Whenever I've socialized with the Gaineys—when they were still married, that is—it had been in Los Angeles or Las Vegas. And when I've seen Derek Lang, it certainly hasn't been here. So there's been no occasion for me to see the two men together."

Michael was nodding. "Just bear with me a few minutes longer, Ms. Crockett, and then I'll leave you in peace, I promise. Did Sheila Gainey ever mention any names, any people she knew through Derek Lang or her ex-husband, anyone at all whom she didn't like, or who was causing trouble, anything at all that struck you as negative or odd?"

Gayle thought for a moment. "There was Freddie Bickford," she told him. "Sheila spoke of him a couple of times, but not necessarily negatively. He's Roger's lawyer—used to be his partner."

"What about him?" Raintree asked.

"Nothing, really. Just that Sheila saw him or spoke to him regularly—they've remained friends despite the divorce. In fact, a couple of times Sheila would speak with Freddie or see him and then tell me that Roger was blaming her for some troubles he was having with the business . . . I don't know what exactly, but I got the feeling that Freddie enjoyed giving Sheila these morsels of gossip and bad news. I guess he wasn't any more thrilled with Roger's behavior toward Sheila than the rest of us."

"It was an ugly divorce?"

"It was an unnecessary divorce. Male menopause, pure and simple." She shot him a blistering look that dared him to argue with her. He didn't.

"Any others, Ms. Crockett? Anyone else Sheila Gainey spoke of—positive or negative—who was involved with both Lang and Roger Gainey?"

"Not really, although she did mention a woman to me . . . kind of an interesting name . . . damn . . . sorry, Detective, I can't . . . wait a minute . . . it was like a jewel . . . diamond . . . no, Diamante, that was it. Marilu Diamante. Sheila spoke of her once or twice, said she was some mucky-muck in Washington, D.C."

Detective Raintree added the new name to his list. "What did she have to do with Derek Lang?"

"Her D.C. job involved infomercials and cable shopping in some way, so they probably knew each other professionally. Again, you'll have to ask Sheila. I did get the sense, though, that there *might* have been more to it."

Raintree stood up, and the performer, slightly taken aback by the unexpected end to the interview, also got to her feet, and shook his offered hand.

"That's it?" she asked, showing her surprise.

"That's it, Ms. Crockett. You've been a tremendous help, thank you."

"I was planning to fly back home to Los Angeles this afternoon."

The detective smiled. "Have a safe flight. I'll be looking forward to seeing your infomercial."

When he got back to the station house, he slowly crossed Gayle

Crockett's name off his list, and underscored the name she had given him: Marilu Diamante. She had been present at the funeral service—that he had determined easily enough by asking. He hoped she hadn't left town yet or he would just have to make her return. At the funeral. Mentioned by name. Definitely a candidate for the short list.

Chapter
Twenty

Scott Brickell hated remembering that evening. He had been beyond desperation. Tahoe was a total bust; he had accumulated another $22,000 in markers. Derek Lang had been his only hope.

"I'm sorry, Scott. I don't have a thing for you."

"But you promised!" Scott bit his lip, ashamed of the whine, ashamed of his need.

"No, Scott, I said if the right product came along I'd think of you, but no one wants you representing their product. You're poison with advertisers."

"Bullshit."

"No, Scott, not bullshit, truth. Your failure to sell stuff on PCE, your reputation as a gambler—this is well known to advertisers and manufacturers. You're a celebrity, and whether your troubles have been magnified or not, the fact remains that you've acquired a reputation as a loser. No one wants their product associated with a loser."

A little run of lousy luck and the bastards were writing him off! Damn him and Roger Gainey and all of them who dared to underestimate Scott Brickell!

"I wish you'd try a little harder, Derek. I know I can give you what you want," he said with a lid on his anger.

"Maybe you can, but I need you to prove to me and advertisers that you're clean. And not just from the gambling."

"What's that supposed to mean?"

"You know exactly what I'm talking about, Scott."

The comic laughed dismissively. "Hey, what's a little coke now and then? Don't tell me you haven't indulged."

"Scott, that's what I mean, that's what's wrong. Your attitude. You think anyone not as fucked up as you is a loser." Derek shook his head with mock pity. "A cocaine-addicted gambler—what a combination. You've got the paranoia of one butting heads with the blind hope of the other. No wonder you're in trouble."

"That's not fair. I've had a run of lousy luck, that's all. And you're going along with the others who think I'm finished, that I don't have what it takes anymore. You're wrong, Lang. You're all wrong, and I'm gonna make you regret what you're doing to me. You'll see, I'm gonna make you sorry you went back on your word."

"Mr. Brickell, you were saying that you had a meeting with Derek Lang to discuss a new infomercial you were doing for him, is that right? Mr. Brickell?"

Scott blinked rapidly to bring him back from the last meeting with Derek Lang, back to the reality of this man sitting on his couch, in his living room. A cop, asking questions about his relationship with Derek Lang. Some smart bastard got to him before he could. Just as well. With the way his luck was going, he'd probably have gotten caught in the act.

"That's right, Detective."

"And it went well?"

"It went as expected."

"Mr. Brickell, please don't make this any more difficult than it has to be. It's very easy for me to check what you tell me. Did the meeting go well?" Michael Raintree pressed.

Scott shrugged. "Not particularly," he admitted. "I need to pay off some bills, and Lang wasn't ready with a spot for me yet. I was disappointed, but not enough to kill him."

"And when was this meeting?"

"I already told you, five, six days ago, I can't remember."

"Did you threaten Mr. Lang?"

Scott's eyes widened with surprise. "Why would I do that?"

"Disappointment can make a man do many things, Mr. Brickell. I'm sure you can appreciate that."

"No, I didn't threaten him," Scott stated. But he had. He had leaned across Lang's desk until he could feel the other man's breath in his face. That's when he had told him he was going to regret doing this to him, he was gonna make him sorry, him and all the others who had written Scott Brickell off.

"Is that a threat?" Lang had asked with laughter in his voice, a sound that had made Scott giddy with rage. He had reached over and grabbed Lang by his necktie, wrapping it around his fist and pulling so hard that the other man was lifted from his chair. But Lang hadn't blinked. Hadn't pushed him away. Hadn't done one damn thing, just waited, staring at him, knowing Scott would release him. And he had.

Lang's laughter as he fled the office was the final humiliation that sent Scott spiraling into a dizzying maelstrom of fury mixed with fear, feeding on gram after gram of cocaine in the days since that meeting. He hadn't even known Lang had been murdered until that sow, Alicia Devon, had called to tell him.

"Where were you between eight and ten o'clock last Thursday night, Mr. Brickell?"

"What? You can't really suspect *me?* Hey, I'm not answering another question without my lawyer."

"As you wish. This is merely a formality," Raintree explained. "We have to ask that question of everybody. It doesn't mean you're a suspect, but if you want your lawyer present, by all means call him and we can arrange to meet down at headquarters."

How the hell was he supposed to remember where he was last night, let alone almost a week ago? Shit, he was either drunk or stoned or both. And he was alone, that's for sure. He couldn't get it up these days if he had the help of a tripod propping it.

"I was at the Gila River Reservation Casino playing poker." He began to nibble hard on a ragged cuticle.

Raintree nodded and wrote on his notepad. "Can you give me the names of any of the people you played with or anyone else who might vouch for your presence there? I'm sorry, Mr. Brickell, I know these questions are insulting, but we have to ask them in order to eliminate all possible suspects."

"How the hell would I know who I played with?" Scott blustered. "Go down there, they'll remember me, count on it. It's not every day a star like me shows up in a dump like that."

"Why did you?"

"Come again?"

"I asked why you went there if it's so beneath you. That is what you're saying, isn't it, Mr. Brickell?"

"Yeah, yeah, I guess. I don't know why I went, needed some action, that's why. What other reason could there be?"

Scott watched warily as the detective put away his pad and stood up. "I'll be checking this out, Mr. Brickell," he said as he walked to the door.

"Be my guest."

"One more thing, Mr. Brickell."

"Yeah? What now?"

"Next time you talk to the police, check to make sure there are no cocaine flecks around your nose. Have a nice day now."

Scott slammed shut the door and hastily rubbed his nose on his sleeve so hard it started to bleed, which had been happening too often lately. Shit, shit, shit!

He went back to his bedroom and slumped on his unmade bed. He had to change his luck, he just had to. He had to get rid of the stench of fear he could smell all over himself. He was even afraid the truth could hurt him. He could have told the cop he had been home by himself. He was innocent of killing Lang, so he didn't have to lie, but his luck was so rotten the cop wouldn't have believed him.

He was glad Lang was dead, served him right. Too bad they hadn't gotten Roger Gainey, too. It was Gainey who had given him bad products and bad time slots and who wouldn't renew his contract when he needed it most and who poisoned his wife against him so she wouldn't find a product for him. Gainey, a pal once, now an enemy who deserved Lang's fate. It was a long shot, but maybe someone else was thinking the same thing. Maybe there was someone else out there the two men had humiliated or angered or disappointed to the breaking point, someone who had killed once and would not find it difficult to do so again.

It was a long shot, yes, but hey, he had played them before and won. Wasn't it about time his luck changed?

What Detective Michael Raintree was thinking about Scott Brickell almost amounted to a stroke of good fortune. He wasn't sure Brickell was telling him the truth about playing poker at the reservation casino—although it was easy enough to determine. Poor slob. He and his wife used to enjoy the comic's routines whenever he was on late-night TV or when he had his specials. They had even seen him in person once in Reno, laughing almost nonstop at his quick, off-color patter. Where had that guy gone? Up a straw and into his nose. Or onto a crap table. Or both.

No, Michael Raintree wasn't convinced Scott Brickell had been playing poker the night of Derek Lang's murder, but he was pretty sure he wasn't the killer. His coke high wouldn't have been strong enough or lasted long enough to give him courage to perform the act. Besides, he was a gambler on a losing streak. Brickell would have known better than to bet on himself.

Chapter
Twenty-one

Marilu Diamante felt herself all jagged angles and sharp edges, glass broken and splintered, stepped on. Derek was dead. Gone was the investment of over four years of her life. Gone was the carefully created blueprint for her future. There was such pain for her loss that she was tempted to pat herself for bruises. But there was anger, too. For whoever had robbed her of hope. For whoever had, in her mind, wrested control of her life by taking Derek's. Anger, too, for the Phoenix police. Of course she had attended Derek's funeral, an appearance that had convinced the police she merited closer scrutiny, but on their timetable. So she was stuck here until they met with her and said she could go, and that could still be another day or two.

The waiting was hell. It left her with nothing to take her mind off what really was making her wince. And that was the irrefutable fact that Derek had no longer been hers to lose.

As she sat now in the air-conditioned dimness of the lounge at the

Camelback Inn, waiting for the vodka to blunt the edges, she recalled their last conversation, at lunch the day he was murdered. She had flown in that morning from Los Angeles, intending to spend the weekend with Derek and then fly back to Washington Sunday afternoon. Things hadn't worked out quite as she had intended.

They had met right here, in this very lounge. That had been Derek's suggestion, and it told her as nothing else really could that it was finally over between them. How could she continue to deny it when for the first time since the beginning of their affair they had not met in a room with a bed. Even though she was not the type of woman to fool herself, Marilu had continued to hope since that weekend at the St. Regis that whoever the other woman was, she'd wear out her welcome. Derek would come back to her, their bond stronger than ever. But by suggesting they meet at the cocktail lounge, Derek had snatched that last positive possibility away from her.

He'd said all the expected things: He cared for her tremendously . . . always would. Respected her. Admired her. Hoped she'd find the happiness she deserved. Hoped they could continue to work together whenever the occasion arose. Blah, blah, blah. He didn't apologize for the other woman. He didn't apologize for causing her hurt. But then, why should he? Marilu asked herself. He had never promised her anything, and she had never revealed how much he meant to her, how much she was *counting* on her meaning as much to him. How could she blame him when she had been so careful to camouflage her true feelings?

She had been about to tell him, too, when his pager went off. He had glanced down at the number, and suddenly grinned. "That's her," he had said with more warmth than she had ever heard in his voice. "I've gotta run, Lu." He leaned over and kissed her cheek. Her cheek! As if they had never been more than business colleagues! She wanted to be angry with him, but she couldn't. It wasn't his fault that after several years with one particular woman, someone else might capture his fancy—fleetingly—which meant casual, unimportant. He was not supposed to fall in love!

And so Marilu's deepest and hottest and most enduring anger was reserved for *her,* for the woman who had tricked Derek into believing he cared more for her than for Marilu. It was this woman who made her gut twist. It was this woman who had stepped on and shattered her mirror of dreams. That's whom she blamed. Not Derek, no. Only *her.*

"Hi. Sorry I'm late."

Marilu looked up as Sheila slid into the banquette and leaned over to peck her cheek. "I'll have what she's having," Sheila said to the waitress.

"Vodka on the rocks? That's not like you, Sheila."

"I don't much feel like me these days."

"Me either."

"It's so awful, Lu. I miss him terribly."

"*You* do?"

"Yes. Why does that surprise you?"

"I don't know. I didn't realize you and he even knew each other that well."

"Lu." Sheila leaned closer to her. "We've been lovers for three months."

No doubt she was drunk. How else to explain the ridiculous words she had just heard? Liquor has a way of hitting fast when your defenses are down. That must be it, Marilu decided, staring at her friend and seeing a stranger with remarkably big and bright dark eyes, beautifully smooth skin and a full mouth, slightly open.

"I thought you knew." The stranger was talking again, more nonsense.

"Sheila?"

"Marilu, what's wrong? What is it?"

"Sheila? What are you talking about? You and Derek? Is that what you expect me to believe?"

"Lu, come on," Sheila laughed nervously. "Of course I expect you to believe it, it's the truth. We'd been involved for a while. I really did think you knew."

Marilu's smile was a sharp red slash. "You didn't tell me and Derek certainly didn't tell me, so how could I have known? I'm many things, but a mind reader isn't one of them."

"Of course not. I just assumed you knew because you're so plugged into our world." Sheila shrugged. "I should have told you."

"Yes, you should have."

Another small laugh. "To tell you the truth, I think I was a little embarrassed. I mean, Derek Lang of all people. Roger's rival, a former boyfriend of yours, a wealthy businessman with a mean reputation as a playboy. I guess I couldn't quite get used to the idea that we were together, myself."

"Former boyfriend?" That was all Marilu heard, caught on it like a fish hooked by bait.

Sheila frowned at her. "Well, yes. Come on, Lu, you told me you and Derek had a fling years ago, that it was over before it began."

"I lied."

"Marilu—"

"I lied. Derek and I have been having an affair for four years. I loved him, Sheila. I loved him."

"Oh my God!"

"I knew there was someone else. He even admitted it, but I assumed she was a casual fling. Not"—Marilu slid her eyes up and down Sheila's face, smearing it with disgust—"not a friend."

"I had no idea, Marilu. No idea at all. Derek never said a word. I swear it."

"Would it have made a difference if you had known?"

"Of course! How can you even question that? Wouldn't it have made a difference if you had known about me?"

"No."

"No?"

"No. I loved him, Sheila. Obviously, you didn't."

"I'm so sorry, Marilu. Believe me, please. He should have told me."

"No!" Marilu quickly shot back. "*You* should have told me. You, Sheila, not Derek."

"But he knew we were friends."

"That wouldn't have mattered. You see, I told him what I had told you—that he had been, as you so poetically put it, over before he began. There was no reason for Derek to tell either one of us that he was sleeping with the other."

"He was still sleeping with you?" Sheila's eyes reflected her astonishment.

"Up to the end." Not quite the truth, but so what?

"That bastard."

"What? How can you blame Derek when it's you who's at fault? You should have told me and then I would have explained about Derek and me."

"Why did you keep him a secret all these years?"

"Why did you keep him a secret all these months?"

"I told you, Marilu, I felt self-conscious about him. And, frankly, I was cherishing my happiness. I hadn't experienced it in so long that I was superstitious about it, knowing how fleeting it could be. I have, after all," Sheila said more sternly, "been burned badly this past year, when I thought I was happy. I didn't want to spoil anything. You're right, though, someone should have told you, only it should have been Derek. Actually, I'm surprised you didn't know, so many others did."

"Well, I didn't, and Derek did tell me there was someone; I never imagined it would be someone I trusted, a friend."

"If you trusted me so much you would have told me about Derek long before. And you still haven't answered that. Why did you lie about him?"

It was Marilu's turn to shrug. "We both thought it was better that way. Might have struck some as conflict of interest, collusion, inside information, who knew. We just felt that discretion was necessary."

"Even with me, a so-called friend?" When Marilu said nothing, Sheila gazed into the clear liquid of her drink for several long moments before turning again, facing the other woman. "He should have told both of us about the other, Lu. It was Derek's responsibility to either tell us or firmly break off with one of us. He did neither."

"It's not his fault, it's yours."

"I know you don't really believe that. You're too smart, too sensible. When you're thinking more clearly, you'll realize there is only one of two explanations. Either Derek was just doing what many men do, and that's score as much as possible, as often as possible, regardless of the consequences. Frankly, I doubt that. I don't doubt that he might have enjoyed the notion that he was having sex with friends, kind of like the thrill of cheating on your wife, I would imagine. But even that seems beneath Derek, don't you agree? If you do, then you'll have no choice but to accept the second explanation. And that is that he gave you all the signals and you simply chose to ignore them. So in the end you can blame Derek or you can blame yourself, but not me, Marilu, not me."

Sheila never knew how she managed to leave some bills on the table and walk steadily out of the lounge and into her car. She certainly counted herself among the luckiest people alive that she was able to drive and get home without an accident.

She tried to make sense of what Marilu had told her. Roger had once said that Derek had no passion for anything but the deal, yet the Derek she had known had been an ardent lover, an attentive listener, a fun companion, an interesting businessman. He had lifted her confidence about so many things, enabling her to look at herself with pride again, enabling her to approach life with assurance again. If she could get all that from a man with no real soul, then she would take it.

But she could not take being two-timed. She wanted very much to believe that Marilu, so in love with Derek, had deliberately convinced herself that she would have him back when this temporary infatuation was over. She could understand that irrational rationalization: she could not criticize Marilu for deceiving herself. Sometimes the only alternative when the truth is that painful is deep denial. Hadn't she done it herself when it came to Roger and their marriage?

Ultimately, no one was really to blame. It was a vicious circle: Marilu keeping Derek a secret, Derek not thinking to tell her, Sheila, about Marilu, Sheila not telling Marilu about Derek. Secrets. Not mean secrets, but secrets that turned mean.

Marilu Diamante wasted no time.

"You're sure about this, Ms. Diamante? Derek Lang had told Sheila Gainey that he wanted to break it off with her. Is that right?"

"Yes, Detective Raintree, that's exactly what happened. He said she went berserk on him, that was the word he used, berserk. Started throwing things at him, cursing him, threatening him that she wouldn't let him get away with this. She had been dumped once and she would never let another man do that to her again. Derek said he couldn't get out of her place fast enough."

"Oh, so this was at Ms. Gainey's house, not his hotel suite?" Raintree asked, pencil poised over notepad. Marilu nodded, watching the detective write. "And when did Mr. Lang tell you about it?"

"At lunch the next day. He and I are . . . were very dear friends, Detective." She paused. "I might as well tell you the truth. Once we were more, but that was a long time ago. We remained good friends, however, and whenever I came to Phoenix we'd see each other."

"So you knew about his affair with Sheila Gainey?"

"Of course."

"I assume you know her, Sheila Gainey?"

"Yes, but not well. My dealings have primarily been with her ex-husband, Roger Gainey. I didn't have much to do with Sheila except to say hello when we were at the same social functions. And once her husband left her, I had no business with her at all."

"I see. Now, when did you say the deceased told Ms. Gainey it was over between them?" Raintree asked, flipping back pages from his pad, looking for the earlier reference.

"The night before he died, Detective Raintree. The night before." Marilu's expression was concern crossed with confusion. "You don't think she . . . no, that's ridiculous. She would never hurt Derek, she loved him."

Michael Raintree smiled knowingly. "A woman scorned, Ms. Diamante? I've found they can be capable of all manner of terrible things . . . in the name of love, of course."

"I suppose you're right." Marilu sighed her reluctant acceptance of such a universal truth. "I must have felt it was possible, otherwise I wouldn't have come down here to see you, would I have, Detective? I guess what Derek described, the savagery of her attack, and those threats, well, obviously they disturbed me enough to bring me down here."

"And I very much appreciate that you did. Saved me a trip to see you. Now just a few more questions, if you don't mind."

"I don't see how I can help any more than I have."

"This is just routine, Ms. Diamante, but we need to know where you were between eight and ten o'clock the night of Mr. Lang's murder."

"I was in my room at the Camelback Inn. Alone. I had flown in that morning from Los Angeles at Derek's request. That's why we had lunch—he asked me to make a special trip. He was really having trouble with Sheila and wanted my advice." Tears welled up in her eyes. "I was so tired that I decided not to have dinner with him. If only I had . . ."

"It's interesting, Ms. Diamante, that a man as sophisticated and experienced as Mr. Lang would seek the advice of a friend when he needed to get rid of a lady."

"Not so interesting, Detective. Men who can run multimillion-dollar empires often find women the most difficult of all challenges they face."

"You do have a point there." Raintree grinned. "Well, I guess that'll be all for now."

"For now? I thought once we spoke, I'd be free to go back to Washington?"

"Again, it's just a formality, but I do have to check out your alibi for the night of Mr. Lang's death. I'm sure everything will be just fine, but I would appreciate if you could stay around until I know for sure—probably another day or two at the outside."

"I don't know how you can check me out, Detective. I was in my room. Alone. Who's going to verify that for you?" Marilu could not help the testiness from lining her voice. Everything had been going according to plan until *this*.

"We have our ways, Ms. Diamante," Raintree assured her with a smile. "Of course you're free to go, but just in case I might need you again, you'd have to fly all the way back here."

Marilu took a deep breath. "I see your point. All right, I'll stay through the weekend, but then I really must leave."

"I'm sure that'll be more than enough time. You've given us quite a bit to go on, Ms. Diamante. I imagine we'll be able to close this case by the time you have to leave."

"That's what I was hoping you'd say, Detective." And Marilu then turned to leave before the detective could see the smug smile on her face.

Detective Raintree did not have to see Marilu Diamante's face to know that she was lying. Not about being alone in her room the night of Lang's murder, probably not. But about Sheila Gainey? Oh yeah, she was lying about her, about knowing her, about Lang breaking off with her, about her going berserk. Michael Raintree's intuition, honed by years of sad evidence of man's basest instincts, recognized pain when he saw it, understood a cry for vengeance when he heard it. What this interview with Ms. Diamante had revealed to him was that if Sheila Gainey was guilty of anything, it was only of having the man another woman wanted.

Chapter
Twenty-two

Michael Raintree's eyelids itched with the grit of fatigue. He had no one but himself to blame for the condition, insisting as he did that there was more to Derek Lang's murder than met the eye. He knew he was right, too, but that didn't make it better, just increased the tension of having to hear what someone wasn't saying, reading body language—the twitch, the blink, the almost imperceptible movement that told him a person was either lying or at least not telling the entire truth. It was exhausting work, and he still had a way to go.

All he was certain of at this point in the investigation was that Gayle Crockett could be eliminated from the list of suspects. The night maid at the Camelback Inn had knocked on the door of Marilu Diamante's room at eight o'clock when she had gone there to turn down her bed. The maid verified that Marilu—or some woman—had called out that she didn't need service and no, she didn't even want the complimentary chocolates. Room service and a bellboy had said that the woman in Room 275 had ordered a light dinner at nine-fifteen, but the tray had been delivered and picked up outside her door, so it was certainly technically possible for Marilu Diamante to have slipped away, gone to Derek Lang's hotel apartment, killed him, and been back in her room without anyone noticing. Michael didn't think so, though.

He still hadn't been able to find out who had played poker with Scott Brickell—if, indeed, anyone had—but he had a hard time believing the cokehead could get it together enough to actually plan and execute a murder, nor did he see Brickell as being clever enough to plant evidence that pinned the crime on someone else. No, that kind of thinking required more patience and control than an addict possessed. Still, he couldn't be eliminated totally until his alibi checked out.

He looked down at his list—several more and not much time left to prove to his lieutenant that his hunch was based on fact, not just gut instinct. He pulled the unmarked car up to the curb now, hesitating briefly before getting out. He had been a longtime fan of Alicia Devon, and it seemed to him that his wife had bought just about every product the singer hawked on those infomercials. She had even been complaining lately that Alicia Devon hadn't been on the air in a while and she missed her. Now here he was in front of her home about to question her about a murder. Christ, sometimes he hated this job.

She answered the doorbell herself.

"It's a real pleasure to meet you, Ms. Devon. My wife and I have been fans of yours for a long time," he greeted her.

"Thank you." Alicia smiled, touching a spit curl. "You must be Detective Raintree."

"Yes, ma'am. I won't take too much of your time, but if I may—" He nodded toward the not fully open door.

"Oh, of course. I'm sorry, I'm not thinking clearly. May I get you some coffee, water, soda?"

"No thank you, this won't take long."

Alicia led him into her den. On the walls were such show business memorabilia as framed gold records, a country music award, photographs of her with celebrities and politicians, photographs of her through the years, the aging process having been unnaturally arrested through the magic of surgeons' skills. Show business. Michael was sure police work had to be easier.

"I don't know how I can help you, Detective," Alicia said. "I wasn't even in Phoenix the night Derek Lang was killed."

"You weren't?"

"No. I was in Atlantic City, performing at the Taj Mahal there. You can check it out with my manager."

"I will, Ms. Devon. I did see you at the funeral, though, and that's why I'm here now. I'm doing a little investigating of people who might have been close with Mr. Lang, people who might have had a motive for seeing him dead."

"I certainly wasn't close with him," Alicia quickly stated, twisting a curl.

"But you knew him well enough to attend his funeral."

"Well, yes, of course. The world of infomercials is a small one. It seemed the respectful thing to do."

Michael looked unnecessarily at his notes. Alicia Devon had not made the A-list because she had been at the deceased's funeral. She made it because he had learned that the Queen of Infomercials, as she was known, had had a serious falling out with Roger Gainey and was shopping herself to other networks. It seemed she was "between engagements," as they said in show business. In other words, she needed work. Michael figured that that could make a person act in any manner of uncharacteristic ways—maybe even murder. He doubted it, though. He imagined Alicia Devon's value to him in the investigation would be as a source of information about the business and the players.

"I understand you're no longer with PCE-TV, is that right?"

"Yes," Alicia confirmed after a slight hesitation. "I decided to look elsewhere, some place more suitable."

"More suitable? In what way?"

The entertainer laughed indulgently. "Why, to my talents, Detective. I would think that would be obvious."

"I'm afraid I still don't understand. Is there really a difference in the networks?"

"Not in the networks, in the head of the network, the person who makes the final decisions on what infomercials to show. For stars of my caliber, Detective, we're as much the entertainment as the product, and we require the right merchandise, the right set design, the right time slot—everything so that both we and the goods we're selling are displayed to maximum advantage."

"And you didn't feel PCE-TV was doing that for you?"

"Not PCE, Detective, Roger Gainey."

"So you decided to look elsewhere."

"That's correct."

"*You* decided, Ms. Devon?" he prodded softly.

"Well, it was a mutual decision between Roger and myself," she allowed. "I assume you've already spoken to him and gotten his warped version."

"Actually, I haven't."

Alicia's blue eyes grew wide. "He should be at the head of your list, Detective. If anyone had a motive for doing away with Derek Lang, it was Roger Gainey."

"You mean because of the relationship with his ex-wife?"

"Oh, so you know about that. No, that was just one issue. Derek was better and bigger at everything, that's why. Roger was madly jealous of Derek, hated him, really hated him."

"Enough to kill him, Ms. Devon?"

Alicia's vehemence retreated. "Well, that I wouldn't know, of course, but if pressed, I'd have to say yes, enough to kill him, that's how much he hated the man."

"Did the deceased feel the same?"

"Excuse me?" Her hand dropped from her curl to her lap, attention warily on Michael.

"Did Derek Lang hate Roger Gainey?" he repeated.

"How would I know?"

"But you hate him, don't you, Ms. Devon?"

Again, the entertainer's eyes went round with surprise, and she nervously began to twist the fabric of her dress in the same mesmerizing rhythm she had worried her spit curls.

"Ms. Devon?" Michael prompted.

"No, I do not hate him. And even if I do, what has that to do with Derek Lang's death?"

"Did you approach Derek Lang for a job?" Michael went on, ignoring her question.

"I might have."

"And what happened?" When she did not answer immediately, he said, "I can check it out easily enough, Ms. Devon, but I'd appreciate it if you'd save me the trouble."

"Derek turned me down," she muttered, not looking at him.

"Oh, I see."

Alicia got to her feet and walked over to a credenza upon which were photographs and mementos from her career. "You don't see anything, Detective," she said softly, her back to him. "You can't possibly. I had a new infomercial produced by Sheila Gainey." She turned now, her face animated, the words flowing. "I thought it was beautiful irony, you see, getting Roger's ex-wife—who happens to be a producer—to put together the spot that was going to prove to Roger he had let go of a major star."

"I thought you said it was a mutual decision to part," Michael knowingly reminded her.

"She turned out to be no better than her former husband," Alicia continued with open bitterness.

"Derek Lang turned down your new infomercial, didn't he?" he asked, his voice gentle.

Alicia stared at him a moment, past him, Michael imagined, to the hurtful memory of the rejection. "Yes he did, Detective. Yes he did!"

"You were angry at him, weren't you?"

"No, no, not at Derek, at her, at Sheila Gainey! At Roger Gainey! Why should I be angry with Derek? He turned down an inferior spot. Who could blame him? I knew it was terrible, all wrong for me, my strengths, but she wouldn't listen."

"When did this happen?"

Alicia put back the framed picture of her and Willie Nelson she had been holding and returned to the sofa, facing Michael. Her eyes were so pale and dull that the detective thought she was going to be ill, but it was pain and anger that had taken life from them.

"Two days before he died," she answered. "I was devastated," she admitted. And then she again looked beyond the detective, beyond the room they were in to that afternoon in his office, sitting there with Sheila and the thick, suffocating silence after Derek had viewed the new infomercial. He had liked the product, but felt she was the wrong spokesperson for it. It was Sheila's fault! She had warned her that no one would believe Alicia Devon in a motivational spot, but that was all Sheila had been able to come up with and Alicia had been desperate. She had made herself believe that Derek Lang would take her on, convinced Nick that he could tell Roger Gainey to go to hell—Alicia Devon would be in the grave before she'd do his graveyard shift! That conviction and hope had sustained her until that moment in Derek Lang's office. She would never forget how Sheila had avoided her eyes or how Derek had said, with all the sincerity of a snake, "I'm sorry, Alicia, I don't see it for us. Try something else, why don't you? I'll always be willing to consider you, this just isn't the right spot for you, not if you want to revive your career."

Was it then the reality of her situation became, at last, unavoidable? Was it the word "revive" that triggered the audible whimper? So humiliating. Everything lately was so humiliating. It was a horrible way to go through life, exposing yourself to people because you needed them and because of that, giving them the power to humiliate you. She really was so tired of them all.

"Detective Raintree," she said, standing, "I'd like you to leave now, please. If you have any more questions, I'll have my lawyer get in touch with you."

Michael slowly closed his notebook. "For what it's worth, Ms. Devon, I think you're tremendously talented and I hope you're back on television soon."

There was the faintest glimmer of life in the blue eyes as they met his, and then it was gone. "Yes, well, someday, Detective. And now . . ."

"Just one more question, if I may?" he added, heading toward the door.

"Yes?"

"You mentioned that Roger Gainey hated Derek Lang. Is there anyone else you can think of who might have had reason to kill him?"

It took so long for Alicia to reply that Michael thought she might not have heard, lost as she was in her own anguish, but then she spoke. "I imagine the list is either very long or very short."

"Meaning?"

"Derek Lang was a powerful businessman with farflung operations and no doubt there were many people he outsmarted along the way. Those people would make up the long list." She eyed the detective appraisingly. "I have a feeling, though, that it's the short list you're interested in, the list of people in Derek Lang's Phoenix world. Am I right?"

Michael nodded. "So who would you put on the short list?"

"Let's see. If you've gotten around to me, then you must already know about Scott Brickell and A. L. Peck, since we are, or rather were, Gainey's biggest celebrities. But when he didn't want us, Derek Lang became the next big game. Now if he rejected them, too—" She shrugged meaningfully.

"Why include Peck with you and Brickell?" Michael asked. "I thought he was hugely successful."

Another shrug. "Hey, I thought *I* was hugely successful, too, and I'm sure Scott did as well."

"Seems to me there was motive to murder Gainey, not Lang."

"Not necessarily. Roger might have caused the pain, but if Derek Lang didn't want you, he closed the door on hope. You tell me which is worse, Detective, you tell me."

"I'm sorry, Ms. Devon, I truly am."

She nodded wearily. "Go see Peck, Detective. He doesn't have Scotty's 'special' problems and he doesn't have mine, either, for that matter."

"What problem is that, Ms. Devon?"

"He's not out of work."

•　•　•

"Thanks for agreeing to have lunch here at the house, Sheila. Sometimes the scene at a restaurant gets to be a little too much."

"A. L. Peck suddenly publicity shy?" Sheila smiled skeptically at him over the rim of her iced-tea glass.

"It's the Lang murder. This town's become Hollywood of the desert—you get the feeling everyone's talking about you and none of it's nice. It's even getting tough to get laid privately."

"I thought you liked an audience for that," she couldn't resist.

"I'm serious, Sheila. They're investigating all of us who had anything to do with Lang. I'm surprised they haven't gotten around to you yet. You've got to be a prime suspect."

"Me? That's ridiculous."

"Jilted lover? Murder has been committed for lesser motive."

"But I wasn't jilted. I—"

Peck held up a hand to stop her. "I don't want to know. It doesn't matter, okay? But don't be surprised when the cops come calling."

"Of course I won't be surprised. I'm expecting them, in fact. I got a call from a Detective Michael Raintree—I'm seeing him later. I'm sure he wants to see me because of my relationship with Derek, not because I'm any kind of suspect." She made a dismissive face. "Honestly, Linc, save your imagination for new infomercials."

"Roger, too," he went on, undaunted.

"Roger, too, what? If you invited me here to discuss Derek's murder, then I'd better leave right now. I miss him, Linc, I miss him a great deal, and I refuse to make him or our relationship a course on this menu."

Jack Rangel had originally invited Sheila over to catch up, enjoy each other's company without a parade of people coming by their table. He had had no intention of talking about Derek Lang except to find out how Sheila was handling it, but it seemed this Detective Michael Raintree was a one-man investigating force. He was coming by later this afternoon, and if anything made Jack jumpy it was dealing with the police.

"I'm sorry, Sheila," he said, nodding at Ricardo, his "man" who had just served them their crab salads. "That detective you mentioned called me, too. I guess the reality that the case isn't closed got me thinking who might have done it."

"Why you?" Sheila asked. "I didn't think you even knew Derek, except for a nodding acquaintance."

"Oh, I knew him," Jack said with a small smile. "He tried on a regular basis to steal me away from PCE."

"If that was a motive for murder, the streets would be littered with dead bodies."

"I didn't like him, Sheila. I didn't kill him, but I'm not sorry someone else did."

"Linc!"

"He was a man totally without scruples, without morality when it came to getting what he wanted. I find it difficult to believe that anyone who could be that ruthless in one aspect of his life was not the same in every area."

Rattled, she tossed her napkin over her uneaten salad and got to her feet, moving out of the shelter of the umbrellaed patio table to a chaise longue, the sun beating down on her head almost soothing compared to the hurtful recollection of the real last time she had been with Derek. She had seen that ruthless side of him, that man who could turn cold and distant, so chillingly removed that there was no reaching him. It was not what she wanted as her final memory of him, and so she had put it out of her mind, preferring their time a week earlier, when they had been planning a weekend away together. But Linc's words forced her to face that last night with him.

They had been in her house, Derek furious with her, demanding that she never again treat him with the kind of cavalier disregard she might have gotten away with with Roger, but that he would not tolerate. And all because she had not called him when she said she would. Sheila had been so stunned by his attitude that she did the truly unforgivable: she began to laugh. But there had been nothing humorous about Derek's outrage, or his absolute seriousness when he told her that unless he had her word she would never do it again, they would have to rethink their relationship.

At first, she explained why she had been unable to call, and for a busy executive like Derek, she assumed that would be sufficient. She assumed wrong; nothing would placate him, it seemed, and although a small part of her realized that he was overreacting because he cared and was unfamiliar with the feeling and how to deal with it, she found the situation unacceptable. She had not come so far only to be treated like property, as far from equals as master and slave. Which she said. One word then led to another, and before she knew it, she was holding open her front door for him at seven o'clock at night, removing him from her home, maybe from her life. He didn't seem surprised or sorry to go.

That had been the night before he was murdered.

In the calm and clarity, and regret, of the days since his death, she wondered if she had been victim to a ruthless man or inspiration for a loving one. She would never know.

Jack joined her now on the chaise longue. "Sorry, honey."

Sheila shrugged. "We're all capable of cruelty under the right circumstances."

"Not you."

"I've been pretty ruthless regarding Media Gains," she said with a knowing smile. "At least Roger would say so. And speaking of dear Roger, I'd call him ruthless, too. Look how he handled Scott Brickell. And Alicia Devon."

"No, those were sound business decisions," Jack refuted, "and even though you might not be willing to view the man who had hurt you in a better light than the man who seemed to care for you—"

"He did care for me."

"—there was one big difference between the two of them. I don't for a minute believe Roger got any pleasure out of those decisions, whereas Derek—" Jack shook his head, tempted to say more, knowing that more would be too much; that more meant reliving how he had discovered what Derek Lang had done to him, reliving the confrontation in Derek's office less than a week before his death; reliving the confrontation that would strike any cop as motive for murder. "Let's just say Derek's conscience wasn't as finely developed as other men's," Jack concluded.

"He was very kind to me," Sheila said softly. "And he was pivotal in helping me get over Roger."

"No, Sheila, it was timing. You were ready to get over him."

"Maybe so," she allowed after a moment's consideration. "Poor Roger, he must be suspect number one. Do you realize how many witnesses there were to that fight? And then—what?—less than a month later, Derek is found dead. If I were the police, I'd haul Roger's ass in and forget about everyone else," she joked, taking Jack's offered hand and going back to the table.

Jack laughed, recollecting the scene at the United Way fund-raiser, a civic charity affair that always brought out everyone who was anyone in Phoenix. Afterward, people would claim it had been the sight of Sheila with her arm locked through Derek's that had set him off, proving that he still cared deeply for his former wife, but judging from the fight, one would be hard-pressed to believe he didn't hate her as much as he did his rival.

"That was the most awful night," Sheila went on. "I couldn't believe what Roger was saying, the accusations. All that anger."

"Hell, Sheila, what did you expect? There you were with Derek, cozy as teenagers, and regardless of the fact that Roger left *you,* it's a man kind of thing to consider even discarded property his own."

"Thanks a lot."

"Besides which," Peck continued, "I hear Roger had been having a couple of setbacks business-wise, so of course the guy was angry. Not to mention he was less than stone sober."

"A lot less," Sheila remarked. "But that's still no excuse for bad behavior."

"Believe me, I'm the last one to defend him when it comes to you, but frankly, I probably would have done the same thing."

As Sheila thought back on that terrible night, she acknowledged to herself that the fight had been inevitable, and that perhaps, in a way, she even wanted it. ". . . Ah, the two lovebirds, thick as thieves, how appropriate." She and Derek had been outside on the pool patio of the Hyatt where the dinner dance crowd had overflowed. They were talking with Linc and one of his two dates, and Freddie and his date. At least thirty people were within earshot when Roger had approached them.

"In this group, you better identify which thief you mean," Linc had joked.

"Why, who else? My loving, loyal ex-wife and her new boy toy, of course."

"Roger!"

"What's wrong, Freddie? Don't you think my description is appropriate?" He came up closer, took Sheila's chin in his hand and kissed her gently on the lips. "Hello, Sheil," he had said more mellowly. "I'm sorry. I didn't mean to insult you."

"Where's your date?" Sheila asked, stepping back.

Roger shrugged. "Somewhere. Anywhere. Who cares. You look terrific." He had turned to Derek. "Doesn't she look terrific, Lang?"

"Yes she does. Roger, maybe you should—"

"Please don't make any suggestions to me, Lang. You're not exactly someone who has my best interests in mind."

Derek had laughed. "You've got that right."

"Freddie was just telling us how successful the George Hamilton spot is—that's great."

"Thank you, Sheil. Fortunately I was able to get that one off the ground in time."

"Roger, come on, let's—"

"It's okay, Freddie. In fact, maybe it's just as well we clear the air. Maybe once they realize I'm onto them, they'll stop."

"Stop what, Roger?" Sheila had asked irritably. "What are you talking about?"

Roger had stared long and hard at her, then at Derek. Up until that moment the situation might have been diffused, but when Derek brought his arm possessively around Sheila's shoulder, pressing her closer to him, there was no turning back for Roger.

"Stop stealing from me, Lang. Stop taking what's mine." He then looked around at the group, smiling, an entertainer waiting for applause. There was none.

"Still don't get it?" he had asked rhetorically. "Let me elucidate. I believe it began when Sheila—no doubt in retaliation for . . . well, we all know what for—"

"Roger, please don't do this," Sheila had urged, but at this point, he was listening only to the insistent need within to blame and accuse, and reclaim some of the control over his life that lately had seemed to slip away from him.

"I'm sorry, Sheila, I am, but I think it's better if we get it all out in the open. Maybe once you and your boyfriend"—the word was spoken as if it were an obscenity—"realize that I know what you've been doing, we can get back to business—at least I can. I suppose he'll just have to steal from someone who hasn't caught on to him yet."

"Gainey, I really think you ought to stop before you say something you'll regret. This is no place to—"

"Lang, Lang, please, I said no advice, not from you. Let's begin with Gayle Crockett, shall we? My former wife, acting out of vengeance which, while I can't completely blame her, still surprised me, went after the one star I've been working to land for years. To make sure the point of the knife she's stabbing me with is really sharp, she then gives the spot to a man she knows I can't stand, sealing the bargain with . . . well, I'd say a kiss, but I've never been one for that kind of understatement."

"Come on, Sheila, let's go," Derek had said. "Gainey, I hope you're drunk, because if not, you have no excuse for acting like such a jackass."

"I'd rather be a jackass than a thief!" Roger retorted, moving closer until he was inches from Derek's face. All conversation dulled as if filtered through a screen, even the band's music flattened. Everyone's attention was on this little circle providing unexpected entertainment.

"Okay, Roger, that's enough. If you have a quarrel with me, we can take it up privately. Now is neither the time nor the place," Derek tried again.

"No, Lang, now will do just fine," Roger said more calmly. "First you take my wife—"

"She wasn't yours to take," Derek stated, making an effort to remain unemotional, although the way he was gripping Sheila's shoulder made it evident that his self-control was slipping.

"She's not yours to have!" Roger tossed back.

"Roger, Derek, stop this, both of you," Sheila had begun, but Roger cut her off.

"Let's try to be honest for once, Lang," Roger went on almost conversationally, the impact of his words thus stronger. "You can't deny that as beautiful as Sheila is, as charming, as talented, my *ex*-wife's appeal to you has less to do with her many attributes and a whole helluva lot with information she feeds you on me and PCE."

"Roger! You've gone too far now. Come on, we're getting out of here." But Roger shook off Linc's grasp and stood stonily in place.

"Oh, Roger." That from Sheila, enough to make him hesitate before going on, but not stop.

"I'm sorry, Sheila, but ask him, go ahead, ask him."

"Gainey, you are beneath contempt. I used to think you knew your business. You were a fool for walking out on one special lady, but at least you were smart about your business." Condescension oozed off Derek. "But now I see I was wrong about you. You couldn't be too smart about anything if you could underestimate me that badly. Do you really think I need to sleep with someone in order to get ahead?" His laugh was more stinging than a slap. "Is that how *you*'ve done it, Gainey?"

"You bastard!" This time his voice was loud enough to bring even the quiet murmur of neighboring voices to silence.

"Roger, calm down, please. They don't know. Can't you see, they don't know?"

"You're such a fool, Freddie," Roger said nastily, ignoring how the lawyer's eyes widened and his lips tightened, his whole body stiffening at the rebuke. "You think they're going to admit they stole my ideas. Christ, man, for a lawyer you can be awfully naive."

"What ideas, Roger?" Sheila asked. "What are you talking about?"

"Nicely done, that innocent act. I'm talking about my showcase concept, that's what. Exactly three people knew about it—you, me, and Freddie. Suddenly BFL has it, I'm playing catch-up, and Freddie is *not* making pillow talk with my competition, so draw your own conclusions."

"Easy there, Gainey," Derek said, jumping in. "You should know better than to blame anyone for the ups and downs of business. A lot of the time it's just dumb luck that makes for success."

"I repeat: exactly two people beside myself knew about my idea for a thirty-minute, three-product showcase for major manufacturers. What happens? I find out that you, *you,* Lang, have signed up Proctor-Silex for just this very format and what do you know? Sheila here is producing. Now you tell me, you call that luck or a leak?"

"No one had to leak the idea to me, Gainey. It was a good one and I'm a good businessman. Now why don't you take your pathetic self out of our way. You've overstayed your welcome."

Sheila remembered looking at Roger at that moment. His gray eyes had smoke in them, his fists were clenched by his side, and the grinding of his teeth was audible.

"I'm going to stop you, Lang," he had whispered hoarsely. "One way or the other, I'm going to make sure you stop taking what's mine."

"Is that a threat?" Derek had asked with that same silky patronization.

"Damn right it is, Lang. Damn right."

"Do you think he did it?"

"Absolutely not," Sheila answered Linc. "I was only joking before when I said the police should haul him downtown. It would serve him right, that's all. But Roger kill? Never."

"Can you really be sure of that? After all, a year ago you wouldn't have thought he was capable of divorce." Linc did not want to be unkind, but the fact remained that everyone had secrets, everyone had facets to their nature they kept hidden, even from themselves . . . unless provoked.

"He would never kill anyone," Sheila repeated. "He might want to, but he would never actually do it. No, Linc, I wouldn't care if they found his fingerprints all over the murder weapon, I do not believe Roger could murder another human being. What happened that night at the dinner dance was just the result of a man reaching his breaking point. Maybe it was seeing me with Derek, or maybe it was seeing *you* and Freddie with us—his best friend, his number one spokesperson, and his ex-wife all enjoying themselves with Derek Lang, the devil himself." She laughed synthetically. "Freddie told me afterward that the business with the showcase for ProctorSilex had been just the latest in a long line of mishaps."

"I heard that, too," Linc confirmed. "I gather Lang beat him to signing up the Festival Cruise Line. A great idea, having a captive audience for infomercials. I can just see me taking my program on a nice, leisurely cruise to the Caribbean." He grinned. "The truth is, though, that Derek is . . . was, a smart businessman and he had smart people working for him. It is possible that he or one of his people could have thought of these opportunities on their own—bad timing, that's all."

"Of course it's possible," Sheila agreed. She grew thoughtful. "That wouldn't explain the computer glitch, though."

"What computer glitch?"

"In PCE's customer service department. Seems customers were being charged double for every returned item."

They both laughed. "Oh Christ, he must have loved that," Jack said, then, more seriously: "You know, Sheila, Derek Lang *was* capable of doing everything Roger accused him of, including—" He broke off, averting his eyes.

"Including using me to get at Roger?" she supplied gently.

His eyes met hers. "The man had no soul, no *need*. The only time I've seen men like that was in—" He cut himself off sharply, again almost going too far. There was something about this woman that brought him dangerously close to trusting.

Sheila's brow creased, but she did not press the issue. "I'm not going to argue the merits of Derek Lang, Linc. He was a complex, complicated man, I will give you that, and so he could have been as cold as you claim, and as kind and supportive, and yes, loving as I knew him to be. But there's one thing you're forgetting."

"What's that?"

"Me. You're forgetting me, Linc. You're forgetting that I might have been using Derek to get at Roger. A woman scorned is a woman seeking vengeance."

"Not you."

She smiled tightly. "Who knows what a person is really capable of when sufficiently provoked?" And Jack could say nothing to this echo of his own sentiments.

Sheila would be devastated if she ever knew the truth about him. She was one of the most decent and least duplicitous people he had ever known. So, for that matter, was Roger. Well, maybe not as decent, but one usually knew where you stood with him. They were both basically honest people. She was right. Roger was not capable of murder. It was not in his nature to hurt another person deliberately; it was not in his nature to fight back, but rather, to fight *for* something he wanted, whereas Derek Lang was a familiar creature to Rangel, a man whose nature it was to take. Sometimes it wasn't even *what* he took that was important; it was the taking, beating the other guy. They were two of a kind.

Suddenly eager to shed the sense of dread knotting in his gut at the prospect of having to face the police, he broke into the famous Lincoln Peck grin, the one that had seduced millions of viewers into shelling out money for promises he could never keep. "Sheila, honey, I think it's time we engaged in a little juicy gossip—it's gotta be better for the appetite than murder."

"Linc?"

"Hmm?"

"You know what your problem is?"

"Too many women, too little time?"

Sheila shook her head. "You distrust too much."

"I do?"

"You do. Makes people suspicious. I'd be careful when you speak with the police, Linc. Wouldn't want them to think *you* had anything to hide."

He stared at her, gauging what she knew, *if* she knew. Then he watched her grin spread wide, her dark eyes brighten mischievously.

"I'm as honest as my namesake," he said, his laughter coming a little too hard, a little too loud.

Chapter
Twenty-three

No, no way. You can't be serious. It's impossible."

Freddie's face was filled with regret. "It's the truth, Roger. I'm sorry, but it is."

"Shit. Hasn't she done enough?" Roger groped absently about his desk, then grinned sheepishly at the lawyer. "I keep forgetting I lost that damn paperweight. I still look for it like an ex-smoker looking for his pack." His smile vanished. "I'm glad it's gone. I don't need any reminders of that treacherous bitch."

"Roger, stop blaming Sheila for your problems. She's not a vindictive woman and you know it."

"I might have agreed with you once, but look what's been going on. It's just one damn thing after another, and now this. It's too much, Freddie. Too many bad things happening to be coincidence. Sheila and Lang were in it together, out to ruin me."

"You sound paranoid."

"Paranoid is when you blame someone else for troubles you don't have the guts to admit you caused. Being a victim is when that someone else is all too real. I know the difference, Freddie, believe me, I know the difference." Again he went searching through the papers on his desk. "Dammit, where's that paperweight? Where in hell's name could it have disappeared to?"

Freddie looked at his wristwatch. "That detective's going to be here any minute. You have your story straight?"

Roger's expression turned quizzical. "My story?"

"Well, he's going to ask us where we were that night."

"So I'll tell him. Big deal."

"No big deal, Roger. I'm just telling you to be prepared for what might turn out to be some tough questions. After all, it's no secret that you didn't like Derek Lang."

Roger laughed. "Jesus, Freddie, you almost sound like a real lawyer."

Freddie lifted an eyebrow, but said nothing.

"Where were *you* that night?" Roger suddenly asked.

"Right here. Working."

"So I'll say I was too."

"But you weren't."

"So what? You gonna tell the cops the truth?"

"Yes, I am." Freddie looked surprised by the suggestion to do otherwise. "We've been together a long time, Roger, been through a lot, but lie to the police for you regarding a murder? No, I can't do that, not even for you."

"I know, I know, I was just talking." At that, his intercom buzzed and his secretary announced that Detective Michael Raintree was here for his appointment.

After introductions were made, Raintree said, "I'll try to make this as quick as possible, gentlemen. We're pretty sure we know who murdered Derek Lang, but I'm asking a few routine questions of some people to make sure we've been as thorough as possible."

"Of course," Freddie said, and Roger nodded.

"I understand you and Derek Lang were not on the best of terms, Mr. Gainey. Would you say that was true?"

Roger looked at Freddie, who wore a blank expression. "I suppose," he conceded. "Lang was seeing my ex-wife and had snared some major infomercial deals that I had been working on, I *thought* in secret."

"So you hated him."

"Hated him?" Roger tasted the word. "No, I don't really think I did. I was mad, angry as all hell because business was not going the way I wanted, and I'll admit it, I was jealous of him."

"Because of your ex-wife?"

"Because of Sheila, yes." Roger, again unconscious of his actions, went looking for the crystal paperweight he used as his worry beads. He snapped a glance in Freddie's direction, turned his attention back to the detective. "I'm sorry, what did you say?"

"Nothing, Mr. Gainey. But I will now. You divorced your wife, didn't you?"

"Yes."

"But it still bothered you that she was with another man."

"It wasn't just any other man, Detective. I think we've already established that."

"You and he had a rather visible and audible fight shortly before his death."

"Is that a question, Detective?" Roger stalled.

"Actually, no, Mr. Gainey, it's a statement of fact. Why don't you tell me about it."

Roger held the detective's steady gaze, then produced a small, self-effacing laugh. "We had a blowup at the United Way thing, yeah. I had had a little too much to drink, and Freddie here had just told me about losing another major deal to Lang, so, yeah, I was pissed."

"You were heard to threaten him, Mr. Gainey."

"Threaten Lang?" Roger repeated, frowning. "If I did, it was in the heat of the moment, it didn't mean anything." His frown deepened. "Hey, you can't seriously be thinking I had anything to do with Lang's death. Yes, the man was a competitor, and yes, I could have done without him in my life, professional and otherwise, but kill him? Never, not a chance. Not my style, Detective. Just not my style."

"Oh? And what would be your style, Mr. Gainey?"

"Tell him, Freddie," Roger instructed, relaxing for the first time since the detective had entered his office.

"Roger can be ruthless, even mean—"

"Freddie!"

"And he has a hot temper at times."

"Jesus Christ, Bickford, you're supposed to be my friend."

"But he's not a killer." Freddie smiled warmly at Roger. "He has two character traits, Detective, that would make it difficult, I think, for him to commit murder."

"And they would be—?" Raintree prompted.

"First of all, he hates details, planning. Prefers to think big picture and leave the nuts and bolts to less . . . well, less imaginative minds."

"Like you, Mr. Bickford?"

"If you will," the lawyer granted with a nod.

"And the other trait?"

"He's rash—sometimes acts without thinking."

"Yeah," Roger muttered, "like when I divorced my wife."

If the detective heard, he gave no indication of it. Instead, he continued with Freddie's line of thinking, but kept his eyes only on Roger. "Murder can be a rash act," he pointed out. "Say, something committed in a moment of great anger and frustration when hostility spills over into hatred, the kind of hatred that's eating you up inside, that compels you to act or go crazy." He paused. "What do you think, Mr. Gainey? Do you think that's possible?"

Roger never got to answer, although his gray eyes were wide and his hair was tousled from having run his hand through it. Whatever brief moment of ease he had felt was now gone.

The detective was speaking again. "Why don't you tell me where you were that night, Mr. Gainey. We'll check it out, of course, but if what you say is true, that puts you in the clear and you'll have nothing to worry about."

"I didn't think I had anything to worry about to begin with, Detective. Didn't Freddie just get finished telling you I'm not capable of killing anyone?"

"Please tell me where you were that night, Mr. Gainey."

"I don't know. Who the hell can remember?" Roger found his appointment calendar and flipped through to the date in question. He hesitated before speaking. "I must have been home," he mumbled.

"You really don't remember, Mr. Gainey?"

Roger shook his head, and he shut his eyes briefly. "I have nothing marked on the calendar. When I'm home at night it's not too memorable, Detective."

The detective nodded with understanding, and had Roger known, a measure of sympathy as well. Not surprisingly, Michael Raintree had discovered yet another person with so much counting for so little.

Softly, he asked: "Did you see anyone, speak with anyone that night who can verify that you were home?"

Again, Roger shook his head, the enormity of his potential problem coming into sharp focus.

Suddenly, the detective made Freddie the object of his attention. "What about you, Mr. Bickford?"

"What about me? I was here, working until about midnight, maybe even later."

"Anyone to verify that, a security guard, garage attendant?"

"Sure, Santiago was on duty that night, he's our security guard, but he's on vacation in his home on Barbados."

"I see. What about closed-circuit camera, any kind of tape record to substantiate your alibi?"

"An alibi, is it?" Freddie remarked, almost smiling. Raintree said, did nothing, just waited. "There's nothing, Detective," Freddie went on stiffly. "I guess we'll just have to wait until Santiago returns—sometime next week."

"How did you feel about Derek Lang?"

Freddie shrugged. "I didn't feel one way or the other about him. I didn't really know the man."

"I see." There was a pause, a disquieting silence, thick with anticipation. "Tell me about some of these business difficulties you'd been having, Mr. Gainey."

"Which one?" Roger asked on a bitter bark of laughter. "The first or the latest?"

"All."

Roger gave him a shortened version of the various mishaps that had been occurring. "Before you got here, Freddie was telling me about the latest—and, I have to presume, the last. Freddie, why don't you fill in the good detective on what the dear departed has done."

"Do you know anything about the world of infomercials, home shopping, Detective?"

"Until now, only what it cost me when the bills came in—my wife's a big home shopper. I'm learning more all the time, though."

Freddie nodded. "Then perhaps you'll appreciate the importance of Roger's concept to create an upmarket channel called LifeStyle where the products would be trendier, more youth-oriented, and most important, more expensive."

"Seems like a natural next step," Raintree acknowledged.

"It hasn't been easy, but we finally found the right location in San Diego where we could headquarter the operation. Roger rightly wanted it to be as separate from PCE as possible. You were even going to hire a separate chief executive, weren't you, Roger?"

Roger smiled. "Actually, I was going to offer the spot to you, with equity. I know you wouldn't have taken it, wouldn't have moved to San Diego, but hell, you deserved at least first refusal for the job."

"Me? You were going to offer it to me?"

"Yeah." A fuller grin. Then, abruptly, his expression soured as his attention shifted back to the detective. "Lang just happened to have signed the lease on the exact spot on Moravia Street in San Diego four days before his death, offering a third more to rent the space where he was planning to headquarter BxB—*his* new upscale home shopping network! BxB—Twice Best—how's that for arrogance! The pirate had inside information and beat me to my own idea."

"Sounds like a solid motive for murder, Mr. Gainey."

"I just found out about it today, Detective," Roger argued. "Freddie and I were planning to fly to San Diego tomorrow. When he called to check that everything was in order, the real estate broker told him what happened. Right, Freddie?"

"I'm afraid so."

"Did your former wife know about this new project?"

"Of course she did. How else do you think Lang found out about it? She told him. She's been giving him all kinds of secret information about my operation in order to get back at me for leaving her."

"You're convinced Lang learned about it through your wife?"

"How else?"

"A spy? Someone in your organization on Lang's payroll? It's been known to happen."

Roger dismissed the notion with a wave of his hand. "Sure it happens, but not here, not to me. Very few people know about these special projects, Detective. Sheila, Freddie, of course, a couple of guys in financial, one or two from marketing, maybe one or two from research and development. All loyal, been with me a long time. Besides, no one but Sheila has any reason to hurt me."

The detective's smile was shallow and knowing. "Oh, don't be so sure about that, Mr. Gainey. People can be real funny about what they decide hurts them, peculiar funny, if you know what I mean."

He put his pen and notepad away in a pocket, but did not get up to leave. Instead, he reached into his other pocket and extracted a large plastic sandwich bag. In it was a crystal paperweight in the shape of a dollar sign.

"Hey, where'd you find that? I've been looking all over for it." Roger was elated, conveniently forgetting his earlier pronouncement to Freddie that he was glad the reminder of Sheila had gone missing.

He began to reach for the bag. "I'm afraid you can't have that, Mr. Gainey."

"Why not? It's mine, isn't it? And why are you keeping it in a damn sandwich bag, for Christ's sake?"

"We found it the night Derek Lang was murdered."

"Exactly *where* did you find it, Detective?" The words came out slowly as Roger realized where this was heading.

"Right by Derek Lang's head, Mr. Gainey. In fact, if you look closely, you'll see blood and hair on it."

"I don't fucking believe this!" Roger's voice crackled with incredulity. "Is that what killed Derek Lang?"

The detective said nothing.

"But I didn't do it! I didn't kill him, I tell you. This is someone's sick joke, it's gotta be."

"A joke, Mr. Gainey? No, I don't think so."

"Then someone hates me a helluva lot, Detective, and has gone to considerable trouble to make me look guilty." As this realization came to Roger, his voice steadied, his posture stiffened, and there was a resolve in the set of his mouth, in the cold flatness of the gray eyes that signified an unspoken determination to find out who this enemy might be.

"Are you arresting me?" he asked quietly.

"No. At least not yet."

"Which means your evidence is not conclusive," Freddie remarked. "I assume fingerprints have been wiped clean?"

Raintree nodded, then turned over the plastic bag. "'To Roger. My million dollar man. Love, Sheila,'" he said, reading the etched inscription. "Kind of like leaving a calling card, isn't it? And that bothers me, gentlemen. It's too easy, and I don't trust a homicide case that gets solved this easily."

"It's hard to believe that that's what killed Lang," Roger commented after a moment's thought.

"What makes you say so?" Raintree asked carefully.

"Well, it's a small paperweight, not that heavy, either. Granted, there's blood and hair on it, but could it really kill someone?

"From repeated blows to the head, it could."

There was something in the detective's voice that alerted Roger. "I'll ask you again. Is that what killed Derek Lang?"

Detective Michael Raintree took his time answering; in that space of time, he thought that either Roger Gainey was extremely clever for posing the question or else very, very innocent.

"No," he finally said. "He died from six shots from a thirty-two-caliber pistol. The blows from the paperweight probably stunned him, but bullets killed him." He got to his feet. "Do you own a gun, Mr. Gainey?"

"Yes, but I left it with my wife."

"I know. She told me. Funny thing, though, she can't seem to find it. I imagine that's because we have it locked away in our evidence room. Found it right there alongside the body."

"What!"

"See what I mean about nice and easy?" Raintree went on conversationally as if he hadn't exploded a grenade in the room. "Bothers me, it really does."

"How do you know it's my gun? It could be—"

"Your gun is registered, Roger," Freddie pointed out. "No fingerprints again?"

Raintree nodded. "What about you, Mr. Bickford? Do you own a gun?"

"No."

"With all this evidence, why aren't you arresting me?" Roger wanted to know, his voice testy with anxiety.

The detective shrugged. "Like I said, lots of evidence that just makes me itchy. Too much points to you, Mr. Gainey, just too damn much. Make sense?"

"Are you telling me I have nothing to worry about?"

Raintree walked to the door, turned. "Oh no, Mr. Gainey, I'd worry if I were you. I most definitely would."

There was no hesitation; it never dawned on him to consider anyone else. The divorce had been thoughtless, selfish. Sleeping with his competition, maybe stealing his ideas . . . well, under the circumstances, how could he fault her? Right now, none of that mattered. Right now, there was only her, the one person he trusted totally.

"Sheil, it's me, Roger. I need to see you. I need . . . you, Sheila. Please."

And because loyalty takes longer to die than love, or perhaps, better put, lasts longer, Sheila said: "I'll be right over."

Three

PART

Chapter
Twenty-four

The ribbon of road seemed endless, despite Sheila's knowing there was less than six miles between her house and Roger's new condominium off Camelback Road. This was not a trip she ever could have anticipated making six, seven months ago. A little more than a year had passed since that unforgettable evening when one life had ended, and though it had been inconceivable at the time, a new one had begun that now felt absolutely natural and right. With time, the discovery of her own untapped strengths, and a man who let her be a woman again, she had taken small steps, then exuberant strides away from pain and confusion, anger and blame, toward the immeasurable comfort that came from self-acceptance. Today she could not imagine ever being that unhappy again, or ever linking her life so seamlessly with another's. She was able to drive these six miles and think only that someone she once cared for, now only cared about, was in trouble and needed her. The rest of the baggage had been emptied out, discarded.

She found parking on the street directly in front of the building and gave her name to the concierge, who buzzed Roger on the intercom. By the time she reached the seventeenth and top floor, he was standing in the open doorway of his apartment, waiting for her.

"You're staring," she criticized by way of greeting.

"I can't help it. You look fabulous." He leaned forward to kiss her cheek, but she slipped past him. They stood in a large foyer, she looking around at his new surroundings, he looking at her.

"Nice," she said. "You can see clear over to the Superstition Mountains. Must be spectacular at sunset." She stepped further into the living room. "Who decorated it for you, one of your girlfriends?"

"Sheila—"

"Touchy, touchy," she said, grinning.

"I hired a professional interior designer," he told her. "Can I get you something to drink? Wine, white, right?"

"Iced tea." His surprise showed. "No, a glass of white wine would be fine," she said, her smile wry. "I just didn't want you to think I'm the same old predictable Sheila."

"Fat chance of that ever happening again," he mumbled, going off to get the wine.

When he returned, he gestured her to sit next to him on the cream-colored sofa, awash with pillows in the typical southwestern color scheme of brick, turquoise, and sand. She chose instead a plump-cushioned club chair similarly arrayed.

"Before I tell you why I asked you over here," Roger began, "there's something I need to know."

Sheila raised her brow in expectation.

"Why did you tell Derek about LifeStyle and the Moravia Street location in San Diego? Was getting back at me so important to you?"

With an extreme of calm that both startled and amused her, Sheila did not exclaim in outrage, did not jump to her feet and head to the door. She merely sipped her wine, her eyes holding a look of such completely cold disdain that the air seemed to shimmer with her contempt for him.

Roger ran his fingers through his thick hair in his typical sign of frustration. "I'm sorry," he whispered hoarsely.

"You damn well should be."

"Then how did he know? Dammit, Sheila, how did he know?"

"How did he know what? I don't have a clue what you're talking about."

"I believe you. Freddie said you'd never sabotage me, but I refused to accept that, I couldn't. Because if it wasn't you who told Lang about the Moravia Street location, that means it had to be someone who works for me."

"Are you telling me that Derek Lang leased the space you had found for LifeStyle?"

Roger nodded. "You didn't know?"

"I had no idea. I didn't even know you had gotten that far with the new network. You've been talking about it for a while, but I didn't realize it was finally coming together for you."

"Freddie didn't tell you?"

"Believe it or not, Roger, when Freddie and I see each other, the conversation does not revolve solely around you and PCE."

"I'm sorry, I just thought—"

"No, Roger, that's your whole problem. You didn't think. To consider that I would ever stoop so low as to deliberately try to destroy anything to do with PCE is not to know me very well at all. Then again, you never really did, did you?"

"So many lousy things happening, one after another," Roger tried to explain, gliding swiftly past her comment. "I figured you wanted to get back at me. Wouldn't *you* think someone had carefully planned the incidents if they had happened to Media Gains?"

She weighed that. "No. I would very carefully look into each incident separately. Like you, I don't believe in coincidence, but I'd have my facts straight before I went around accusing anyone. Especially someone I had spent twenty years with. Yes, I wanted to get back at you, but I had already accomplished that. Hadn't I?"

He looked at her curiously. "You mean because of your relationship with Lang?"

"That and getting Gayle Crockett first."

He grimaced, remembering that stroke of oneupmanship. Then he smiled. "You got paid back for that one, though."

"Oh?"

"You got stuck with Alicia Devon's turkey."

"True, true." Sheila laughed. Then, more seriously, she said, "I'm confused about something, Roger. If you thought I was so duplicitous and disloyal, why in the world did you call me over here tonight?"

Of course, they both knew she knew the answer; both might even have known that she needed to hear the words, hear them from Roger himself.

"Because you're the only one I trust," he gave her.

Sheila's delight in watching him squirm through the idiocy of his il-logic was not yet sated. She sat back in the club chair, forefinger tap-ping her lip as if in deep contemplation of his revelation. "Let me see if I've got this right. You accuse me of passing on trade secrets in order to get back at you for leaving me, yet when you're in trouble, you call me because I'm the only one you trust. Am I missing anything?"

"You've made your point, Sheila."

"I certainly hope so." She grinned broadly. "Now, what's going on? What's happened?" All lightness had vanished.

"Remember that crystal paperweight you gave me for my first mil-lion?" Roger asked. "The one inscribed—"

"'To Roger. My million dollar man. Love Sheila.' Of course I remem-ber it. What about it?"

"It was found by Derek's head the night he was murdered. His hair and blood were on it."

"Oh my God!"

Roger nodded, utterly abject. "I'm the police's prime suspect, Sheila. You've got to help me find out who's framing me."

Sheila could have been no more stunned than if the police had de-cided *she* was their prime suspect. She still maintained that there was no way Roger Gainey could kill another human being, no way. Yet the police had his paperweight with Derek's blood and hair.

"How convenient," she murmured, thinking aloud.

"What is?"

"To find a weapon with your name on it. Certainly helps the police do their job. Was *it* the murder weapon?"

"No. The police think, that is, Detective Raintree—"

"Michael Raintree—he's the one who came to see me, too," she interjected.

"I know. He told me. Thinks the evidence is just too tidy to be for real. Thank goodness, since it's *my* paperweight with *my* name on it."

The color drained from Sheila's face as she said, "And mine. Were your fingerprints on it?"

"No. Besides, that's not what killed Lang. The real murder weapon was a gun." Roger slumped back on the couch, his eyes on the ceiling as if reason could be found there. "Six shots from a handgun killed him. Six shots from a thirty-two—the same caliber as *my* gun." He focused again on Sheila. "Talk about premeditation. This murder has two victims—a dead man and a live one who needs to clear his name or else. Someone's been very clever at my expense."

Sheila felt sick. "Roger, Detective Raintree asked me about the gun, but when I went to get it, I couldn't find it."

"That's because he has it." Her eyes went round and shiny like the bottom of a glass. Roger pushed ahead with the entire story. "My gun was recovered from the crime scene. No fingerprints, of course, but ballistics matched the bullets, and the serial number checked out as registered to me. Whoever did this is clever *and* thorough."

He frowned at her. "You didn't know the gun was missing?"

"No. I told you, I discovered it when Detective Raintree asked to see it."

A silence came briefly between them, Roger pinching the bridge of his nose as if that stinging pain would help him get at the truth. "Sheil, why don't you tell me everything that was said between you and the detective. Maybe we can learn something that'll help."

She thought for a moment, remembering the meeting, anxious to include any details that might help. "It was yesterday afternoon," she began. "I had been over to Linc's for lunch when we discovered that this detective had made appointments with both of us for that day. Mine was first."

"Thank you for taking the time to see me, Ms. Gainey," Detective Raintree had said. "Unfortunately, murder investigations don't stop on the weekends."

Sheila had led him to the den and then sat across from him on the loveseat while he took a chair, flipping back the cover of his notebook, and glancing through pages long ago committed to memory.

"Forgive me for being somewhat indelicate, Ms. Gainey, but am I correct that you and the deceased were involved?"

"You mean were we having an affair? Yes, Detective, we were. We had been together for about three months when he . . ."

"And it was going well?"

"Going well?"

"No end anticipated?"

"What an odd question, Detective." Sheila's short, dry laugh was without amusement. "Are you asking me if a breakup was imminent?"

"Yes, ma'am, I am."

Sheila studied him a moment, thinking. "You've been speaking to Marilu Diamante, haven't you, Detective?"

Michael Raintree nodded.

"I see," Sheila continued. "So you think I might have had a motive to kill Derek because he wanted to break up with me?"

"Ma'am—"

"The truth is that Derek and I did have a very serious disagreement the night before he was murdered. He wasn't happy with my . . . I guess, my attitude, my approach to the relationship. He wanted more commitment, I think. Although . . ." And here she smiled softly at the recollection of a man so unused to caring that he had to fight with the person causing him that discomfort. If only they had had more time together, time to understand and deal with the fears.

"Ms. Gainey—?" the detective prompted.

"Sorry, where was I? Oh yes, we had this argument about my not being as devoted or some such nonsense—although I don't think he realized that's what we were arguing about."

"Was it enough of a disagreement to cause a breakup?"

Sheila looked steadily at the detective, remembering Derek's words. "He thought it was," she admitted in a voice suddenly small and hollow with the realization that to some people, she had a very strong motive for murder.

"I'm sorry, Ms. Gainey, but I have to ask this next question. Where were you—" and he proceeded to question her whereabouts the night and time span of Derek's death.

"I was here, alone. I was exhausted from work, Detective. My social life, even with Derek, consisted mainly of evenings at home. And no, before you ask it, I spoke to no one and saw no one who could vouch that I was here. I'm sorry—you have only my word for it."

Detective Raintree stood up then and went over to the glass doors leading to Sheila's patio. Without turning, he asked, "Is there anyone who comes to mind, Ms. Gainey, anyone you think might have killed Derek Lang?" He then faced her, watching for all the nonverbalized responses.

Sheila frowned with concentration, her eyes focused inward. Someone hiding something would have met his probing look, and answered quickly by either naming a particular individual or claiming ignorance of the issue.

Finally, Sheila spoke, her attention again fully on him. "I'm afraid many people come to mind. Derek Lang wasn't particularly beloved."

"I've heard. You strike me as a relatively sensible woman, Ms. Gainey, someone who would think twice before putting her hand in the fire. Yet you enjoyed a relationship with this man. Can you explain that?"

Sheila's laugh reverberated with ruefulness. "I don't know how much you've heard from other people you've spoken with, Detective, but Derek Lang was my ex-husband's staunchest competitor in the infomercial business. Divorce can compel a person to do the strangest things."

"But it became more, didn't it?" Raintree asked gently.

"Yes, it did."

"What about Marilu Diamante?"

"What about her? I thought we were friends—not close friends, mind you, but the business brought us together and we enjoyed each other's company without delving too deeply into personal matters. I knew she had had an affair with Derek, but she had told me it was long over and unimportant at that. I had no idea it was still going on—or so she claimed."

"Didn't that upset you?"

"I didn't believe it."

"No?"

"No. I think Derek had broken things off with her shortly after he and I began to see each other seriously. I may be wrong, of course, but that's what I choose to believe. Marilu was desperately in love with him, it seems, and so she refused to accept that he had found someone else." She paused, measured the detective a moment. "You know, Detective, love is an investment. When we don't get the return on our investment that we had been anticipating, well, we make excuses and we lie." She smiled tightly. "What do you think, Detective?"

"I think you'd probably have made a great detective, Ms. Gainey," Raintree admitted. "It's a job that combines legwork and brain work, and a whole lot of hunch. Anyone who understands human nature the way you seem to would make one helluva detective."

Sheila smiled her appreciation of his compliment, and Michael Raintree returned to the chair. "You produced a tape for Alicia Devon, didn't you?" he asked.

"Against my better judgment," she admitted. "Derek rejected it. I was pretty sure he would. Of course, Alicia blames me totally for that. Why do you ask?"

"Do you think she's capable of murder?"

"Yes," Sheila answered without having to think about it.

Detective Raintree let his surprise show, and Sheila explained.

"Alicia Devon is one of those desperate individuals who cannot accept responsibility for her own failures. Lots of people are like that—

especially in show business. They have to blame someone else, have to perceive themselves as victims or else it would mean facing up to the fact that their talent was no longer significant." Sheila paused, waiting to see if the detective had anything to say, any questions, but he was wooden in his silence, and she went on. "Alicia Devon had to blame me, and no doubt, my former husband, for her failures—her waning popularity, her wrongness for the video we produced—a motivational spot for which she was totally unsuited. But it was her desperation that rejected reality."

"You don't think she'd blame Derek Lang?" the detective finally spoke.

Sheila shook her head. "No, at least not enough to kill him. Roger— my former husband—Roger would be first on her hit list; I'd probably come next."

Raintree then asked her about Scott Brickell.

"Never, absolutely never," she said with conviction. "He doesn't have the guts to kill—another eternal victim."

Detective Raintree put away his pad and pen, and smiled warmly. "You're a very intelligent woman, Ms. Gainey."

"Thank you."

"And refreshingly honest."

"Well, I'm certainly glad to hear you say *that*."

"By the way," he added offhandedly, "do you have a gun?"

Sheila jerked, surprised by the unexpected question. "Why, yes, I do. Actually, it's Roger's gun, but he left it here when he moved out, thought I might feel better with it around for protection."

"Do you know how to use it?"

"Not really. I mean, I know how to cock the trigger and pull, but I've never seriously practiced for aim and accuracy."

"May I see it, please?"

"Excuse me?"

"The gun. I'd like to see it."

Sheila got up and left the room. When she returned she was scowling. "It's not here."

"Are you saying it's missing?"

She nodded, confused. "I keep it in the night-table drawer by my side of the bed. It's not there; it's not in the other night table, either, or any of the dresser drawers. I can't find it, Detective."

"Did you give it back to your husband?"

"Ex-husband," she corrected automatically. "No, I haven't seen Roger in weeks. This is so strange. I don't understand it." She studied the detective's face, searching for an explanation. "The newspapers haven't said, but was Derek shot to death?"

"Thank you for your time, Ms. Gainey," Raintree said by way of not answering her question. "You've been very helpful."

"Detective, please, can't you tell me how Derek died?"

"I can tell you this much, Ms. Gainey," Raintree answered. "He died violently. And prematurely."

"And now you're saying that it was your thirty-two-caliber handgun that killed him?" Sheila asked Roger. "What are you going to do? What can I do?"

"You're going to help me clear up this mess, that's what."

"I'm not looking exactly like Miss Clean and Innocent myself, you know. After all, if the police want to believe that Derek was breaking up with me and that that's a good motive to kill, I suppose they could consider me a prime suspect, too. Don't forget that the paperweight has my name on it as well as yours."

"Than we'll help each other clear up this mess," Roger amended.

"We should get ourselves lawyers," Sheila suggested.

"No. Not yet."

"When then? When one or both of us gets indicted? Roger, a lawyer. Now."

Roger got to his feet and went over to the vast picture window that looked out on the majestic Superstition Mountains, now obscured by night. "Come here a minute, Sheil, please."

"Roger—"

"Please." When she was by his side, he pointed to the mountains and beyond. "Out there is freedom, Sheil. I'm not about to give that up or trust some lawyer to make sure I keep it. You're the only one, Sheila, only you."

"But what can I do? The police could arrest you any minute now. No, you need a lawyer, not an ex-wife."

"And I'll get one if it comes to that. But meanwhile, I need you, ex-wife, but not ex-friend, or you wouldn't be here now, would you?"

She didn't answer, just watched how the earnestness in his expression turned ironic. "Who would have thought Derek Lang would end up bringing you and me together again?" he said.

Sheila gazed into the familiar gray eyes, wondering if this were madness or the only reasonable way out of a bad situation. As if in a flash, their history together rolled before her, and her conviction deepened that this man was incapable of killing. Sadly, she had to admit that had the situation been different, she would not have been able to say the same of Derek.

Someone had hated him enough to kill him. Someone hated Roger even more, enough to frame him, make him endure a living death.

"I guess you're many things, Roger—like selfish, self-absorbed, self-centered—"

"Vivid choice of words, thank you."

"—But you're not a murderer. You may have entertained fantasies of killing Derek, maybe doing away with me as well—I certainly have come up with a few creative scenarios for ending your life."

"You have?"

"But imagination and action are two very different things. I'll repeat what I said to Linc about you—even if your fingerprints were found all over the murder weapon, I wouldn't believe you're a murderer. So yes, Roger, I'll help you prove your innocence provided you keep one very important fact in mind at all times."

"Which is?"

"We're not together again, Roger. Don't for a second forget that."

"But, Sheil—"

"Not for a second."

Chapter
Twenty-five

On the drive back home from Roger's, Sheila felt as if she had been at the epicenter of an earthquake and had survived. There was damage and it would not be easy to repair, but it could be done.

By the time she was inside her home, she was trembling from aftershock.

What Roger was proposing was completely preposterous, and unbelievably, she had agreed to go along with him. What had she been thinking? Obviously, she hadn't been or else she would not now be playing Nancy Drew to Roger's Hardy Boy. It wasn't as if *she* had anything to hide. Then again, that was exactly what Roger was claiming. The fact that neither of them had checkable alibis, combined with another fact, that if someone wanted, they could twist the yin and yang between any two people into motive. Sheila and Roger were vulnerable, no question about it, but there was a world separating vulnerability and guilt. Exacerbate vulnerability, though, with some pretty damning evidence—like *their* paperweight with *his* blood and hair; *their* gun's bullets in *his* body and the result was the kind of mess that required a highly competent criminal lawyer.

Instead, they were relying on each other because Roger had this romantic notion about freedom, and she had . . . ? What, Sheila, what do you have? she asked herself, leaning back against her loveseat, eyes shut. Was it some subversively unconscious desire to be with Roger again? she wondered. Was it the challenge—dared she admit it?—the excitement of the chase? Was it a deep-rooted longing to find Derek's killer herself, as if that would somehow enable her to close that chapter in her life with less regret than she feared might linger within her, given their last time together? Or was the reason she had agreed to help Roger no more complicated than that she believed he was innocent?

On a hunch that Detective Raintree might be willing to buy some time for Roger, might even be willing to share some information, since the detective had no one helping him with his investigation and he did not trust simple solutions, Roger was going to the stationhouse to see if perhaps the detective would give him a list of possible suspects—other than himself. It would at least be a place to start, Roger had told her. Sheila wasn't sure a policeman's list was really necessary. She had a theory that whoever had killed Derek had been someone she knew, someone local. Derek was not in Phoenix so often that were the killer not from the world of infomercials, the crime could have been committed in any number of other places Derek frequented.

That thought had Sheila reeling. It was bad enough that the man she had been involved with had been murdered. Bad enough that it was her ex-husband who was the prime suspect. Now, it seemed, the killer had been one of them, a colleague, maybe even a friend. The concept was horrific to contemplate, yet it felt right, uncomfortably right.

She got up from the couch and wrapped her arms around herself as if with sudden chill, and she did feel cold, through and through, the kind of numbness she had experienced after Roger had walked out on her; the kind of stunned disbelief that her world, as she had come to know it, was falling apart, again. Before, she had turned to the shelter of work. Later this week she was supposed to have her Internet infomercial finished for Freedom Travel, an international franchised travel agency that was eager to test the buying power of the twenty-five million potential trip takers who were current Internet subscribers. Getting this spot to produce had been a major coup for Media Gains, as was landing Steve and Edie to host it; they were the perfect has-beens to lure retirees to give up their money for travel. The spot was due its final edit and that was a part of the process she usually insisted on overseeing herself, yet this major professional opportunity was being ignored in favor of a murder investigation! It was all too bizarre.

Then again, she reminded herself, she might be fighting for her own freedom as well as for Roger's. After all, her name was on that paperweight; she and Derek had had a serious falling out; she couldn't prove she had been home alone; and the gun that had killed Derek had been taken from her home. Her home! The theft was such an invasion that she felt sickened to her soul from it.

Right then she decided she needed to see a friend, the one person whose support had never wavered, who never let emotion cloud good judgment and logical thinking.

The Freddie Bickford Sheila was eager to talk with was unavailable to her. When she drove by his house, there seemed to be no lights on, at least none that she could see. The truth was that Freddie was in his home office at the back of the house, a desk lamp of no significant wattage illuminating the immediate area, but casting no light beyond, offering no play of shadows on his desert sand and cactus backyard that could be noticed from the front of the house. So Sheila drove away, heavyhearted, and Freddie never even knew she had been there. Just as Sheila did not know that the Freddie she had gone to see was not the man sitting at his desk in the dim light.

Freddie sat back in his desk chair, a hard-seated wooden chair designed for pain; there could be no other explanation for such uncomfortable furniture, yet Freddie had had it since high school—it went everywhere with him, including his two marriages. When they were over, he had had to give up a great deal, but not that chair. Then again, who else would have wanted it? He obviously needed the uncompromising hardness as a reminder that reality is never cushioned or, at best, wears padding that can be removed or become worn out, like the permanence of the partnership with Roger that Freddie had once actually believed would last forever. Instead, Roger Gainey had picked his brains, taken credit for his ideas, downplayed his importance, and then bought him out, adding insult to injury by offering him a job.

Every time Freddie Bickford mentally ran down the laundry list of offenses committed against him by Roger, his heart tightened and his fingers cramped into fists. Yet he had never needed to accept Roger's job offer. He could have walked away at any time but chose not to; he made the conscious decision to accept what Roger dished out. It was, for the longest time, a passivity that filled him with self-disgust, much as a compulsive overeater is sickened by his inability to push away a platter of food. The truth was that, for this same long time, Freddie did not believe that Roger had done anything wrong. Ever since their days together in Los Angeles, Freddie had been Roger's satellite; it seemed only fitting, given that he was a lawyer and Roger was the "creative" type. Which was why he so rapidly agreed to transplant himself to Phoenix. Felt such inordinate pride when Roger took as his own Freddie's concept of selling the "hot" merchandise on their game shows. Understood Roger's need to "go it alone." His own lack of self-esteem made him Roger's ideal foil, and by the time Freddie had grown up enough to accept and like and value himself, their roles were irreversible.

Still Freddie did not leave. By then, he had alimony and child support, and Roger paid him well. That, of course, only built on the foundation of resentment that had existed, unnurtured, for years, so that, by the time Derek Lang entered the picture, Freddie Bickford had developed the kind of rage that could, in time, turn murderous.

Derek Lang had then done the unforgivable. He had underestimated Freddie; had genuinely believed he knew Freddie better than Freddie knew himself. Lang had thought, for so long, that he was manipulating the lawyer, and Freddie had allowed him that little pretense, much the way he had come to let Roger believe the fiction that he was in control of his fiefdom. In every relationship there exists the dynamic of inequality, usually with basically benign results. For years, quietly getting even with Roger by giving his archrival inside information had redressed the balance for Freddie. Even though he knew he had only himself to blame for maintaining the imbalance, Freddie had grown soul-weary of his own weakness. Betraying Roger restored his strength.

And then he decided he wanted out. He had even been considering retirement, taking an endless journey to play at every major golf course in the world. After giving Derek the Moravia Street location, Freddie had told him this was his last time, no more, he was finished, done. Again Derek had smugly asserted that Freddie couldn't stop, the rush of power he got from stabbing his best buddy in the back was too intoxicating to give up. And to make sure Freddie understood that there was no quitting unless he, Derek, decided so, he had then threatened the lawyer, told him that if he ever brought up quitting again, Derek would not only tell Roger what his trusted attorney and best friend had been doing, but he'd make sure the American Bar Association, the SEC and NIMA knew as well. He'd be disbarred, disgraced; in other words, Freddie Bickford would be destroyed. Derek Lang did not take kindly to being the one dismissed.

It was after this that Freddie's rage escalated. The idea of ever again being controlled by another human being was unacceptable. Fake passivity had grown to be weighty camouflage that he needed to shed once and for all. Derek Lang had underestimated him. Roger Gainey had undervalued him. Both men had been using Freddie as their pipeline, fueling their power. The time had come to show them who really had control.

With the same careful, methodical, patient thoroughness Freddie brought to all his endeavors, he created a murder scenario that was both elimination and punishment.

He had tried to figure out a way to avoid involving Sheila; not for anything would he intentionally hurt her, but there seemed to be no other way, not if the paperweight and the gun were to be used to maximum advantage. He hadn't particularly liked himself when he had let himself into Sheila's house with the spare key he knew she kept taped to the inside of the barbecue cover by the pool. There had been no alternative. He wouldn't have felt one tic of genuine regret over the rest of his actions if Roger had not gone and mentioned his plans for LifeStyle, making him, *him* head of the new network! He would have been independent; he would have had people reporting to him; he would have the public acknowledgment of his power, strength, ability. He hated to do it, but he had to ask himself the question: Had he made a terrible mistake? Had Roger finally realized the full extent of Freddie's value to him, acknowledging it with this gift of his own network?

It was too late now, though. Certainly too late for Derek Lang. Too late for the truth. Too late for Roger.

Just then the telephone rang, and he automatically reached over to answer, then he changed his mind. He was in no mood to talk to anyone, let his machine pick up.

"Hi, Freddie, it's me, Sheila. I drove by earlier to see you, but you were out. If you get home before ten, please call me. If not, first thing tomorrow morning, please. I really need to talk to you, Freddie. You're the only one Roger and I can trust, and we both need your help. Love you."

Freddie Bickford squeezed his eyes shut, hard, pain riddling him. What did it matter if he had succeeded brilliantly in killing one nemesis, planting irrefutable evidence to frame the other? In the end, he knew, it was most of all too late for him.

Chapter
Twenty-six

There were so many motives in this case that Detective Raintree felt like a prom queen, trying to decide which date to choose; he didn't want to select the wrong guy. Or woman, it might well turn out. Somehow, though, he didn't think a woman had killed Derek Lang. From what he had been able to piece together, the deceased had been a man who had inspired many different feelings in people, and a woman might even have experienced a murderous anger toward him, but Raintree didn't think she would ever kill him, not if there remained the slightest chance that alive, Derek Lang might want her—professionally *or* personally.

No, Raintree was just about convinced a man had perpetrated the crime, but this man had not been Roger Gainey. In fact, Raintree was more than convinced that killing Derek Lang had been almost secondary to framing Gainey. Which meant that whoever had done it was someone who did not act rashly. And this someone could, indeed, have been a woman.

Time was running out. Just this morning his lieutenant had been griping about the heat he was getting from the captain to arrest Roger Gainey and be done with it. How often did the Phoenix Police Force get to close a murder case this handily? It would be good public relations, he pointed out—not an unimportant factor for a city heavily reliant on its tourist trade. But his lieutenant trusted Raintree and so was giving him a little more time, emphasis on *little.* Which is why Raintree went and slipped the list of possible alternative suspects to Roger Gainey this morning. He needed help—Gainey needed to clear his name. The captain would have his shield if he knew, but hell, Gainey was guilty of nothing more than jealousy and somehow he was going to prove that. Gainey was not angry or frightened enough to kill. He might be frustrated by professional setbacks, but he wasn't scared of losing his business. And he might regret walking out on a woman he still had feelings for, but he wasn't angry, at least not angry enough, at the man who had her, even if that man had been his fiercest competitor. No, Roger Gainey's feelings were not swollen enough to burst into a kill.

But the others on that list? Who knew? In Raintree's experience, murder—whether premeditated or impetuous—happened from a seemingly innocuous provocation that ignited a long simmering, sometimes even subconscious, anger that stemmed from a variety of feelings the person wished to end: fear or frustration, manipulation, shame, loss of power, love, or loss of it, even death of someone could incite the living to a murderous anger that had to be taken out on someone, the death blamed on someone who had to be punished. Raintree was no psychologist—the police department had several of them and they were fine to consult, he supposed, but he'd go on hunch and experience and plain old common sense. They had proven reliable in the past, and he was confident they'd come through for him again this time. Whoever had killed Derek Lang had probably been scared; he, or she, had definitely been angry, very, very angry. And not just at that one man. There were two victims in this case, and the one who was still alive wanted to stay that way, alive *and* free.

At first they were going to divide the list to save time, but then they reconsidered, deciding there was not only strength in numbers, but the added value of the surprise factor when people saw them together again. The reaction of people as they walked down the corridors of PCE toward Roger's office confirmed it.

Roger told his secretary who was expected, then he and Sheila settled themselves in to wait. "By the way," he said, "I found out something interesting from my buddy Raintree."

"Oh, so now he's your buddy, is he?" Sheila was not amused. "The man probably has a warrant all but signed for your arrest, and you call him buddy." She shook her head. "I still can't believe he actually agreed to let you help, and gave you that list. The guy must want to end his career prematurely."

Roger shrugged, cockier than he actually felt. "Why not? I told you he wasn't convinced by the evidence, and I'm better than no help at all. I mean, *we*'re better," he quickly amended.

"How much time did he give us?" Her voice was soft, the seriousness of the question weighing it down.

"He didn't say."

"Guess."

"I don't know, Sheil. Not too long, I'd imagine. Unless he really does want to lose his job."

"Then we're wasting time. We've got to get you a lawyer, Roger. Please. Enough of this nonsense, we're not professionals, we don't know what to do."

"One pass at all of them, just one. Then, if it comes to it, I'll get a lawyer, I promise."

She stared hard at him, then slowly nodded.

"Don't forget you might be a suspect, too," he reminded her.

"Then we'll get me a lawyer as well," she answered. "Although if your buddy Raintree is all that smart, he knows better than to concentrate on alibi when motive opens up so many more possibilities."

"I always thought that if you can prove where you were during the time a crime was committed, that clears you. Besides, I thought you needed motive, opportunity, and means to be found guilty."

"First of all, there are all kinds of ways to fake an alibi," Sheila told him. "More importantly, it's motive that is the purest clue. The rest can be manipulated."

"You've given this some thought, haven't you?" Roger asked with evident admiration.

"Haven't you?"

"Not really," he admitted. "I just wanted to be doing something. I didn't really have any idea what."

"Typical—leave the details to someone else while you concentrate on the big picture."

"Sheil, come on, be fair. At least I'm helping." As he had not been able to stop doing since it went missing, he fumbled around his desk for his paperweight, then grinned self-consciously, remembering its whereabouts.

"Raintree's eliminated a couple of names from his list," Roger went on.

"Specifically who?"

"Gayle Crockett, for one."

Sheila was surprised. "She was a suspect?"

"I don't know if she was a real suspect—more a source of information, I'd guess."

"Who else?"

"Your pal Marilu is pretty much in the clear."

"Too bad," Sheila grumbled. "What does 'pretty much' mean, exactly?"

Roger explained about the room service left outside her hotel door, the sending away of the night maid.

"Not exactly proof of anything," Sheila remarked. Then, with curiosity in her voice, she said, "Raintree really did tell you a lot, didn't he?"

"I couldn't very well go off blind, could I? Then I wouldn't be much help to him or us."

Sheila nodded, genuinely pleased with the confidence the police detective had shown Roger. He knew Roger was innocent and had to prove it—what a twisted process justice could be!

"Who else?" Sheila prompted. "What about Freddie? Was he on the detective's list?"

Roger was taken aback by the perception of the question. "As a matter of fact, he was. Obviously, you're not as surprised by this as I was."

"Roger, we're dealing with a finite world here. Try to keep that in mind. I'm sure Detective Raintree is concentrating on Derek's Phoenix life—" And she told him her theory. "It would only make sense to have Freddie on the list."

"Well, he was here, working."

"At night? Since when does Freddie work past six o'clock?"

"It was for our new deal with Vikki Carr."

Sheila frowned. The name was vaguely familiar, and Roger was visibly displeased with her lack of immediate recognition. "You must remember her, Sheila, she's that singer from the sixties and seventies. She's Mexican, has lots of albums in English and Spanish. Kind of the Hispanic Dionne Warwick."

"Don't tell me—you're planning to use her for a Spanish Psychic Network?"

"You got it—and that's just the beginning," Roger went on enthusiastically. "I'm hoping to sign José Feliciano and Linda Ronstadt, maybe even the Menudos—start a whole new network—with crossover stars. What do you think?"

"Will the infomercials be in Spanish or English?"

"We'll test-market both. There are plenty of Spanish-language cable stations around, though, so I'm more inclined to go with English."

"Impressive," Sheila commended him, then added, "Did Derek know about this?"

Roger looked at her as if she had cursed him. "No, of course not . . . shit . . . I'm not sure. Lately he seemed to know about everything before I could get it off the ground."

"Would Freddie know?"

"He might. He'd know if Feliciano or Ronstadt had been approached, anyone I didn't have a contract with yet."

"Felicity Carr was a done deal?"

"*Vikki* Carr. And yes. That's what Freddie said he was doing that night, reviewing her contract before giving it to me for signature."

"Can he prove that?"

"Does he have to?" He laughed. "Come on, Sheil, be serious, this is Freddie we're talking about."

She sighed. "You're right, of course. I'm guess I'm getting a little nuts over this. By the way, I tried to reach him last night, but he wasn't home. Must have a new lady friend," she said with open affection.

"What did you want him for?"

"Oh, I don't know. Just to get his thoughts on this whole mess."

"That sounds suspiciously like trust, Sheil," Roger pointed out, his tone teasing. "Yet you just asked if he could prove he was working late the night Derek got it. Can't have it both ways, kiddo."

Sheila weighed the contradiction, then, with a fluttering in her stomach as the words were involuntarily wrenched from her, she said: "*Can* he prove it, Roger?"

"So it's going to be like that, is it?"

"I guess it has to be unless you enjoy being the prime suspect in a murder investigation," she whispered, ashamed.

"Point taken. Anyway, yes, he can prove it. There was a security guard on duty that night—he's on vacation but due back in a day or two. Raintree can question him them."

"And meanwhile we'll talk to Freddie ourselves."

"Sure, but he has no motive—if we're to go by what you think is important."

"That's true," Sheila confirmed. "I don't think Freddie knew Derek much beyond saying hello to him at a social function." She suddenly looked beyond Roger, remembering back to a partnership that was bought out. "Then again," she dared, "there's you."

"What about me? Come on, Sheil, Freddie's my best friend. Don't even think it, okay? Just don't."

"You're right, sorry." But Sheila was not convinced. They were in no position to eliminate anyone, not even someone she had turned to just the night before because she could think of no one else she trusted as much. Yet in the clear light of day, and the harsh reality of Roger's possible arrest, no one, not even one's most trusted friend, could be excluded from consideration, at least not without substantial proof. And if, as she believed, motive was key, there was a time when Freddie Bickford had that and then some, when it came to Roger. Sheila could only assume that the years had mellowed him. As for his lack of relationship with Derek Lang, well, that too would bear further looking into, but of all this she said nothing to her ex-husband.

"Anything else the detective shared with you that I should know about?" Sheila asked.

"Just that Brickell—yes, he's on the short list—anyway, seems his alibi can't be proven. Claims he was in a poker game out at the Gila River Reservation, but he doesn't know the names of any of the players. Probably too stoned to remember his own name."

"Maybe there wasn't even a game. Seems to me our ex-host's alibi is as weak as ours."

"He had motive too, it turns out," Roger informed her. "Scott wanted Lang to hire him, but Raintree told me he'd turned him down."

"I'd call that motive all right."

Roger brushed his fingers through his hair. "No one is completely clear of some suspicious implication. I'd say we have our work cut out for us."

"And *I* say get a lawyer and let the professionals do their jobs," Sheila stated, glowering. Just then Roger's intercom buzzed, and he nodded to Sheila.

"It's time," he announced.

When Roger had called her personally to ask for this meeting, Alicia had experienced a wellspring of hope that made her buoyant with possibility. He had reconsidered her worth to PCE. She was going back on prime time for him. He was giving her a major showcase. She was still the queen of the infomercial.

The minute she stepped into the office and saw *her*, hope fizzled flat like the last days of a permanent wave.

"Well, this is a surprise, seeing the two of you together," she said by way of greeting, clenching her teeth so hard her lips barely moved.

"Sit down, Alicia," Roger said.

She looked warily at Sheila, whose expression was blank.

"Why is *she* here? Don't tell me the two of you are an item again? What happened, Sheila—Derek's death really move you?" Stop it! Stop! she warned herself. Don't antagonize them, they could still help you. But it was too late, and she knew it; too late to channel the fear. She fluttered her spit curl, then forced her hand to sit quietly in her lap.

"Sorry," she muttered unfeelingly.

Still Sheila said nothing, her dark eyes measuring, assessing the tension coming off the singer like heat waves off tarmac. She was counting on her silence to bring Devon to a degree of nervousness that would somehow reveal important information.

"Roger, what's this all about? When you called, I thought you had reconsidered my position with PCE. That's not what this is about, is it?"

"No, Alicia, it's not."

The performer glanced from Roger to Sheila, back to Roger, her face a study in concentration. "It's about Derek's death, isn't it?" she guessed. Roger's nod was slight. "Rumor has it that you did it, so why am I here?" She frowned. "Come to think of it, why are you here— shouldn't you be in jail or something?"

Both Gaineys ignored her probing look, her insulting question, forcing her hand.

"Well, I wasn't even in Phoenix the night it happened, so I'm afraid I can't help you—if that's what I'm supposed to do." She screwed up her face into an expression of disbelief. "Then again, you didn't really think I would, did you?"

"We know you weren't here," Sheila finally spoke, her voice soft, gentle, deceptively so, given the steel of her posture, the flatness in her eyes.

"So, then—?"

"You could have arranged for Derek's death."

"Don't be ridiculous!" Alicia laughed, a dry, unpleasant bark. "Believe me, if I wanted someone dead, I'd do the job myself."

"You certainly had motive," Sheila stated.

Alicia's face began to darken with hate, a hatred so intense that it brought out all the age and desperation in her face, creeping into the crevices of flesh, pulling down her mouth, making pinpoints of poison of her eyes.

"Motive to kill Derek Lang?" she repeated softly. "No, I had no reason to kill him. In fact, he was far more valuable to me alive—he was a possible job. No, it's you"— she pointed at Sheila—"and you, especially you, Roger, who deserved to die, not Derek, he wasn't to blame for what's happened to me. Derek had taste—he recognized a stupid, terribly produced spot when he saw one. He rejected it because *it* was inferior, not because *I* was."

"I'm very impressed by your revisionist memory, Alicia," Sheila said, her outward appearance belying the rapid beating of her heart. "You were desperate. I warned you not to do the spot, but you wouldn't take no for an answer, you didn't care what you did as long as you had something to show. Desperation made you inferior and desperation might have driven you to arrange for Derek's death."

"Damn right I was desperate!" the singer erupted. "Because he"— and now the full force of her venom was directed at Roger—"made me that way. If it weren't for him, I wouldn't have had to work with a second-rate producer on a second-rate spot!"

"You didn't think Sheila was so second-rate when she did your shows at PCE," Roger reminded her.

"Bullshit!" Alicia spat. "She was bad then, too, but what choice did I have—she was fucking the boss! Why else do you think so many of my shows failed at the end—you weren't banging her often enough!"

The crudeness shocked both of them, an unexpected attack of evil that echoed in the room, circles of ugliness assaulting their senses until, after what seemed like a long time, they finally faded.

"You hate us that much?"

"Yes, Sheila, I do." The singer could no longer control it; her fingers flew to a spit curl, a useless pacifier. "Yes, I hate you. I wish it had been either one of you who had been murdered instead of Derek." Her lips spread into a malicious smile for Roger. "But maybe dying slowly in jail will be even better."

"I think it's time you left now," Roger said.

"And believe me," Alicia went on as if Roger had not spoken, "if I had arranged for a murder, I would have made sure the right person got killed!"

"Get out, now, Alicia, before I call security and put what's left of your pitiful self into the garbage where it belongs."

The singer opened her mouth to retort, thought better of it. Mustering the tattered shreds of her pride and dignity, she stood up, looked from one Gainey to the other. "I hope the two of you rot in the same kind of hell you've put me in," she cursed, then left, slamming the door so hard it missed the catch and swung back open.

Neither Roger nor Sheila could possibly know what it cost Alicia Devon to walk steadily past Roger's secretary, down the familiar halls of the PCE offices to her car. Her stomach kept lurching as if with dry heaves, and her eyes were stinging with tears she would not let herself shed.

Neither Roger nor Sheila could possibly know that as much as Alicia Devon loathed them, the depth of her hatred she reserved for someone else, someone who, in the darkest hour of night, when there was no relief from the truth, insisted she face the real enemy, the one person, the only person deserving of her hatred: herself.

But they were both so dumbstruck by the malevolence of a person they had once considered if not friend, then warm colleague, that they could not utter a word. That she had distorted and warped her own sense of importance, her talent, her value to such an extent that anyone, everyone else was to blame for her fall from grace, sickened them into silence.

Then again, they did not know that ultimately, Alicia Devon was sickened by the distortion herself.

It was Sheila who spoke first, tentatively, as if after a long illness. "I don't think I can go through this with you, Roger. I'm sorry, but I can't bear that much hatred."

"I understand, Sheila, and it'll be okay, you'll see." Roger went to crouch down in front of her, not daring to do what he most desired—touch her, with assurance, with caring, with affection. He did not want this woman hurt again, not because of him.

"I'll take care of this, Sheil. I'll get a lawyer like you want. Don't you worry about it, okay? This was a stupid idea. I'm sorry."

It would be difficult to determine who was more surprised when Sheila put her hand against Roger's cheek and just held him like that.

"Does that mean you forgive me for everything?"

"No. It only means I'm not giving up." She stood, forcing Roger to do the same. She briefly shut her eyes as if clearing away the shackles of dread that threatened to hamper her from doing what was necessary.

"I'm sorry, she was just so awful, but if you're serious about that lawyer—?" She smiled faintly as he shook his head. "I didn't think you really meant it. And that's okay, Roger, I'll go through this with you. In a sick, perverted kind of way, it's actually interesting, although I could do without such an intimate view of people's dark side," she added with a shiver.

"Do you think Alicia had anything to do with it?" Roger then asked, going back to his desk while Sheila went over to a window, gazing out for a moment, before turning and answering.

"No, I don't. Even if she has a moment of clarity when she sees the truth, Alicia Devon is able to function only by blaming us. No, she might have framed you, Roger, but she wanted Derek Lang very much alive."

Roger nodded his agreement. "That leaves Scott, Linc, or Freddie."

"You left out Marilu."

"I know, because even if her alibi isn't ironclad, I don't think she would have killed the man she loved. She'd sooner have killed us."

"Seems like that's a familiar theme," Sheila muttered. "So you don't buy the woman-scorned theory?"

"Not with her," Roger explained. "She always struck me as the kind of woman who understood that everything has its price and if she wanted something badly enough, she was willing to pay it." He looked thoughtful, remembering times he had been with Marilu, spoken with her both as a friend and as an important player in the cable shopping community.

"Patience was the price she had to pay to be with Derek, but when that failed, couldn't she have been hurt and angry enough to punish him?"

"No, Sheila, I really don't think she did it. It was you she was after, that's why she went to Raintree with that cock-and-bull story about you obsessing over Derek breaking up with you. No, I don't see anything to be gained by questioning her, at least not at this point."

"Okay, then let's tackle Mr. Personality. We know he had motive, maybe opportunity. Now if we find out he somehow stole my gun, we just might have our man."

Chapter
Twenty-seven

Snot dripped down his nose. He swiped at it, missed, tossed his head back in a peal of shrill laughter as inappropriate as the tears streaming down his cheeks.

He brought his head forward, leaned over the hand mirror, finger pressing hard against the nostril to blow in more coke, but there didn't seem to be any more. How was that possible? He had had three grams delivered two days ago. Or was it four days ago and only two grams? He couldn't remember. He moistened his forefinger with saliva, traced the entire surface of the mirror, the dresser top, nothing. He even tore apart the straw to get the last coke dustings.

No more coke.

No more job.

No more money.

Soon, no more Scott Brickell.

He held the murky hand mirror up to his face, saw dissolution. He leaned over the dresser, peered into the far clearer mirror hanging above it, and saw selfishness and waste; a man of straw about to go up in flames.

Scott Brickell placed bets on horses and dogs, athletes, cards, dice, wheels of fortune. His biggest bet, the one he had mortgaged his future against, had been himself, his belief in his superiority, his luck. No one could win when Scott Brickell came to play.

He had had it all once. The women. The fancy cars. The best tables at the best restaurants. Shit, there had been a time when they'd clear the tables for him, let him play by himself, playing for four, five hands at a time. He had had it all. Once.

Now he was running on empty, and *they* were coming to pick over his bones.

At exactly that moment, the doorbell rang. Scott's eyes bulged with fear and he started to whimper like a baby, clutching his stomach, letting the coke snot drip unchecked. Maybe, if he didn't move, didn't breathe, they'd go away. Then, he swore, he'd enter a clinic for detox, join Gamblers Anonymous, do it all, clean and sober, clean and sober. He was young. He had talent. He swore he'd never make another bet in his life if they'd just go away! He began to chew furiously on a cuticle.

The doorbell rang again, a death knell.

"Be right there," he called out, going into the bathroom to splash cold water on his face. It was ineffectual against the pallor, the stubs of unshaven beard, the crusts caught in the corners of his watery eyes. If only he had a couple of lines to help him bluff his way through this . . .

He opened the door, gaped, then began to laugh hysterically with relief at the sight of Sheila and Roger Gainey.

"Come in, come in," he said expansively. "I was expecting someone else, but I'm sure glad to see you guys."

Sheila and Roger exchanged a wary look as they followed Scott into the house.

"What brings you here, and together no less?" Scott was rubbing his nose, smiling too brightly, sitting too straight.

Roger spoke first. "Brick, you okay? Maybe we should call you a doctor, huh?"

"No, hey, I'm fine, fine. Not to worry." He laughed, as false as his posture. "If you two are together again, that would be great for yours truly, wouldn't it? I know you wanted to produce a new show for me, Sheila—you turned me down out of some stupid sense of loyalty to Roger, but now you don't have to worry about that, you can—"

"I told you then and I'll tell you now—I won't produce for you until you clean up your act and change your attitude. And—not that it's any of your business—we are not together again."

The comic's face lost its fake amicability, as did his tone of voice. "Then why the hell are you here?"

"We understand you and Derek Lang had a fight shortly before his death," Roger said.

"Fight? No, man, we didn't fight. The bastard wouldn't hire me. He had given me his word, and reneged. But fight? No, no fight. I could have killed the bastard, but hey, no, there was no fight." Suddenly, Brickell realized what he had said.

"Hey, I told the cops I was playing poker that night and they seemed cool with that. What business is it of yours to be asking me questions?"

"Roger is the police's number one suspect in Derek's death, Scott," Sheila explained, her manner curt, unfriendly, disgusted by the terrible waste before her. "We're trying to clear his name, help the police if we can."

"No shit?" Scott said, grinning with genuine glee. "Roger a murderer, who would have thought you had it in you, Gainey? Did you do it?"

"Did you?" Roger immediately boomeranged the question.

"Me? Hell no, I told you, I was playing poker."

"With no one the police can find to verify your claim," Roger said.

"Oh, get the fuck out of here, will you? I don't have to listen to this crap or tell you one damn thing. You stopped being important to me the day you fired me. I hope they nail your ass to the wall for this."

"You hated Derek for not hiring you. You can't prove your whereabouts." Sheila leaned forward, her elbows on her knees, her voice a relentlessly steady drone of accusation. "Did you shoot him, Scott? Did you shoot Derek and make it look like Roger did it to get back at him? Did you? *Did you?*"

Brickell stared at Sheila, transfixed as if by a master storyteller, then, slowly, he pushed himself to his feet, went to a small bar set up on a side table, poured and drank down a shot of tequila before turning back to them. "I wouldn't pick up a gun if my life depended on it. I hate guns." He spoke with more sobriety than the Gaineys had ever heard from him. They glanced at each other, confused.

Scott poured and tossed back another shot, then took his place on the sofa again, calm, sad, but calm. "When I was eight years old, I came home to find my parents shot to death in our kitchen."

"Oh Jesus Christ," muttered Roger. Sheila could only shut her eyes and take several long, shuddering breaths.

"My father would have shot me, too, I guess, but I had been in school." His expression turned achingly bittersweet. "I've never been able to decide if that was lucky for me or not." His eyes had lost their immediate focus, seeing instead that scene that never left him, not when he was on top, and never when he felt the devil calling.

"I'm so sorry," Sheila whispered.

"He was a gambler, too," Scott went on, back in the present. "He didn't have any problem with controlled substances, though," he added. "His idea of recreation was to go out in our backyard and shoot at empty bottles, beer cans, anything. He had a whole target range set up back there."

"Scott, you don't have to—"

"Hell, Sheila, you came here to ask questions, so now you're getting the answers. Besides, I have nothing to hide, not anymore. I'm so exposed I need full body root canal." Even now, there was a flimsy thread of his old humor.

"Anyway, the day it happened, my father had lost a bundle on the ponies or some sports game, who knew, it didn't matter to him, it's never mattered to me. It's the rush of the bet, not what you're betting on that matters," he explained. "I guess my mother had had enough, at least that's what my aunt told me afterward. They found my mother's suitcase in the hallway. She had one for me, too, both fully packed. She was leaving him, and he couldn't bear that. He always claimed he gambled to make money for *her*." Scott's laugh was wise with knowing. "So he shot her. Better dead than gone, I guess. Two shots to the head. Then he ate the gun himself." Scott frowned with the memory, then pasted on a dead man's grin. "I never much cared to go near guns after that." Suddenly, he looked straight at Roger. "Although it's been tempting with you, Gainey."

"What are you going to do, Brick?" Roger asked, shaken by this shell of a man, by his story. "Let me help. Let me do that much for you." Roger was as startled by the words as were the other two.

Scott laughed harshly. "Guilt, Gainey?"

"No, Scott, friendship. Remember how that used to feel?"

The comic said nothing, staring at Roger, letting tears fill his eyes. "It's too late," he managed. "I appreciate the offer, but I need a helluva lot more than friendship right now."

Roger looked over at Sheila, who nodded, as he knew she would. "I'll take care of the debt, Scott. All of it."

Scott scowled with disbelief. "Why would you do that?"

"You used to make me laugh. I'd like you to be able to do it again," Roger answered, too casually.

"What's the catch? If I have to be in your debt, I'd just as soon have my kneecaps broken."

"Detox, that's the catch. Gamblers Anonymous, too. Clean yourself up, Brick, that's the catch. Clean up so you can get back on top where you belong."

Scott took his time responding, digesting Roger's words, tasting them for the lie. "You're serious?" he finally asked.

"He's serious," Sheila assured him, getting up to leave. "And if you are, too, go pack a bag and come with us now. We'll check you into the hospital and make all the arrangements."

"What do you say, Scott? It's your call."

"That sounds suspiciously like a bet, Gainey," but Scott was smiling.

"I guess it is. I'm asking you to gamble on yourself. Think you can do it?"

The comic gazed at Roger, then at Sheila. "This is the last wager of the day, isn't it?"

"Of your life."

"Right. Of my life." Slowly he nodded. "Well, then, I think I'll take it. After all, that's exactly what I have left to lose."

Sheila and Roger had just finished telling Detective Raintree about their meetings with Alicia and Scott. They were in Sheila's den, having coffee and sandwiches.

"I'm exhausted," Sheila admitted. "All this emotion coming out. It's not easy to deal with."

"You get used to it," the detective told her. "Besides, these are people you know, that makes it harder."

"As it turns out, we didn't know them that well," Sheila said.

"I'm sorry we have to rush this, but the pressure is really on me to bring you in, Mr. Gainey. Time has just about run out."

"I appreciate the leeway you've given me, Detective. Freddie and Linc'll be here in a few minutes. You have no problem waiting until we see them, do you?"

The detective shook his head. "No, that was our arrangement, Mr. Gainey. You get to question them on your terms. If nothing new comes out, I'll take you in."

"And you'll get a lawyer," Sheila reminded Roger.

"Detective Raintree?" Roger caught the policeman's eye. "Sheila's in the clear, isn't she?"

"Why do you ask?"

"Well, her name's on the paperweight. The gun was taken from her house. And she can't prove where she was that night." Roger's brow creased. "Sounds dangerously similar to my predicament."

"Then maybe she should get a lawyer, too."

"Is that your answer?" Nerves made Sheila's voice crack.

"Look, Ms. Gainey, Mr. Gainey, I really don't think a female committed this crime, and of those females who might be involved, I'd say you had the least motive, Ms. Gainey, and motive counts for a lot with me." The detective spotted the quick exchange of eye contact between them, but went on. "I also don't think that if you did do it, you'd incriminate your husband . . . ex-husband, sorry. From what I've been able to learn about you, Ms. Gainey, you're not the vindictive type."

"So it's me, then," Roger pronounced with grim finality.

When the doorbell rang, Sheila answered, leading Linc back to the den, but did not get to sit down before the bell rang again. This time she returned with Freddie.

"Detective Raintree? Linc?" Freddie looked puzzled. "What's this all about?"

"Sit down, Freddie," Roger invited. "Linc, Freddie, indulge me, if you will. It turns out that Detective Raintree is about to arrest me for Derek Lang's murder."

"Oh shit," muttered Linc.

Freddie frowned and remained silent.

"But before he does that, he very graciously has allowed me the opportunity to ask a few questions of some people who might have wanted Derek out of the way. Might want me out of the way too," he added on a laugh as empty of mirth as a wound.

"That's highly unorthodox, isn't it?" Freddie commented.

"Maybe so," Raintree granted, "but I don't think Mr. Gainey here is going to run out of town, so no real harm done."

"How can we help, Roger?" Linc asked, avoiding the policeman's eyes.

"Well, to start," Raintree said, "someone with a prison record has a lot more experience in the commission of a crime than a man who's been clean his whole life. Wouldn't you agree, Mr. Rangel? Jack Rangel, isn't it? Former address Joliet Prison?"

Lightning electrified the room, thunder boomed stereophonically— and the sun was setting in a desert-clear sky, but not for Jack Rangel, who felt as if the clouds had burst and his past was pouring down, drowning him.

"Oh shit," was all he could manage.

"That's right, Joliet, I had forgotten about that." Roger spoke so conversationally that Rangel's Phoenix tan turned corpse-white as it suddenly dawned on him that all this time, all these years, Roger had known!

"You knew, too, Sheila?"

She nodded.

"But—" To see the glib Abraham Lincoln Peck sputtering inarticulately leavened the atmosphere as efficiently as if a toddler had entered the room.

"Did you really think I'd accept you at face value?" Roger asked rhetorically. "You show up out of nowhere with an amateur though highly effective video that had Sheila convinced you were PCE's answer to Richard Covey and Anthony Robbins."

"And she was right," Rangel put in.

"Yes, she was. But I did check you out."

"How? Where did you know to look?"

"Roger, and Freddie, actually, have an interesting variety of acquaintances," Sheila told him. "Besides, you had a hunch about him, didn't you, Freddie?"

The lawyer nodded, a smile flying on and off his mouth like a decal with insufficient glue.

"So a few questions here, there," Roger picked up the narrative, "and we found out about your record. Frankly"—and he laughed—"knowing you were a con was the best recommendation for your future success I could imagine."

"Let's get back to Derek Lang, Mr. Peck. Or do you prefer Rangel?"

Rangel shrugged his indifference. "What about Lang, Detective? I already told you when you spoke to me the other day that my relationship with the deceased was a courtship. He was always trying to hire me over to BFL and I always turned him down. Does that strike you as a reason to kill a guy?"

"That bastard!" Roger burst out. "Trying to steal my star!"

"Don't play the outraged husband, Roger. You would have done the same if Derek had a star of Linc's caliber," Sheila reprimanded.

"Well, still . . ." But the bluster was already waning.

"Derek knew about you, too, didn't he, Linc?" Sheila guessed.

Rangel nodded. "Threatened to expose me," he admitted.

This made no sense to her. "Why? If he wanted you for his network, what possible reason would he have to want to destroy your reputation?"

Jack Rangel let his eyes survey the various faces surrounding him, faces expectant for a logical explanation. But that explanation meant the admission of behavior so foolhardy it made him ashamed of himself, and Rangel never in his life, at least hardly ever, experienced shame. Still, there seemed no way out of this mess but the truth.

"I was drunk one night," he began, "and I did something seriously stupid. Derek Lang was a man you never, ever showed vulnerability or weakness to." He glanced over at Sheila. "I told you once the man had no soul. I recognized him for what he was," he said to the room at large. "He was as passionless and morally cold as the convicts I did time with."

"No, that's not true," Sheila tried, then stopped, tired of defending the Derek she had known, eager by now only to put an end to the entire ordeal.

"I'm sorry, Sheila."

She waved away Linc's apology, and he went on. "It was our semi-annual dinner, when Derek tried to hire me and I drank his wine, ate his food, and then, like a virgin, passed on the goodnight kiss."

"This the first time you got drunk with him?" Raintree wanted to know.

"Yeah," Rangel grumbled, recalling the night. "I was excited about this new idea . . . drank too much . . . blurted it out. It was an idea I had been researching for some time. My plan all along was to bring it to you, Roger, as soon as I had all the loose ends tied up."

"Instead you get drunk, tell Derek Lang, and that's the end of it for me and PCE. Right?" Roger probed, disgust etching his face, his voice. "Right?" he pressed.

Rangel nodded, miserable. "About four, five days before he was killed, I read in the newspapers that he was launching the BFL Buyers

Card. That was my idea, Roger, *my* idea. I wanted PCE to have a home shopping credit card—it was a brilliant concept, a natural money-maker. Lang gave me his word that anything said when drunk would not be held against me." His bark of laughter rang hollow. "For a con, I sure got taken, didn't I?" He turned all his attention on Roger now. "Believe me, Roger, I never would have said anything if I weren't drunk. I may not have the morals of a saint, but if there's one thing I believe in, it's loyalty. I'm under contract to you; it's you, and Sheila, of course, who gave me the chance to be what I am today. No way was I going to let Lang get away with stealing my idea."

"Did you threaten him?" Raintree asked.

"No! I already told you, he threatened me!" The infomercial star got up and began to stride nervously around the room, touching objects, his tall frame, his impressive presence dwarfing all else.

"I confronted him that same day," Rangel explained, not looking anyone in the face, just walking and touching and going back in time to his last conversation with a dead man. "I read the papers and went to Lang's office. I was furious, livid, and he laughed in my face, just sat there laughing at me. I was so angry I could have killed him." He immediately caught himself. "Oh shit, that's a figure of speech, nothing more, a figure of speech."

"Go on," the detective urged.

"I told him that he had to cut me in on the deal. If he insisted on stealing my idea, then be a gentleman thief and share. He kept laughing at me, said I had no legal document proving the idea was mine, and nothing in writing meant nothing, period. Said it was his word against mine, and who would believe an ex-con. That's when I knew he had me. Up until then, I figured he was just playing hardball. I mean, the guy didn't get where he was wearing velvet gloves and making nice-nice, but I figured I could deal with that. It was when he revealed he knew about my background, hell, that's when I knew I had nothing to fight him with."

He finally focused on Sheila. "I'm sorry, honey, I know you cared about him. I tried to warn you, though."

She nodded. "You warned me about a man I didn't know, Linc. The Derek Lang you're describing was not the man I knew."

Linc shrugged, hearing her, his silence saying that he did not really believe there were two such distinctly different sides to the man; his silence saying that someday, had he lived, Derek Lang might have laughed at Sheila, too.

He then turned to the detective. "I didn't kill him, Detective Raintree. I wanted to, believe me, I wanted to, but I don't kill. I cheat and con and lie. Put all that together, and I guess you could say I steal—but I don't kill."

The detective gazed steadily back at Rangel, using the instincts, the experience, and the plain old common sense that he relied on in his investigations. Rangel's alibi for the time in question had been weak—women, forgettable women. Still . . .

"No, Mr. Rangel, I don't believe you do."

"Then that means—"

Chapter
Twenty-eight

Yes, Sheila, I killed Derek Lang."

"Oh, Freddie, no, no!"

"Why? Oh, man, Freddie, why?" Roger groaned, running his fingers through his hair.

"You, Bickford?" Rangel said. "Don't tell me he had the goods on you, too. But what? You're a starched-collar, creased jeans kind of guy. You're a lawyer, for Pete's sake. What could he threaten you with?"

Freddie was oblivious to everyone in the room but Roger, his eyes holding fast to the man whose trust he had betrayed repeatedly and with gusto.

"You gave him our secrets, didn't you?" Roger said, choking on the words.

Freddie nodded.

"Why? Didn't I share everything with you, Freddie? Weren't you in on every deal, every thought, every project? Hell, man, I was going to make LifeStyle yours—and you sabotaged that, too. What were you thinking? Hell, did you hate me that much?" he asked with sudden, blinding understanding.

He glimpsed over at Sheila, seeking from her an assurance that this was all a mistake, that his trusted best friend could not have been this false, but what he saw in her sad eyes was confirmation of the bitter truth.

"I tried to stop it, Roger," Freddie was now saying. "I really did try. He threatened me. Said he wouldn't just tell you, but he'd go to the ABA, have me disbarred. He wasn't finished with my usefulness, so I couldn't be finished with him."

"How long had it been going on?"

"A long time."

"The cruise line, the ProctorSilex idea—you gave all of them to him, didn't you?" Freddie's silence gave Roger the answer he dreaded.

"What about the Spanish star concept?"

"No, not that."

"Not yet," Roger muttered. "Was he paying you a lot?"

The lawyer shook his head. "The money didn't matter. I did it to hurt you. After you bought me out, made your former partner a job offer, I couldn't bear the humiliation. I needed to get back at you, show you what real manipulation was all about."

"You could have left me, you could have said something. Why didn't you ever say anything?"

"It doesn't matter now. In the beginning, it wasn't so much big-concept projects I leaked as much as how the business ran, what made a deal good, special contracts I made for him. Then, when you walked out on Sheila"—he glanced shame-facedly over at her, and she stared back, her heartache showing—"well, I started doing a lot of it then. You were so cocky, Roger, so sure of yourself. This was my way of letting you know you didn't have the absolute control you thought you did."

Roger's laugh bled sarcasm. "So you ran to my competitor and gave *him* control."

"Killing Derek Lang wasn't the only thing that mattered, though, was it, Mr. Bickford?" Detective Raintree spoke up. "You wanted to get Mr. Gainey in the process, didn't you?"

Freddie nodded. "I wanted him to feel the kind of claustrophobia that comes from being locked into a situation and not knowing how to get out. For years that's how I've felt, passively accepting Roger's decisions, Roger's leadership. I never wanted it all for myself, I just wanted to share, just share, like the partners we once were."

"You stole my paperweight."

"That was easy. Getting the gun from your house, Sheila, that was a bit more complicated. I knew you kept an extra key taped to the inside of your barbecue cover. When you were in San Francisco a few weeks ago, I took it and had a duplicate made. It was easy enough to get in and find the gun."

"Would you have let me go to jail?" Roger had to know. When Freddie said nothing, Roger said, "I don't believe you would have. I'm going to believe you confessed now because you knew you had wronged me and wanted it stopped."

Freddie held Roger's eyes a long beat, then concentrated on Detective Raintree. "I confessed because I was about to get caught. I hadn't counted on a smart detective." Suddenly he smiled, a tight and bitter expression. "See what happens when you underestimate the next guy, Roger? Learn this lesson well."

Rage and Fear, the devil's disciples for murder. That was Detective Raintree's thought as he put the cuffs on the lawyer and read him his legal rights.

Epilogue

H ey, guys, nice to see you two together without a murder convic- tion hanging over anybody's head."

"We're not together," Sheila said as if by rote, lifting her cheek so Linc could kiss it. "Roger thought lunch would be nice, that's all. Don't make more of it."

"Right, Linc, don't make more of it," Roger repeated, grinning. "Sit down, sit down. What'll you have?"

They ordered lunch, and while they waited, they made small talk about what had been happening in the month since Roger's name was cleared and Freddie had been indicted in the murder of Derek Lang.

"Actually, business has been great," Sheila confessed. "It's that tabloid mentality, I guess, but it's working. I hear Alicia fired her man- ager and is doing a local cable talk show outside Galveston, Texas."

"How the mighty have fallen," Linc remarked.

"And I got a please-forgive-me letter from Marilu."

"Too little, too late," Roger decreed.

"Well, we'll see," Sheila told him.

"All this is very nice," Linc said, observing her closely, "but what about you, Sheila? How are you doing, really?"

She looked self-consciously over at Roger, who also was watching her carefully. "Me? I'm fine, Linc, why shouldn't I be? Roger's name is clear, as is mine, I might add. Business is good. I'm saddened by how things have turned out for Freddie, but that's—"

"Are you saddened by what you learned about Derek?" he cut her off.

"Linc—"

"It's okay, Roger."

In the days and weeks since Derek's death, when she learned how cruel he could be, she had to force herself to remember how much he had given her, how restorative his presence in her life had been. Had he lived, would they have gone on to become something important and vital together? No, Sheila did not think so, and that truth did not dismay her, did not diminish what they had had. Was she saddened by what she had learned? No, not really. She was sad it had cost him his life.

Both men saw the way her eyes squinted, not from sun, but from a sheen of tears.

"Linc, see what you've done!"

Her laugh shimmered weakly. "I'm fine, Roger. Come on, you guys, I'm fine, really. And in answer to your nosy question, Mr. Peck, no, I'm not particularly saddened by what I discovered of Derek's character. I wasn't too surprised by any of it. But people come together for all kinds of reasons. He came into my life, Linc, and he was kind and good to me. Let's leave it at that, okay?"

Linc nodded. "Okay, Sheila, okay."

Sheila's face immediately brightened. "There's some really good news to tell you. Scott's making terrific progress at rehab. And he's been attending Gamblers Anonymous regularly. I hope he doesn't backslide."

"He better not," Roger said sternly. "I didn't pay off his debts so he could accrue them again."

"You paid off his debts?" Linc was incredulous.

Roger shrugged with embarrassment. "Someone had to."

Peck laughed. "Next you're going to tell me you're paying for Bickford's defense."

"Not hardly," Roger said. "Although I still have trouble understanding how much the guy resented me. All those years and I had no idea."

"I don't think even Freddie knew himself," Sheila offered. "That kind of bitterness needs time to fester into the kind of hatred that can kill. I don't think he knew how much he hated you, Roger, until Derek triggered it with his own mishandling of him. He murdered *you* when he killed Derek, then hedged his bets by planting the evidence pointing back to you. He wasn't going to let you get away with anything ever again."

"Enough of this macabre conversation," Peck said, electric with excitement. "I want to tell you about my new infomercial. It's going to make us millions."

"We already have millions," Roger reminded him.

"I don't," Sheila said.

"You could if you married me again."

"Roger!"

"Hey, don't tell me you two—"

"No, Linc, we won't tell you because there's nothing to tell," Sheila snapped, skewering Roger with her eyes. "Now, about that infomercial—?"

"It's called *Steps to the Soul.*"

"No," Roger moaned.

Peck went on to describe his new six-step program to "spiritual" freedom, a natural follow-up to *Ladder.* "I'm tapping right into the New Age junkies," he said. "You'll produce it, won't you, Sheila?"

She glanced at Roger, eyes twinkling. "That all depends. I'll have my media buyer contact Roger and see if we can strike a good deal. If not, I'm sure there are plenty of other producers who would do a good job for you."

"I don't want any other producer. I want the best, and that's you, Sheila."

"Linc's right," Roger concurred. "Besides, I'll make sure you get a great time slot."

"Of course you will—what else would you do with a Lincoln Peck spot? Besides, every time Media Gains makes money, you do, too, so save your altruism, Roger, it doesn't wash." She was laughing, enjoying herself with Roger as she hadn't for . . . for well over a year. Working together on the murder investigation had broken down barriers, but it certainly couldn't be described as fun. *This* was fun.

"I'd be pleased to produce your new spot, Linc," she said.

"Great. Now what's this I hear about BFL being for sale?"

"Roger? Is that true?"

He glanced at Linc who shrugged and said, "I thought she knew."

"You're buying it?" Sheila guessed.

"I'm thinking about it. Would you like it if I did?"

"Me? What does it matter what I think?"

"It matters a great deal. I'd like you to run it."

Sheila jerked back, eyes blinking away the absurd words she must have imagined hearing.

"I'm serious, Sheil."

"Oh. Oh my. Oh."

"Is that a 'Great, Roger'? Or a 'You can't be serious, Roger'? Or a 'Tell me more, Roger.'"

"All of the above."

Their food arrived, and no further mention was made of Roger's idea. Just as well, Sheila thought, since the prospect filled her with such exhilaration and, truth to tell, anxiety, that she wouldn't have been able to swallow a morsel if he presented her with all the details now.

Linc did not stay for coffee. "Gotta run. I'm flying to Cancun for the weekend. I'm giving a seminar—and there are these twin sisters and their mother—"

Sheila held up her hand in a stop signal and Roger laughed. "Have fun," he said.

Linc looked from Sheila over to Roger, then grinned. "You two have fun, too."

Sheila glowered, but said nothing. It was Roger who broke the silence.

"You know, Sheila, I was serious about what I said before."

Excitement flushed her face with a youthful glow. "About running BFL? Oh, Roger, it would be so great. I really appreciate your confidence that I could—"

"I meant about marrying me again." He reached across the table to grasp her hand. "It'll be different this time, Sheil, I promise. I made a terrible mistake, a stupid male mistake. Give me another chance, Sheil, please, you won't regret it, I promise."

Feelings cascaded in and on and through Sheila, making her breathless. Disbelief. Pride. Smugness. Contempt. Hate. Love. Regret. Pain. Hurt. Anger. Relief. Delight. So much turmoil, so much growth.

Gently, she removed her hand from his.

"I take it that means no?"

"But thank you, Roger. Thank you for asking, and more importantly, thank you for accepting responsibility. For the longest time I thought I had only myself to blame. That's what hurt the most."

"I had to try," he said with a half-smile. "On the off-chance you would have said yes."

"I'm very glad you did."

"Friends?"

She was startled by the word, its implication coming from this particular man. She began to smile, an expression radiant with understanding and acceptance of how truly far she had come, how far they had both come, that he could ask the question, and she could answer with, "Yes, Roger, friends. Always that."